FUNGI

edited by

Orrin Grey and Silvia Moreno-Garcia

Published by Innsmouth Free Press

✝

ISBN: 978-0-9916759-1-3 (hardcover)
ISBN: 978-0-9916759-3-7 (paperback)
ISBN: 978-0-9916759-4-4 (e-book)

✝

Edited by: Orrin Grey and Silvia Moreno-Garcia
Cover illustration: Oliver Wetter
Interior illustrations: Bernie Gonzalez
Cover and interior design: Silvia Moreno-Garcia

✝

Published by Innsmouth Free Press, December 2012
Visit www.innsmouthfreepress.com

TABLE OF CONTENTS

✦

INTRODUCTION

IT ALL STARTED WITH a voice in the night …

The question, of course, is always, "Why do a fungus anthology?" And the shortest answer is probably that nobody had ever done one, at least not that we were aware of. There's a small but persistent fungal thread that runs, mycelium-like, through the history of weird fiction. It's a thread that's firmly rooted in the decaying hulks and weed-choked seas of William Hope Hodgson's nautical horror stories, especially "The Voice in the Night," which may be *the* tale of fungal terror. It has produced a rich crop of fruiting bodies through the years, from authors like Lovecraft, Bradbury, King, and Lumley, as well as the writers whose work appears in this anthology.

We found early on that we shared a fascination with fungi in general, and weird fungal fiction in particular, when discussing an unusual 1963 Japanese film adaptation of "The Voice in the Night" from *Godzilla* director Ishiro Honda, best known as *Matango*, but also called variously *Attack of the Mushroom People* and *Fungus of Terror*. One of us was terrified by the film, the other delighted, and we figured that was an appropriate combination for assembling an anthology of fungal stories.

More closely related to animals than plants, but fundamentally different from both, the members of the kingdom *fungi* are a diverse and mysterious lot. While putting together this anthology we ran into several fungal stories including: a recently discovered fungus in the Amazon rainforest that can break down the common plastic polyurethane, a study detailing how the evolution of a fungus known as "white rot" may have ended a 60-million-year-long period responsible for coal deposition, and a company in New England that is creating biodegradable packaging material out of mushrooms. In short, our fungal friends can be the source of many wonders … or terrors, as evidenced by the sight of "zombified" ants under the thrall of a strange parasite.

With so many possibilities to draw from, we knew that we needed something more robust than just a series of pastiches. We wanted to go beyond body horror and Hodgson-esque mushroom people to explore the range of possibilities offered by fungal fiction. Our authors have flung their spores far and wide, and within these pages you'll find all kinds of fungus, playing all kinds of roles, in all kinds of stories running the gamut from horror to dark fantasy. The result is an anthology with mushroom submarines, fungal invasions, mind-altering mushrooms, alien *fungi* — and yes, some mushroom monsters.

✦

HYPHAE

By John Langan

↑

John Langan's most recent collection, *The Wide, Carnivorous Sky and Other Monstrous Geographies*, will be published by Hippocampus Press in early 2013. His previous books include a novel, *House of Windows* (Night Shade 2009), and collection, *Mr. Gaunt and Other Uneasy Encounters* (Prime 2008). With Paul Tremblay, he has co-edited *Creatures: Thirty Years of Monsters* (Prime 2011). His fiction has appeared in *The Magazine of Fantasy & Science Fiction* and in anthologies including *Blood and Other Cravings* (Tor 2011), *Ghosts by Gaslight* (Harper Collins 2011) and *Supernatural Noir* (Dark Horse 2011). He teaches courses in Creative Writing and the Gothic at SUNY New Paltz. He lives in upstate New York with his family.

↑

THE HOUSE WAS IN worse shape than he'd anticipated, the roof warped, the siding faded, the window frames clearly rotten. The yard was a mess, too, grass grown hay-high and yellowed, the ornamental bushes either gone or overgrown. The driveway had never been the best — his father had refused to blacktop it, insisting it was perfectly passable — and the rain and snow of the last fifteen years had only deepened its ruts. The bottom of his Subaru scraped an exposed rock and James winced.

Who knew if his key would fit the front lock anymore? He rolled to where he remembered the driveway ending and shut off the engine. His father had not taken his mother's departure especially well; it would not be a surprise for him to have swapped out the locks. James stepped out of the car. If he couldn't enter the house, then that was his obligation fulfilled, right? He could imagine what his sister, housebound following her C-Section, would say to that.

His key slid home easily; the lock released without struggle. With a sigh, he pushed open the front door.

The smell that rushed out made him step back.

"God …."

It was the rotten milk-and-mold stench of strong cheese left to liquefy in the sun. He leaned towards it, recoiled, tried again.

"Dad?"

The smell flooded his sinuses. He breathed through his mouth.

"Hello? Dad? It's James." *Your gay son*, he almost added, but decided to forego the hostilities for the moment. Was his father even here? Cupping his hand over the lower half of his face, he entered the house.

He expected to find the living room littered with months of dirty dishes, the putrefying remains of half-eaten meals the source of the odour his hand did nothing to shield him from. It was clean, as were the dining room and the kitchen, his father's room and the bathroom. His and Patricia's old rooms had been repurposed to TV room and sewing room, respectively, but neither held anything worse than mild clutter.

"Dad?"

He opened the refrigerator. Except for the water jug, it was empty, as were the oven, the toaster oven and the microwave. Did he need any more proof that his father was not here — had been gone, from the looks of it, for some time? But, but … he ducked his head into the bathroom. His father's toiletries were ranged around the sink. Not out of the question for him to have purchased new ones, of course, if it weren't out of keeping with a lifetime's parsimony. A rummage through the closet in his father's room revealed no gaps in its shirts, slacks and jackets, no ties missing from his accumulated father's day and birthday presents — which appeared to lend weight to his father having stayed put.

"In a house with no food," he said, returning to the kitchen. The basement door was closed, but he supposed he should check downstairs, too. His father's workbench was there, behind the furnace, the home to a collection of power tools that had frightened James when he was younger, in no small part due to the lurid cautions his father had given him about each one. *This'll slice your hand clean off. This'll burn the eyes out of your head. This'll take the flesh from your arm before you know what's happened.* Strange to think James had wound up living with a carpenter.

At the basement door, he paused. Downstairs had been his father's retreat. After a bad day at IBM or especially after an argument with James' mother, he would throw open the door, tromp down the stairs and clatter about his workbench. Sometimes, James would hear the power tools screaming, smell sawdust burning, as his father threw himself into one project or another, cutting wood for the new mailbox he was always on the verge of building, or fashioning a new trellis for the front porch. He had spent ever more time down there in the couple of years prior to James' departure for Cornell and, from what Patricia had told him, before their mother had walked out, he had practically been living in the basement.

The conflict that had come to define his parents' marriage had had a single subject: his father's health, specifically, the horrible state of his feet. It was beyond funny; it was absurd to think that such a topic could have undone 25 years together, but, in all fairness to his mother, there had been something seriously wrong with his father's feet. The toenails had been thick, jaundice-yellow, like bits of horn sprouting from the ends of his toes. The toes, the sides of his feet, had been fish-belly pale, the heels gray and traversed by cracks from which thin, almost ghostly fibers projected. Nor had their appearance been the worst of it: Their smell, an odour of stale sweat mixed with the muddy reek of mildew, had made sitting next to him when his feet were uncovered an act of endurance. Mention the condition of his feet to him and he would flare with anger. James had not understood how the man who insisted on taking him to the doctor for the slightest sniffle could not tend to a part of himself so obviously unwell, and the sight of his father's bare feet had stirred in him an obscure shame. As he had grown older, adolescence had curdled his shame to contempt, as it had dawned on him that his father was afraid of what a visit to the doctor would tell him about his feet. In the last few years, contempt had mellowed to something like pity, though it was difficult not to feel a modicum of anger at his father's inertia.

He opened the basement door and was pushed back several steps by the fresh wave of reek that rushed over him. Gagging, his eyes watering, he threw his hand back over his mouth, his nose. "Jesus," he said, coughing. This was too much. He stumbled into the dining room, to the back door. He fumbled with the locks and flung the door wide, pushing the screen door out of the way and stepping onto the back porch and fresh air.

Wiping his eyes, his nose, he crossed to the other side of the porch. The smell clung to him. He inhaled deeply. Something caught in his throat and bent him double, coughing. He straightened, only for a second round of coughing to convulse him. His mouth filled with phlegm. He spat and what spattered on the porch was grey. "Shit." He remained hunched over until his lungs had calmed. His chest felt bruised, his throat raw. He stood, gingerly, and something in the tall grass behind the porch drew his notice.

It was a car, his father's car, the same red Saturn he'd been driving when James had left for college. Descending the porch's steps, James approached the car. The thick layer of pollen lying yellow on it, obscuring its windows, testified to its having been parked here for some time. James felt a momentary surge of panic that his father might be seated in the car, dead of a heart attack or stroke. Heart pounding, he opened the driver's side door, bracing for the sight of his father's desiccated corpse. The car was empty. He sagged against it.

He dug his cell phone out of his jeans, flipped it open. No bars. He held it up, rotating slowly. Nothing. Terrific. Was the phone in the house still working? And what was he planning on saying to his sister if he reached her? "Dad isn't here and there's a weird smell coming from the basement"? He folded the phone and returned it to his pocket.

Maybe his shirt … he unbuttoned, untucked and removed it, then folded it into a rough scarf that he tied over his nose and mouth. Already, the faint odor of rotten milk and mold had attached to the fabric. It was bearable. James climbed to the porch and returned inside.

At least the basement light was working. He descended the stairs slowly, on the lookout for … what? Whatever was producing that smell. He'd never dealt with black mold; maybe that was the culprit. The odour pressed on his improvised mask. He concentrated on breathing through his mouth.

At the foot of the stairs, the water heater stood in its recess, closeted from the rest of the basement by a dark-brown door whose upper half was laddered with slats that allowed him to see the off-white cylinder and not much else. As a child, James had felt a prickle of unease at the base of his neck every time he'd passed in front of that door. Perhaps due to the design of the slats, each of which was set at a 45 degree tilt, light didn't reach very far into the alcove, leaving the walls of the recess invisible and giving the impression that the water heater stood at the near end of a large, dark space. When he was 14, he'd helped his father replace the tank and, although the closet had been well-lit by a pair of worklights his father had hung on the walls, James still had judged it unusually spacious for its purpose.

He was almost past the recess when his eye caught something through the slats, a wooden pole resting on the water heater. He slid his fingers under the lowest slat and eased to door open. It was the handle of a shovel, its blade rusted except for the edge, which was bright from use. On the floor beside it, a pickaxe had fallen over. The points of its head shone. Bracing his hands on either side of the doorway, James leaned into the alcove.

To his left, a sizable hole had been chopped into the wall. Three feet wide by four and a half, maybe five feet high, its margin ragged, it appeared to extend into the earth behind the wall. James released the doorway and stepped around the water heater, in front of the hole. It was too dark for him to see into. He fished his cell from his jeans, unfolded it and turned the screen toward the blackness. Its pale light revealed a rough, narrow tunnel receding to an uncertain destination.

"Dad?"

Was that a reply? He called to his father a second time, stood listening for a response. None came. Holding his cell out before him, he ducked his head and advanced into the tunnel. It was a bit of a tight fit — his father was smaller than James by a good six inches and thirty pounds — but passable. The floor slanted down, while the walls curved gradually to the left. He looked over his shoulder. Already, the water heater was almost out of view. The passage appeared to have been hacked out of solid rock. He didn't know what type lay beneath the house, but his father had cut his way through it.

Where had he been going? Had he been building some kind of underground shelter? From what? His father had always been a man to follow his own impulses, to a fault and to extremes. Of course, there was the example of his feet, which James' mother had told him had become infected from something he'd picked up while on a business trip to Paris. A French colleague had taken him on a tour of the catacombs, during which he'd stepped into a deep puddle of foul water. His socks and shoes had been soaked. Who knew what had been swimming around in there and decided to hitch a ride on his father's skin. No doubt a treatment for Athlete's foot would have taken care of it, but the most his father would do for his feet was soak them in a basin of warm water. James could remember the expression on his father's face as he lowered his feet into their bath, agony that dissolved into something like pleasure.

Beyond his feet, and what he called his thriftiness and James his stinginess, there was his father's refusal to leave this house, despite what must have been a decade-and-a-half campaign by James' mother to have them move. While James and Patricia had lived at home, their mother had argued that the house was too small, the school district substandard. After they'd left, she had insisted that the house was too much trouble to maintain, its location too remote. No matter her line of attack, his father's defense had been the same: This was their *home*, the emphasis he placed on the word substituting for hours of reasoning. From his mother, James knew that his father's early life had been rootless. Only son of a master sergeant in the Army, James' father and his mother had moved from New Jersey to what was then West Germany, from West Germany to Washington State, from Washington State to Kansas, from Kansas to Japan, from Japan to New York, where his grandfather had been killed in a car accident when James's father was thirteen. Afterwards, James's father and his mother had continued to wander, living with this relative or that until James's grandmother fell out with them and they went in search of a new place to stay. Even knowing the little he did about his father's early life — because the man refused to discuss it in any detail with him — James could appreciate what must have been a profound longing, a need, to have a home of his own. To insist on remaining in that spot at the expense of your marriage, however, went beyond need to pathology, a layman's diagnosis that appeared confirmed by the tunnel down which James was moving.

How far did this thing go? The air had grown noticeably cooler and damper. How deep did you have to dig for that to happen? The spoiled-milk-and mold-odour had grown strong enough to force its way through the fabric of his mask. Were the walls growing narrower? What would happen if he couldn't turn around in here? Dread pooled below his stomach, started to rise. *Relax. Relax.* He stopped, concentrated on breathing slowly and deeply. *You're fine. Relax.* The fear subsided.

He swept the cell phone up and around the stretch of tunnel he was standing in. Its blue-tinged glow showed only rock, nothing to account for the smell. Could it be some species of microorganism residing within the rock? Holding the cell phone in front of him, he continued forward.

Maybe fifteen feet ahead, the tunnel ended in darkness. Some kind of rock? Coal? Was there coal in these parts? It wasn't stone, he saw as he drew nearer. The light went out into it, as if he were looking into space, which, he realised, he was. His father's tunnel had broken into a cave.

At the end of the passage, James halted, shining the cell phone back and forth. The light revealed a low ceiling arcing over something shining — water, a subterranean lake whose margins lay beyond his light's reach. Directly before him and to his right, a rock shelf gave the lake a shore. James set a tentative foot onto it. The rock held. He brought his other foot down beside it and, when the shelf did not crack and spill him into the water, began moving along it.

This must be part of the aquifer that supplied the house's well. Had his father been trying to reach this? How had he known about it?

To his right, a white rectangle lay on the floor. Bags — large bags made of heavy white plastic, a dozen or more flattened and stacked neatly. There was green lettering on the top one: "Ammonium Nitrate", under the words a percentage, "34.40% N", under that a measurement, "Weight 500kg", and finally, under that, "Produced in Ukraine." He knelt to check the other bags. More of the same. Wasn't this what the Oklahoma City Bomber had used as the active ingredient for his home-made bomb? Was that what his father was doing, planning to blow up the house from below?

No, that was ridiculous. One thing was certain: Whatever his purpose, his father had been here. James stood and continued along the shore, keeping close to the wall. Who knew how deep that water was? There couldn't be anything living in it, could there? An image of an eyeless fish, its skin translucent, flashed across his mind's eye. *Thanks,* National Geographic. When he came upon his father, it was almost anticlimactic. Back braced against the wall, he was standing with his hands in his trouser pockets, the casual pose of a man passing the time. Were it not for the detail that his pants were rolled above the knee, presumably to avoid dirtying them on the white fertiliser heaped most of the way up his shins, he might have been acting the punchline to an elaborate and overlong joke: *Oh, hi, son. What brings you here?*

"Dad!"

His father's eyes were closed, his lips parted. He did not respond to James' shout. James drew near the edge of the pile of fertiliser and stretched his free hand to his father's chest. Through his shirt, his skin was distressingly soft. James waited. The rotten-milk-and-dirt smell was overwhelming; he could feel it filming the surface of his eyes. Under his fingertips, his father's chest stirred, barely enough to register. A thrill ran up James' arm. "Hang on, Daddy," he said. "I'm getting you out of this."

Dementia: That was the only answer that made any sense of ... this. No doubt, his father had been sliding into it for far longer than any of them had realised. His refusal to depart the house suddenly seemed less stubbornness and more anxiety. A surge of pity swept over James. Placing the cell phone on the floor with its screen angled towards his father, he stepped into the fertiliser. He slid his hands between his father's arms and sides, bringing them up and around his back, hugging his father to him. God — there was nothing to him. How long had he been standing here? "Hold on, Dad," he said, lifting and stepping back. His arms sank into his father's back. His father's chest flattened against his. He tilted towards James, but did not come loose from the fertiliser. Grunting, James strained upwards. Between his arms and his chest, his father's trunk shifted, as if his bones had grown, not just brittle, but spongy. The reek of bad milk and mold clouded the air around them. He leaned back, pulling as hard as he could. Sweat tickled the sides of his face.

There was a sound like wet cardboard tearing and his father was free. Overbalanced, James fell, pulling him on top of him. The base of his skull cracked on the stone shelf, detonating fireworks in front of his eyes. A host of sighs escaped his father. Taking him by the shoulders, James gently rolled him onto his back. "Hold on," he said as he struggled to his feet, swaying with dizziness. Pressing the back of his head with one hand, he retrieved the cell phone with the other. He turned the screen to his father.

He did not scream at what the light disclosed. For a long time, his brain simply refused to register the gaps below his father's knees, insisting that he must be confusing the fertiliser caked on his father's skin with blankness, absence. In the same way, his brain would not acknowledge the long rents in his father's neck, the top of his chest, as anything more than shadows. The pale fronds pushed out of the ends of his legs, the vents in his neck and chest, the front of his shirt, were hair, dust, cobwebs. Not until his father's eyelids raised and revealed a pair of orbs speckled with rust-colored patches did James make a sound, and that was a low moan, the utterance of an animal when it understands that the jaws of the trap have bitten deep into its leg and will not release it.

His father's mouth opened. The tip of his tongue appeared, trying to moisten his lips. His voice was a thin wheeze forced out. "Who?" he said.

James did not answer.

"Light," his father said, his eyelids lowering.

James did not move the cell phone.

With the weak, tentative motions of something very old or very sick, his father twisted from side to side. He was trying to flip over onto his stomach, which he could have accomplished more easily had he removed his hands from his pockets or if his legs had extended below the knees. Instead, he relied on his elbows and hips. It required several attempts. Once he had succeeded, he raised his head as if scenting the air and started a half-crawl towards the mound of fertiliser. His body scraped on the rock floor.

What sent James running from the cave and what had become of his father was seeing the things he was leaving in his wake and identifying them as pieces of his father, chunks of flesh that more resembled the pale meat of a large mushroom. That, and the white threads that rose out of the place where his father's legs had been immersed in the fertiliser, and that inclined towards him as he worked his way back towards it. When what had been his father shoved itself up onto the pile of fertiliser, it exhaled, the sound of something come home.

Cell phone in hand, James fled up the tunnel to the basement, roughing his hands, his head, on the rock, not caring, concerned only with escaping what he had witnessed. The knot of emotion in his chest was indescribable. He scaled the basement stairs three at a time, emerging into the kitchen and daylight that stung his eyes. He stumbled across the living room, out the front door to his car. As he was reversing up the driveway, he realised he was still wearing his improvised mask and breathing in the odour that had saturated it. He clawed it from his face, rolled down the window and flung it into the tall grass beside the driveway.

When he was almost home, James pulled to the side of the road, shifted the car into Park and screamed until the cords on his neck stood out, slamming his hands against the steering wheel until it cracked on one side. When he could scream no more, he picked his cell phone up from where he'd flung it on the passenger's seat and dialed his sister's number. Her answering machine picked up. Voice hoarse, he told her he had changed his mind: He wasn't going to visit Dad, after all.

For Fiona

↑

THE WHITE HANDS

By Lavie Tidhar

♦

Lavie Tidhar has been nominated for a BSFA, British Fantasy, Campbell, Sidewise, World Fantasy and Sturgeon Awards. He is the author of *Osama* and of the *Bookman Histories* trilogy, as well as numerous short stories and several novellas.

♦

CLITOCYBE RIVULOSA — FOOL'S FUNNEL

ON THE ISLAND OF CHANTERELLE, there are extensive mangrove swamps in which thrive the CLITOCYBE RIVULOSA, or FOOL'S FUNNEL mushroom.

It is a pleasant island, Chanterelle, located in the South Seas, and prior to the HUMAN-FUNGI ACCORD of 945 AF, it had remained unexplored. It is a mountainous island, thickly forested, with white, dazzling beaches scattered amidst the dark and cool lagoons in which the mangroves spread out, their endless roots feeding into the shallow water where a plethora of fish live and die.

Amidst the roots of the mangroves, there sprouts the Fool's Funnel, a white, flat thing, about a body's length across, lacking obvious beauty, but possessed of a certain porousness and longevity which were to prove of great use when discovered.

There are no native humans on the island, nor sentient fungi.

The first humans to arrive on Chanterelle did so in large canoes, dug out of the trunks of MIGDAL trees, with as many as fifty rowers to a boat. The human expansion of 1015-1230 AF led from the main human continent of ADAM, across the South Seas, colonising many of the islands. It was on Chanterelle that they discovered the *Clitocybe rivulosa*, but it was not until two centuries later — in or around 1354 AF — that the first FLOAT, or FUNG-RAFT, was built and launched.

There is a small island off Chanterelle, called PADDESTOEL, where humans have made their base — one stepping-stone of many in their great migration across the South Seas. Children born there played often in the shallows and the more adventurous built their own, small canoes to explore the nearby "mainland" of Chanterelle. There, no doubt while innocently playing, in the manner of human children, they discovered the properties that make the Fool's Funnel so interesting.

The children used the Fool's Funnels as stepping stones, discovering that the fungus could easily bear their weight. Later on, they began severing the fungal cord from the mangroves it fed on. To their no-doubt-obvious delight, they discovered that the maimed mushrooms continued to function, not only in carrying their weight, but now — free-floating — could also act as miniature boats.

Shortly after that discovery, the famous PADDESTOEL ISLAND RACE began, which has been celebrated annually ever since. Contestants attempt to circumnavigate the island using a freshly-harvested Fool's Funnel as their vehicle. No engines or paddles are allowed.

A passing marine enthusiast, the soon-to-be-famous GOBALAK YIGMAQ, traveled to Paddestoel in early 1351. On witnessing the children at play, he realised the immense importance of what they had discovered. Obtaining funds from the island-nation of ONDDO, Yigmaq began an ambitious ship-building program on Paddestoel — the first such we know of in human history.

What Yigmaq had discovered is that, by lashing several of the floating fungi together, he could create a marine vehicle to rival — and soon surpass — the fragile human canoes. Within only a few short years, the island-nation of Onddo had built — and armed — the world's first-ever fleet of fung-rafts. In equally short order, they had conquered nearly a quarter of the known world, in the process ending the short-lived Human-Fungi Accord, which had lasted just over four hundred years.

HYGROCYBE COCCINEA — SCARLET HOOD

This tale comes to us from pre-empire Onddo.

It tells of a rebel — a vigilante — called "Scarlet Hood".

He was born of a human-fungal love affair that shook the court of Onddo. His mother was a human, a princess of the court, by the name of 'Agatha'. His father was the notorious pirate captain, AGARICUS AUGUSTUS — THE PRINCE.

Scarlet Hood was thus born of royalty, yet out of both wedlock and polite society. He was delivered on the pirate holdout of PLAT UITZETTEN, a floating fungal island. A poem written of his birth said:

He was human-shaped, yet porous,
Deathly-pale but for his hooded head!
Scarlet like a pirate's wrath.
Scarlet like an executioner's mask.
Hygrocybe Coccinea!
To live is to want.

His father was captured shortly after by the AMANITA PHAL-LOIDES and executed horribly. His mother killed herself when she received the news. He grew up in poverty, reared by human and fungal pirates, and learned to wield a sword before he learned to write.

He returned to Onddo a dashing young captain. Men desired him. Women found him irresistible. He was welcomed for a time at the court, a curiosity, an aberration, yet a charming one. But soon, he fell afoul of the authorities. The Scarlet Hood saw first-hand the injustices of the court, the poverty of the people and he decided to fight. Before long, he was running wild on the island, robbing and killing, yet only the rich. It is said he distributed their wealth to the poor. He fomented revolution. For a time, he seemed likely to actually win, to bring down the dynastic monarchy on Onddo.

For a time.

ARMILLARIA MELLEA — HONEY FUNGUS

The HONEY FUNGUS, or ARMILLARIA MELLEA, is a non-sentient fungus originating on the island of ZBOHATLÍK, but cultivated extensively elsewhere. It is now a prohibited substance on all islands and land-masses. Cultivation, distribution, smuggling and use can result in heavy fines, imprisonment and the death sentence.

It is said the notorious vigilante, SCARLET HOOD, had become addicted to the honey fungus during his time on ONDDO. He became its main distributor on the island, importing the drug through his connection with the pirates of PLAT UITZETTEN.

The drug creates a feeling of well-being, as though "drowning in honey". It is highly addictive to both humans and sentient fungi. The Zbohatlík Cartel is said to control 80% of the market share and is the most powerful criminal organisation known to this editor.

MAMARANG AND SUMULPOT

A tale come to us from the fungi-continent of UYOGA.

Like most pure fungi narratives, its interpretation and retelling into human terms is uncertain. It has been transcribed as a poem, which goes:

> Mamarang, she fleshy good
> Spore-bearing age she come!
> Sumulpot, he handsome, handsome gilled (and/or) hooded.
> Thinker-poet, love (find attraction/spore-connect)
> Together, together.
> Mamarang and Sumulpot
> Go into dark forest.

The tale, then: Mamarang and Sumulpot fell in love (SPORU-LATED), but, being of different fungi-clans, ran away into the DARK FOREST, a mythical place in FUNGI MYTHOLOGY where rebel fungi traditionally run, something like our equivalent of a PIRATE ISLAND. There they had many adventures, until, at last, they reached a giant MIGDAL tree (though these only grow, to our knowledge, on the human continent of ADAM). There they grew onto the roots of the giant tree, producing many spores which grew into a new phylum, of which both humans and fungi, to this day, speak only in whispers ....

AGARICUS AUGUSTUS — THE PRINCE

Pirate lord of PLAT UITZETTEN, father of SCARLET HOOD, heir to the Uyogan dynasty of RUSULA. Died at the hands of DEATH CAPS by administration of POISON PIE.

HEBELOMA CRUSTULINIFORME — POISON PIE

Non-sentient fungi originating in a forest area on UYOGA, used primarily by the DEATH CAPS, who are immune to their effect. Cause slow and agonising death in both humans and fungi.

ONDDO, FALL OF

The Maritime Empire of ONDDO stretched, at its zenith, over an entire quarter of the world, including significant holdings in both the continents of ADAM and UYOGA, as well as numerous islands. It controlled the island of CHANTERELLE, where the rare FOOL'S FUNNEL fungi grows, and from where its fleet originated.

By the 1600s AF, the empire had reached its apex and, early in that century, first encountered the DEATH CAPS.

"They seemed to come from nowhere," the historian GLJIVA wrote in his *Rise And Fall of Onddo*. "They wore no armour, they had no human features, they used no rafts. Their superiority lay in control of the sky itself."

The Death Caps rode the semi-sentient LEPIOTA PROCERA, or PARASOL MUSHROOM. The Death Caps were parasites. When they landed on human lands, they attached themselves to human hosts, burrowing into their flesh and minds, controlling them and feeding on them, discarding each human like edible fruit and moving on to the next.

"The Reign of Terror lasted for centuries," wrote Gljiva. "They could not be stopped. They bombed the fung-rafts from on high and glided on the winds to pass any defense. They leeched secrets from our minds; they turned our sons and daughters into cattle. They were unremarkable to look at, ruthless in their actions, and sometimes excellent poets."

Gljiva records a rare visit to the court on Onddo:

"I came into the harbour. The sky was dark with Parasols. The fung-raft was crewed by docile humans. We came to land. The city, once great, sprawled before us. It was transformed.

"In place of stone walls, stout houses, now grew fungal houses, expanding and contracting softly, as though breathing. The roads were slimed with spores. I saw a man hanging from the rafters of a colonised Migdal tree, thousands of exotic fungal breeds leeching its life, growing on its roots and branches. The human, a male, was hanging motionless, fungus growing over his naked body, his fingertips, his penis, his nose.

Only his eyes were clear. He saw me and blinked. Our eyes met. He was aware. He knew what was happening to him. I turned my eyes.

"I came to the court. The palace rose before me. Enormous, bulbous, breathing, porous, it was hideous and beautiful at once. I came to the throne room. It was dark, warm, moist. I fell to my knees. I offered myself up to be used and discarded. I felt the way one feels in a place that is holy."

GLJIVA (NO SECOND NAME)

Minor human historian in the SECOND ONDDO EMPIRE period. HONEY FUNGUS addict. Disappeared on a voyage of discovery to the northern continent of FONG. Presumed dead.

LANGERMANIA GIGANTEA — GIANT PUFFBALLS

Non-sentient fungus native to the island of CENDAWAN. The Giant Puffball is an airborne spore the size of several humans. They are not to be confused with the LEPIOTA PROCERA, or PARASOL MUSHROOM.

It is a tradition — begun with the 372 AF FESTIVAL OF RISING — to hook one's self onto the stalk of the Giant Puffball during its sporal release period, which occurs annually. The passengers, usually younger children, are borne away to the skies with the rising spores. Some descend early; some are lost at sea; and some find themselves, by the luck of winds, arriving, like the fungus itself, on new lands, new worlds to explore.

A poem from the HUMAN-FUNGI ACCORD PERIOD describes the phenomenon:

Taking flight
Spores
Rise
Children

Rise
Wind
Calls
To wind.
Beyond, beyond
New horizons
Beckon.

TREMELLA MESENTERICA — YELLOW-BRAIN FUNGUS

Species of intelligent fungi from the northern continent of FONG. Destroyed DEATH CAP CIVILISATION/SECOND ONDDO EMPIRE by 2015 AF. Disappeared in 2113 AF, at the same time as the sinking of the island of KULAT.

FONG

Northern fungal continent. Became inaccessible in or around 2113 AF. It is now surrounded by a repellent force that prohibits both maritime and airborne passage.

LACCARIA LACCATA — DECEIVERS

Fungal-based cult, but popular amongst both humans and fungi. Most active during SECOND ONDDO EMPIRE, where it was practiced by rebel forces. Believed to have originated on the floating pirate island of PLAT UITZETTEN centuries before.

XYLARIA HYPOXYLON — CANDLE-SNUFF FUNGUS

A tiny mushroom rising out of the bark of a tree, a black sleeve followed by a white hand, reaching out, as though waving. It is the traditional symbol of the DECEIVERS CULT (See LACCARIA LACCATA) as well as the final mark of a sentence in the hieroglyphic-based alphabet of the YELLOW-BRAINS CIVILIZATION. A children's ditty, recorded by the historian GLJIVA on the island of CHANTER-ELLE, goes:

Look at the white hands
Waving to you from the shore.

Goodbye, goodbye, they're saying
We shall see you and yours no more.

↑

HIS SWEET TRUFFLE OF A GIRL

By Camille Alexa

✦

Camille Alexa is a dual Canadian /American author living near a Pacific Northwest volcano in an Edwardian home filled with fossils, broken shells, dried branches, and other very pretty dead things. Her poetry has been nominated for the Rhysling and the Dwarf Star awards, while her short fiction collection *Push of the Sky* earned a starred review in *Publishers Weekly* and was an Endeavour Award finalist. Complete bibliography and contact info at camillealexa.com.

✦

MOREL LOOKS AWAY FROM the thin membranous portal in the giant puffball's exterior and studies again the daguerreotype cradled in his hands. The image is of a young woman, a tomboy really, uncomfortable sitting still for the photographer in her starched white ruffles and careful curls. He prefers to remember her pale limbs as always in motion, playing tennis with him on the lawn of her father's estate, or gamboling with the newborn whippet puppies in the barn while sunlight glinting off stray bits of straw clinging to her white, white cap. Closing his eyes, he can practically hear her soft moans as he takes her in his arms, presses her against him, her aromatic oils and delicate juices filling his mouth as he latches it hungrily to hers.

Yes, Amanita is a sweet truffle of a girl. He misses her sorely.

A wail echoes down the rubbery passageways of the underwater vessel, bouncing dully off the puffball's spongy interior surfaces as it makes its way to him. Morel slides the beautiful Miss Virosa's likeness into his vest pocket and, ignoring the cramping of his empty stomach, makes his way from the chamber to see if he might ease his colleague's agony.

Mr. Shiitake is as Morel left him, lying hunched and miserable against an interior chamber wall. The man's hands are red and raw where he's been chewing on them. The soft yellow meat of the puffball is turning a necrotic brown where Mr. Shiitake has been gouging fistfuls of its rotting flesh, shoving them in his mouth. His lips beneath his thin black moustache are blue, almost as rubbery as the flesh of the organic submersible in which they drift along the sandy bottom of the sea.

Morel kneels by the man's side, rolls him into a more comfortable position and uses a less-than-clean handkerchief to dab at the profuse sweat dotting the man's face, past the unpleasant effluvia leaking from the corners of his colleague's ragged mouth. "Is that better, Mr. Shiitake?" he asks.

"Oh yes, Mr. Morel. Thank you." Shiitake's hands shake where he grips Morel's lapel. "Sorry to be such a bother."

For the hundredth time, Morel wishes Dr. Crimini had not already succumbed. It surprises him that a doctor wouldn't know better than to consume the decaying flesh of the modified *Calvatia gigantea*, no matter how hungry he became, particularly as he'd incorporated no small amount of the highly toxic *Clitocybe rivulosa* into its making. "For the gills, don't you know," the Doctor had been fond of telling Morel. "For the enormous gills."

But it was madness that made him do it, of course: the madness that comes of being trapped leagues under the sea in a deteriorating hollow gasterothecium the size of a house. No propulsion, no food, no light other than the eerie phosphorescence emitted by the foreign fruiting bodies grafted to the puffball's exterior, anchored by stringy stalk tethers to dimly illuminate the black ink of deep ocean several meters in every direction, orbiting their giant puffball with slow underwater undulations like glowing globular planets orbiting a drowned moon.

It's enough to drive any rational man to irrational measures.

↑

Morel's portal window is beginning to cloud. He presses his face against the once-clear membrane, peering into the stygian deep. Between the dangling, floating globes of luminescent phosphor fungi swim fantastical creatures. Once, Morel would have eagerly run to fetch his sketchbook. He would've tried, with quick light strokes of charcoal, to capture the weird unearthly flutterings of the animals' gills, the huge round marbles where eyes would once have been when such creatures had lived closer to the surface, closer to things Morel can barely remember, like fresh air and sunlight. The air he pulls into his lungs now is thousand-times-recycled stuff, run through the abundant added gills of the giant puffball — a biological invention of the late Dr. Crimini — and filtered back out for another breath. How many times, Morel wonders, has he drawn these same particles into his body, only to expel them again and to draw them back? He can taste the staleness of the air on his tongue like a solid thing. It makes his mind feel foggy, stuffed with spores and cotton.

And sunlight may as well be something he imagined ever having existed, rather than something which last struck the surface of his skin with such unappreciated familiarity just a few days earlier. Can it really only have been a week since he entered Mr. Virosa's study, announced his intention to the Captain of Industry regarding the man's only daughter? *I will make my fortune, Sir*, he had said. *I will make my fortune and then I will make her happy, forever.*

It is for her he put together this small expedition. Only a trial, it was to be, and yet it would have paved his way to a fortune with Her Majesty's Navy. A subsea vessel, cultivated and equipped on shore in record time and rolled into shallow inlets when fully grown. Shortlived, yes, but an endlessly renewable resource which, with practice, could be adapted to land use — even to air! Dr. Crimini had used Morel's sketches of flying puffballs — enormous hollow caps filled from beneath with heated gases and equipped with gondolas and ballast — to shape his experiments with fungi growth in his laboratories on the continent. Morel would get the credit, of course: He was the visioneer.

But the visioneer needed the engineer and the engineer needed the financier: Morel, Dr. Crimini, Mr. Shiitake. Together, the three of them would've revolutionised travel in all its modes, turned the course of history irrevocably and made their fortunes in the process. And in the middle of it all, her white dress belling from her pale perfect form like an angel's spreading wings, would be his darling, his beautiful Amanita Virosa.

The looming shape again catches the edge of Morel's vision and he in vain wipes at the membrane sheath separating him from all the waters of the world. Just beyond the perimeter lit by the illuminated sporocarps at the ends of their stalks, something large waits. Morel can feel it waiting, has felt it for the last couple of days, though day has less and less meaning as time passes in the depths. If only they hadn't rushed to test the project. If only they'd prepared for a possible failure of the propulsion system, that ingenious organic innovation of Dr. Crimini's design that equipped the giant puffball with gill-powered expulsion, whereby water was drawn and expelled from the fruiting body's lower chambers, much as air was drawn and expelled and redrawn within its upper. Installing backup locomotion methods had seemed too costly at the time, though Mr. Shiitake will almost certainly have regretted his veto of such planning a thousand times by now, a million; must've heaped upon himself all the recriminations Morel could've thought to heap, though Morel himself had been most responsible for pushing the undertaking forward more hastily than it should've been. He'd simply wanted Amanita with an impatient ardour borne more of passion than of sense. He sees that now.

A change in the shape of the watery darkness outside Morel's portal makes him gasp. In the eerie, blue-tinted light of the long-stemmed drifting globes, Morel catches a simultaneous glimpse of all the massive creature's elements at once: stumpy fanning tail and fins, not graceful at all; rough, warty hide, looking like some diseased, waterlogged, leathery thing destined never to touch the sun; bulging, round, milky globes of eyes, their cataract blindness the colour of curdled milk gone sour in the bottom of a petri dish ... and the teeth. Heavens help him, he'd not bargained for such teeth from a thing best classified as a mere fish. The teeth are needled, straight and sharp, each the length of Morel's forearm where they flash past his membrane window.

↑

Morel is jolted from sleep with that sensation of falling off a cliff that makes one's legs jerk like a puppet's on its strings. His head snaps up, hunger-fogged brain trying to focus, pressure-clogged ears and phosphor-numbed eyes trying to make sense of the momentarily unrecognisable rubbery chamber in which he lies curled. He pushes off the pliant fungal floor and stands on shaky legs. He can feel creases in his face where it rested in sleep against the daguerreotype of his lady fair, clutched in his hand.

After waking to the sensation of falling, Morel is left with the vague notion of motion, as though something large had bumped or rocked the submersible. He shakes it off, returning Amanita's likeness to his vest pocket and rubbing his head to clear it. When the second jolt comes, it is an abrupt, noiseless quake that leaves the entire vessel quivering, leaves the motion of impact reverberating up from the living floor into the meat of Morel's legs, the jelly of his kneecaps and the hollow of his empty stomach.

He runs to the portal, wipes uselessly with his sleeve, makes out the shapes of teeth as the enormous creature of the depths outside takes

37

another bite, drags at the vessel's lower basidiocarp propulsion chambers with horrible elastic slowness, until the flesh gives, the tear sending another shockwave through the subsea craft.

"No!" shouts Morel, face pressed to the cataracted portal. "Off with you! Be gone!" He pounds dully with both fists against the wall. The surface is considerably less elastic than it had been, not springing back into shape after he lets his hands drop to his sides. He stares with horror at the new dents in the wall of his underwater vessel, hard, crescent-moon depressions with delicate crenulations the exact size and shape of his knuckles.

The monster outside tears another bite off the thick exterior shell and the entire submersible lurches hard to Morel's left as it rebounds from the attack. A keening wail wafts from the passageway to the other upper chambers and Mr. Shiitake's voice, thin and high and frightened, calls: "Mr. Morel! Mr. Morel!"

Morel pounds through the empty gasterothecium passages, averting his face from the doorless study where Dr. Crimini lies, bloated and blue. Entering Shiitake's chamber, he makes his way quickly to the man's side. Ignoring the odours of vomit and other, even more unpleasant matter, Morel kneels, supports his investor's shoulders as another shudder shakes the giant puffball from without, another mouthful of the fruiting body's flesh torn free in the terrible jaws of the leviathan.

"What's happening?" asks the financier, his thin moustache practically disappearing between the swollen, runny mucous membranes of mouth and nose. With a glance at the chamber wall, Morel notes that at least the man has stopped eating the poisonous flesh of their vessel. He quickly suppresses a second thought following hard on the heels of the first: that it might be better if he hadn't.

"A bit of a hiccough, I'm afraid," says Morel, feeling inane. What of this trip from the moment their propulsion failed and they sank stonelike to the depths has not been a bit of a hiccough? It's his habit to soothe investors, his method to always present the possibilities, the upsides of a project rather than its pitfalls. Soon, the giant fish will eat its way into the soft fleshy interior of the puffball and then it will eat Morel and

Shiitake, though they won't notice, having already drowned. Might such a fate not at least be seen as better than starvation? No, that probably isn't the spin he wishes to put on the event of their impending doom.

Another reverberation shakes the submersible, like the ringing of an enormous silent gong embedded in its springy walls. The puffball lurches sharply again. Mr. Shiitake groans and buries his sweaty face in shaking hands. "Do something, Morel. For the love of Jupiter, *do something.*"

And it *is* Morel's job. He is the visioneer. The first day after the Doctor's demise — Crimini having been their pilot as well as their engineer, the only man alive with intimate knowledge of the unique vessel's workings, inside and out, from the minutest level to the grandest — Morel had worn himself to a frazzle tugging every lever-shaped protrusion in the engineer's room, twanging every elastic organic band and depressing every knobby outgrowth where they studded the wall like common toadstools on a rotten log ... but all to no avail. Dr. Crimini himself had not tried harder when the propulsions abruptly halted and they'd sunk lower, ever lower. The man had panicked far more quickly than Morel would've imagined he would, though the mettle of one's fellows is often tested only in crisis, too late, too late.

But if Morel could make the subsea puffball a reality, find a way to bring together all the circumstances which, when combined, allowed them to traverse the ocean in such an unlikely vessel, then by Jupiter, he should certainly be able to bring about the circumstances of their escape from a watery grave. Before, he'd simply mimicked the poor Doctor's final efforts at the helm, not understanding what else he could do, hoping in some small part of his characteristically optimistic brain that they'd find themselves buoyed to the surface despite their increasing heaviness as the craft's spongy tissues absorbed water and moved closer to the sporing phase, growing increasingly sluggish and dull. Once upon the surface of the water, reasoned Morel, they'd be spotted by a passing liner and towed ashore, and rescued, and reunited with their lady loves.

Through the fine fabric of his shirt, he feels in his vest pocket the firm edge of the daguerreotype, pressing into his chest near his heart.

Easing the shaking Shiitake to the floor, he says, "Do something. Yes. I will."

Striding down the passageway toward Dr. Crimini's room, Morel tries to assimilate the brief bits and bobs of the Doctor's endless explanations of spores, of gills, of splicing one species of sporocarp to another at the microscopic level. Words tumble through his brain, some with half-remembered explanations attached, others with just the sounds of the syllables rolling around inside his skull like pebbles in a tin cup: *basidium, gleba, statismospore, ballistospore*. He thinks he remembers that *Calvatia gigantea* can easily contain several trillion spores, and he thinks he remembers the Doctor telling him the modified lower *rivulosa* gill propulsion systems gave rise to a new, hybrid spore expulsion apparatus.

Morel had never paid much attention to such information; He'd expected a short trip from the shore after rolling into the ocean. He'd envisioned a few hours jetting through the shallow waters of the channel and then Mr. Virosa's hearty congratulations when he returned to the man's estate with news of his success. And finally, ultimately, he'd envisioned the slender pale limbs of Amanita entwined with his, silver in the moonlight as he kissed her sweetness. What he'd *not* envisioned was that their buoyant vessel would sink so rapidly to the depth it had, nor that it would be caught in swift channel currents and carried deep beneath the surface of the water quickly out to sea. His visions of success had had no room for the Doctor's panicky ingestion of his own creation's interior walls before the third day was out, nor the man's immediate and fatal seizure in the muscles of his heart. He'd not imagined the wails of his financier in the throes of a similar poisoning and he'd certainly never made any contingency plan for a hostile mammoth of the deep rending the rubbery flesh of his vessel bite by tooth-studded bite until the puffball's shell ruptured and saltwater flooded in to replace the air trapped in its upper chambers, the air Morel and Shiitake needed to remain alive.

Entering the engineering room rocks Morel back on his heels. Though the Doctor didn't suffer the physical indignities Mr. Shiitake endures, he has been dead now for days. The stench hits one like a solid thing, not improved by the already-stale air.

Morel swallows hard and steps over the prone figure on the floor.

The membrane portal in the engineering room is larger than the one Morel has been haunting at the rear of the vessel. This portal, too, is clouding, a milky blue tinting the corners, spreading inward as hoarfrost on a winter morning spreads over the windowpanes of Morel's modest flat above the bakery. But the centre is still clear enough to see the edge of a massive fin as it swivels by.

Swallowing hard again, Morel looks deliberately away from the window. He kneels by Crimini's bloated body and, with swift, silent apology, thrusts his hand into the Doctor's waistcoat pocket.

Doctor Crimini, in life, was inseparable from his tiny notebook. In death, it's not so very hard to tug the thing free from its owner. Morel retreats to an only minutely less unpleasant distance from the corpse. An enormous shadow swishes past the big engineering portal again, and again, Morel averts his eyes. The giant fish has stopped rending the thick exterior of the puffball, but clearly has not lost interest. Morel curses himself for his morose inactivity these past days, blaming despair and that bizarre combination of hopefulness for an unlikely rescue and hopelessness that he'd tried everything he could think of to take them to the water's surface.

The Doctor's little notebook is difficult to read by the dull phosphor light coming from everywhere and nowhere all at once. The tethered globes outside are brighter, but not by much. Page after page of the notebook is crammed with tiny arcane symbols, mathematical calculations, and botanical recipes and formulae. Everything is written in a cramped, undecipherable shorthand. Morel stares at the lettering, trying to make sense of the scrawls and scribbles, the dashes and dots and twisting helices of the Doctor's sums and diagrams.

As Morel stares, peering at each page he flips as though hard scrutiny can force the jumbled lines and ill-formed notes into some comprehensible whole, the sketches and patterns and lines do begin to impart meaning. Flipping, flipping the death-damp pages, he finds drawings less linear than the others, less formulaic and more descriptive.

The puffball shudders, rebounding from another bite torn from its smooth, round hide. Morel braces himself with a hand on the wall near the viewing portal, then quickly withdraws that hand when it sinks into the fungus's softening flesh. This time, the resounding bounce is upward, the recoil of tearing free sending them away from their attacker, toward the surface. Morel feels the upward motion in the pit of his stomach, a brief lurching rise, before they slowly drift down again.

Looking back at the notebook, something Morel scarcely dares recognise as hope quickens in his chest under the daguerreotype in its pocket. Though the shorthand labels on the Doctor's diagrams are no more readable than before, the lines sort themselves into recognisable drawings: *Here* is the gillwork filtration system which regulates the air of the vessel's upper chambers; *here* is the gillwork which manipulates water through the lower chambers, designed to be directed from the very room in which Morel stands and in which the notebook's author expired; and here, *here* is the spore-bearing tissue of the gigantic puffball, vastly modified, far larger and more powerful than anything before documented in Nature's fungal flora.

Modified, yes, and a ballistospore rather than the typical puffball statismospore. And enormous: as enormous compared to other fruiting bodies as the leviathan outside is compared to the common trout. But it still has trillions of spores waiting to discharge as they mature, waiting to be expelled from the hybrid craft in a process Morel never cared to study, thinking he'd be back safe on dry land by then, thinking it a mere biological process of interest only to Naturalists and other enthusiasts of the life cycle of *Agaricus bisporus* and its copious cousins.

Trillions of spores. Trillions upon trillions, waiting for dispersal. Waiting in the lower chambers of the vessel Morel helped become a reality, waiting to be shot off like the Great Imperial Emperor's fireworks under his chair.

Clutching Crimini's notebook, Morel pounds through the decaying passageways back to the chamber where Mr. Shiitake sits slumped against the wall. The man's breathing is shallow and rapid, his eyes closed. Sweat drenches his grimy cuffs and collar. Morel drops to the spongy floor. After a final glance at the diagram, he shoves the notebook into his hip pocket. He draws the daguerreotype from his vest and, after a kiss to its surface, uses its sharp corner to slice a deep diagonal cut into the chamber floor. The puffball shudders, but Morel knows the motion is the vessel's nonsentient rebound from the jaws of the giant fish outside, not a reaction to his violation of its skin.

When the slit is big enough, Morel grips the edges and tears with all his strength. Even a day ago, the skin of the vessel would've been too resilient for such an act, too tough and too strong. But now the compromised flesh tears easily in his hands, almost willingly peeling back to allow him access to its lower chambers more bell-shaped than spherical. By the soft phosphor light of the walls, Morel sees the water less than an arm's length from where he kneels, hears its lapping echoes against the now motionless gills. Carefully he slides the lovely Amanita's image back into his vest pocket and, casting a fleeting look at the insensible Shiitake, plunges headfirst into the ocean-filled lower chamber.

The cold is a shock. Morel surfaces and gulps air, ignoring the iced agony flooding his every pore. Knowing he must work fast, he plunges again and, with eyes wide open, grabs the nearest gill with its countless, corrugated basidia. He shakes the gills, pounds them, kicks the nearest basidium repeatedly, hoping beyond hope it will trigger a reaction, and another and another, until all the trillions of spores shoot off in a glorious eruption that will propel the hollow submersible all the way to the surface.

The last strength is leaching from Morel's limbs into freezing water. He kicks again, thinking he sees a quiver of the gills that is neither a reaction to the fish's nosing from outside the vessel, nor Morel's kicking from within. He gives a final kick with his angled foot, knowing it for his last if he wants enough strength to pull himself up out of the water into the chamber above. In response the basidium erupts, its gigantic spores shooting off in all directions, careening into other basidia with other spores, the chain reaction Morel hoped for making the puffball shudder and the water roil. Even as Morel hoists himself up through the jagged hole with shaking arms, he feels the puffball rise. He anticipates the twisting in his stomach that will come from rapid ascent, senses the first tiny stirrings in his blood he imagines are its gases boiling.

He staggers to Shiitake's side, grips him under the arms and hoists him to his feet. The man's skin burns where Morel's icy fingers clamp to it, shimmers where coated with sweat and tears and muscarine mucous. With the release of its spores, the puffball is collapsing. Small rends appear in the walls as Morel watches, the ocean trickling, then gushing through the widening rifts. But they are moving upward: Morel feels it in his lurching guts, imagines the surprised monster below staring blindly after the rapidly ascending undercarriage of the departing vessel, thousands of spores swirling in the agitated waters of its wake.

When the water in their chamber is chest-level, Shiitake stirs from his senseless state. "Mr. Morel?" he says, hands flapping feebly at the rising water.

"Never fear, Mr. Shiitake," says Morel, optimism flooding him like ecstatic delirium. "Merely a minor hiccough. It'll all be better soon, when we reach the surface. Fresh air will do you good."

Shiitake nods gratefully before his eyes flutter shut again and his chin slumps to his chest. Morel lifts the unconscious man's head to keep it from the water, paddling with his other arm as their feet leave the chamber floor. The agony coursing through his veins and innards has been replaced with a buoyant lightheadedness, not at all unpleasant after the days of gloom and despair. When the rapidly filling chamber takes them close to the ceiling, Morel uses the arm not keeping Shiitake afloat to punch through the soft material of the collapsing vessel. He imagines the giant puffball deflating like an enormous bladder emptying of air. When his fist breaks through, quickly and more easily even than he'd hoped it might, water and their swift upward momentum does the rest, tearing the puffball asunder like the skin sloughing from an overripe melon, so it splits open, releasing its travelers inside as though they, too, number among its seemingly infinite spores.

The water nearest the sunlight is a beautiful turquoise azure, reminding Morel of his Amanita's fine flashing eyes. They are so close to the surface he can even see the sun: a brilliant ball of light-green fire shimmering in the few hands-breadths between Morel and the flat top of the ocean. Lugging the inert Shiitake with him, Morel beats at the water, beats and beats and kicks. As the fiery green ball grows dimmer, Morel grows stiller. Beneath him, the white spheroid remnant of the puffball, compromised beyond buoyancy, beyond redemption, sinks into darkness. All around, the water shimmers with the trillions of spores. Trillions and trillions, glinting in the so-close sunshine like the myriad fishes which appear to feast on the sudden bounty. Light glints off the bright silver schools of fish, and off the multitudinous spores, and off the daguerreotype Morel fumbles with numb fingers from his vest pocket as he sinks, gripping the motionless Shiitake with his other arm, gazing into the rapidly dimming face of his beautiful Amanita.

↑

LAST BLOOM ON THE SAGE

By Andrew Penn Romine

✦

Andrew Penn Romine lives in Los Angeles where he works in the visual effects and animation industry. A graduate of the 2010 Clarion West workshop, his fiction has appeared in *Lightspeed Magazine* and *Crossed Genres* as well as in the anthologies *Broken Time Blues: Fantastic Tales in the Roaring 20s* and *Rigor Amortis*. He's also contributed articles to *Lightspeed Magazine* and *Fantasy Magazine* and blogs at Inkpunks and at Functional Nerds (as the Booze Nerd). You can also find him online at andrewpennromine.com

✦

DUKE WINCHESTER PEERED THROUGH the sight of his rifle to confirm what his ears had already told him — a plume of luminescent smoke snaked its way through the San Padrós Pass, tangling on the spiky fungal growths that enveloped the pines. A long, lonely whistle echoed off the toadstool-dotted hills of the Colorado backcountry.

The L&W 445 out of Zohar City roared out of the tunnel, spot on schedule. It had taken Duke two bottles of Black Goat Whiskey and a quarter-brick of Aztec Manna to bribe a Lemuria & Western Railroad butch and obtain the timetable. Expensive, yes, but as the buzz of the great iron beast's aetheric carriages reached his eardrums, Duke congratulated himself on a shrewd bargain.

Legs McGraw, his partner, squirmed next to him, tentacles squidging trails of slime across the lichen carpet of their hilltop lookout. The pungent tang of rotting mushrooms came not from the landscape, but from Legs. He was upset, Duke knew; the beyonder's emotions wafted on the breeze in an odiferous equivalent of a scowl.

"What's spookin' you, friend?"

L&W had kidnapped the best mind in mycotic science, so Duke expected a heap of trouble. According to his man, the L&W guards were well-armed with hellfire shot and rifles that spat green lightning like a Texas space-time twister. The professors from Zohar City were paying Duke well, but he still had a few doubts about fooling with all that scientifical business. The West had surely changed since he'd come up in shortpants.

Professor Karlowe. Legs' mind-voice tickled Duke's thoughts, something between hay and grass: there one moment but not quite there the next. Legs had lived at least one hundred of Duke's lifetimes in the sunken cities of the South Pacific, and so possessed a preternatural sturdiness in most things. The beyonder had been twitchy all the way from Zohar City, though, and that worried Duke.

What if the Professor planned his own kidnapping?

Duke sighted the metal-clad car through the divination crystal in his rifle. The thing looked more akin to some sea-going vessel than a train car, with its rounded hull and discharge fins. The image was blurry, revealing a chromatic smear of wardings and counterspells. The eyepiece had cost Duke a fortune in gold dust, but it couldn't disprove what he already felt in his gut: Legs was right.

"Well that changes the plan a mite." Duke searched the swirling folds of shadow and slime of his friend's face, careful not to look into his compound eyes. Legs couldn't help it if his gaze drove Duke mad for an hour or two.

Karlowe has a devious mind. Plus, they've got Van Schjin's eldritch weave in that hull. I can't touch it.

Legs' hesitation was a country for which Duke had no reckoning.

"So, you worry about the gunmen, then. I'll get that car open. There's gotta be a safety switch in the locomotive. You draw their fire and I'll converse with the engineer about springing the lock." Duke patted the handles of his Colt Hexmakers to show Legs what sort of talking he figured to do.

It was easy banter, but the beyonder still roiled with his hidden thoughts, tendrils of shadow flickering at the edges of Duke's vision. His polecat stench sharpened into something like vinegar before mellowing to burnt, buttered corn.

Perhaps we shouldn't have taken this job.

"Don't be such a croaker, Legs," Duke chuckled. "How long we been doin' this now?" He strapped his rifle loosely across his saddlebags, trying not to count the years. His horse, Shiloh, whickered softly, flames dancing from his hooves, just as eager to get on with the affair as Duke.

Since Adam got his apple, Legs replied with the old refrain.

"Then get yer wiggle on, McGraw. We got us a train to rob."

The air thickened with the reek of the slaughterhouse as Legs rose up on a column of sea slime. Duke watched his partner race down the hillside, trying to shake the feeling there was something else the beyonder wasn't telling him.

↑

Maribel de Miedo watched the bleak shadows of the Colorado mold country through the slits of the Van Schijn car, suppressing another coughing fit. The ache in her lungs receded with a nip from her silver flask. *Feeding the worms.*

The city doctors called it "Pacific Pneumonia", though most folks knew it as "fog-lung" for the crawling miasmas that swirled out of the ocean and blanketed coastal cities for days at a time in impenetrable olive shrouds. Breathing that air sometimes caused little black worms to grow in your lungs. They ate the rest of your insides, eventually. Maribel's flask of tequila and laudanum helped with the slow dying.

She could ill-afford to have another episode now. The train was coming out of the hills into a wide valley scattered with anchorite death-caps, just as night was falling. The tall, scraggly toadstools made good cover — and the best place for a bushwack. She felt helpless, trapped in the armoured car with no room to wiggle.

Maribel wasn't completely alone, though. The Van Schijn car stank of *zombi* — four trigger-happy Deadbeats in ill-fitting L&W uniforms sat cradling their aetheric long-rifles. Overconfident but loyal to the railroad, they were convinced in their fungus-colonised brains that their scientifical armaments and chitin-reinforced flesh would substitute for real experience in a firefight. Maribel knew better.

She didn't like their passenger much, either.

But if they delivered Professor Karlowe safely to Fort Derleth, all would be well. The *zombis* would likely burn their pay on Aztec Manna habits, but, in addition to a very large bonus, Maribel planned to collect on L&W's promise of a cure for her fog-lung.

"Hey, Calico, you're looking peaked."

Marsh, the *zombi* sergeant, lurched over and laid a gentle hand on her shoulder. He wasn't a half-bad shot, the only one of the Deadbeats really worth his pay, but he was terrible in the sack.

"Stop calling me that," she snapped, shrugging him off — and more quietly, "Not here."

"Hey, *Señora de Miedo*, don't take me on so," he grinned, his voice thick as wet leaves in a gutter.

"Night's falling and we're in hard country, Marsh. Keep your eyes skinned." She glared into his fuzzy, spore-soft eyeballs, daring him to get riled at her joke. She wished she hadn't fucked him back in Zohar City.

Marsh just grinned and shrugged his shoulders until the bones poked up from his uniform, flaking spores and bits of flesh. So, Maribel started giving orders to him and a pair of *zombis*.

"Watch the north side of the car. Shoot anything that gets close. I'll take the south port-holes."

Maribel pointed at the fourth *zombi*, the one with eyes leached white by colonisation. "You look after the Professor. Make sure everything stays put if there's a fracas."

The *zombi* gulped, glancing at their cargo. Covered with a heavy velvet drape stitched with orichalcum runes, Professor Karlowe was secured against the jostling of the train by cords of India rubber. Under that drape, in a thick glass jar the size of a barrel, Karlowe's brain dozed, throbbing with mycotic pustules and psychic fruiting bodies. It was all that remained of him after his experiments, the kernel of a grasping and fiendish mind. As long as the warding cloth stayed in place, the Professor would remain asleep.

And if he didn't, well, then, Maribel reckoned fog-lung would be the least of her worries.

↑

Duke rode down from the hills and parallel to the tracks a good quarter-mile distance from the train, eyeing the sparks that flew from the carriage beneath the locomotive. All that fuss blazed down the length of the train: locomotive, two crew cars, then the Van Schijnn car, 12 more freight cars and a caboose. There were no lights on the train besides the electric sparks. *Zombis* didn't need much light, but something about the empty windows gave Duke pause. It was as if the train was driving itself.

Maybe it was. Duke had seen a lot of strange things working for the professors in Zohar City. "Inventors of the Age," the papers called them, as they adapted beyonder ways to cope with the spore-changed West. Rivals like L&W, desperate to profit in this new world, weren't above stealing secrets. With the competition, though, a new era was dawning that Duke barely recognised. He couldn't keep up, not even on a nightmare steed.

Legs had ridden his plasm north — out of sight — intending to double back on the L&W 445 as soon as the last car had passed. It was a cloudy night, at least, and there'd be no moon to betray their ambush until at least midnight. Duke hoped the clouds would stick around until well past the Witching Hour. The full moon might give Legs a brisk up, but Duke would rather skedaddle in the friendly dark once they'd grabbed Karlowe. He'd stopped thinking about this as a rescue, too. If Legs was right and the Professor had arranged his escape, then he was certain to raise some hell to keep from going back.

Duke patted the scales of Shiloh's neck and the nightmare picked up speed on the flat ground, angling towards the train. Shiloh's fiery hooves raised a cloud and Duke pulled his charmed bandanna tight against the possibility of infectious puffballs.

As he neared the train, a tongue of fire lanced from the reinforced window of a crew car behind the locomotive.

Saints' Balls! That was close!

Another blast of sulfurous brimstone hurtled past and the L&W bellowed like a sea-leviathan, a challenge to Duke and a warning to the rest of them that rode the train. His blood surged through him like molten copper. Relic or not, Duke knew he was born to rob trains. Beneath the bandana, he smiled as an inky patch of dark glimmered near the caboose.

"All right, Legs," he said, knowing the beyonder would hear his thoughts even at this distance, "let her rip!"

↑

Maribel saw the flashes of hellfire arc out from the front of the train across the desolate fungal plain. The worms in her lungs churned to the deep call of the locomotive's whistle. Bushwhacked, then. Nothing less than she'd expected.

She opened the view-slit. The glare from the carriage's discharge and the damned clouds made a murk of the Colorado night. But there, just past a stand of anchorite toadstool, she saw him — a lone rider, an inkblot against the velvet hills. Dim flames shot from his horse's hooves, the tell-tale sign of a nightmare. Maribel's breath caught. Whoever was aiming to bushwhack the L&W 445 Express was no ordinary rip. Nightmares were mighty difficult to break; most who tried got eaten. Maribel knew only one to have done it and she hoped to hell it wasn't him out there now.

Marsh nudged her in the kidneys with the butt of his rifle.

"Road agents?" The earthy stink of his mold-ridden flesh filled her nostrils and desire shuddered through her. Marsh was an unwelcome distraction, idiot or no. But Maribel hadn't survived the Awakened West by giving in every time any old fungus-veined chucklehead leered at her sidewise.

"A lone rider. I expect he's aiming to draw our attention elswh—"

There was a sound like waves crashing over the train and even the Van Schijn car rocked from the impact.

"Shit and brimstone!" Maribel cursed as the air fouled with the stink of polecat.

"Close the fucking portholes!" she screamed at Marsh and the rest of the Deadbeats. Dread throbbed through her; the very air reverberated with an abyssal despair. Marsh felt it, too.

"A beyonder!"

Maribel nodded, steeling herself against the alien will that probed the armoured car. Thank the Goddess for Van Schijn's weave, or they'd all be gibbering corpse-suckers already. Beyonders didn't usually truck much with road agents, but there were a few powerful deuces that took to the outlaw life. Maribel thumbed through the possibilities like a poker hand. *The Taos Lightning? Shoggoth Jr.? Legs McGraw? Oh, shit, not Legs.* He was supposed to be up in Wichita.

She shoved Marsh out of the way and headed for the ladder that led up to the car's cupola. Maribel pointed to the heavy door at the fore of the car, all levers and knobs like some grotesque bank vault.

"Watch that door. Don't open it for nobody 'less I tell you to."

Marsh nodded, gripping his rifle until the green veins in his hands turned white. Maribel climbed the ladder into the cupola platform. There was a Van Schijn Gatling there. Its eldritch bullets could chew up anything you aimed it at, even a beyonder.

She heard muffled yelling and thunderbolt discharges outside. The shouts quickly turned to screams. Maribel ignored the thumping rain of *zombi* parts against the cupola and jerked open the porthole.

Deepest night engulfed the car behind her, with a swirl of stars like the rainbow at the bottom of a glass of laudanum. Her eyes ached from the sight and the slaughterhouse stink of the beyonder crept into the cupola, soothed her mind, willing her surrender before it tore her apart.

Maribel jammed the barrel of the Van Schijn gun through its special hatch. She shut her eyes against the unearthly vertigo.

Maribel?

The alien mind brushed against her own and as quickly recoiled — but she'd already squeezed the trigger.

"*Madre de noche,*" she shouted. *Legs!*

She swung the gun wide and green fire stuttered behind her eyelids, the air ripping like wet carpet. A thousand vultures clawed at her brain and the stink of the beyonder vanished. Maribel wondered if she'd scored a hit.

Another violent jolt shook the car. The swivel-mounted gun tore free from her hands and flung her from the cupola. She tumbled into one of the Deadbeats and the pair of them crashed onto the velvet-draped jar. The floor quaked beneath her and she rolled. Her heel crunched something and the scent of old things, musty and virulent, filled her nostrils, smothering her until the world was dark.

✦

The train had been easier to stop than Duke had reckoned. The engineer was not much more than a pile of human-shaped mold, grown fast to the boiler with thick, ropy tendrils blossoming with purple buds. It had only quivered silently when Duke blasted it out of space-time.

Legs had taken care of the rest of the *zombi* guards. Now Duke banged the underside of the Van Schijn car with the butt of his pistol. It made for a good show. He'd also wedged a single stick of implosive dynamite between two stanchions on the wheel carriage and another against the armoured door. Not enough to destroy the car, but it would scare the hell out of whoever was inside.

What are you doing?

"Just gonna get 'em good and streaky," he thought back to Legs. There was a smell of rotten eggs and compost as Legs approached.

I see you stopped the train. Nice job. The beyonder had a hitch in his wiggle and his voice was faint.

"And I see you got shot. Nice job."

Gatling gun with Van Schijn cartridges. Guess who?

"Someone we know?"

Maribel. She's guarding Karlowe.

"Aw, shit." Duke avoided thinking about Maribel de Miedo every chance he got. It only led to whiskey and long one-sided conversations with Shiloh.

"Isn't 'Bel supposed to be in Wichita?"

Legs turned away and didn't answer for several moments.

Remember that fandango down in Mexico, Duke?

The first symptoms of her fog-lung had just come on and 'Bel and Duke had fought like Kilkenney cats the whole time. Their last evening started with a dance, but it ended in a drunken shootout where nothing died but their mutual affection. Maybe he shouldn't have asked her to wear that Spanish dress. Still, something in Legs' tone gnawed at him.

"Wait. You ... and 'Bel?"

Yes. You left her. I was trying to treat her infection.

"I bet you were," Duke muttered, feeling around and finding the old wound still raw. "And I didn't leave her. I just got pretty roostered up on all that *cerveza*."

After Maribel told him she was dying, Duke had sequestered himself in a cantina for three days. The world was Awakening, sure, but why it had to get so personal and take Maribel from him, he didn't understand. After Mexico, he just kept going through the motions, just until he could scrape enough together for a little place in one of the sealed cities back east. But he'd started working for the Professors and somehow just never quit.

He climbed out from under the bulbous panels of the Van Schijn car, trailing the fuse. He glared at Legs as he squirmed in the darkness, a deeper nightmare against the horrors of the Awakened prairie. Duke admitted to himself why he hadn't gone back east. He didn't want to leave Legs behind.

I suspected she might be on this train, Legs admitted, expelling a musk of dirt and iron. *I saw her with an L&W zombi at the Cosmic Eye Saloon in Zohar City.*

"You should've told me, Legs."

I didn't know for sure.

"Well, what the hell are we going to do now?" Duke replied, wiping dust and gravel from his backside. Karlowe, they wanted dead or alive, but Maribel? Maribel was always a complication.

Karlowe will fight us, too. I can feel his mind straining to escape.

"I could always blow the whole damn Van Schijn car, then."

Not with Maribel inside.

Duke rubbed his face in his hands and sighed.

"Then we'll just have to ask her to come out."

↑

Maribel woke to Marsh's toothy grin, a blur of stupid and spite.

"You got him, Calico," he cackled.

She staggered to her feet, relieved to see the drape was still safely secured around Karlowe. The *zombi* she'd fallen into wasn't so lucky. His face was stoved in, a mess of puffballs and oily slime. The lamps flickered like dying stars; the glyphs on Karlowe's drape glimmered. The Van Schijn car was still.

"The road agents."

Marsh frowned. "Yup. What next?"

Maribel was streaked, the fluid darkness of the beyonder still swirling in her thoughts. Would she have shot if she'd known it was Legs? The pain of memory swelled until it became indistinguishable from the ache in her lungs. The worms churned and a fit of coughing gripped her. She turned away from Marsh so the *zombi* wouldn't see the blood dripping from her shaking hands.

Stars burst in her eyes and Maribel thought about Mexico — and Legs. And Duke. Shit. Duke was out there, too.

"All we got to do is wait 'em out," she muttered, half to herself. "L&W's mediums have to know already we've stopped. They'll send someone."

Maribel sat down on one of the velvet-cushioned benches and pulled a flask from her boot. A little tequila, a little laudanum. The pain in her chest dulled to an ache.

"Wait?" Marsh gave her a doubtful look and made a show of checking the cords that kept the drape secured to the floor. Three sharp clangs sounded from the door.

"Evenin', folks," a muffled voice called from the other side. "Reckon I could come in and set a spell?"

Maribel slid the flask back into her boot. It was Duke, all right.

"Best back away from the door, Duke," she replied. "It's wired."

"Don't think so, 'Bel," Duke called. "No demons left in your boiler."

He was right, the lamps were almost out and the battery wouldn't last much longer.

"You try to come through that door, Duke, we got enough lead and lightning to cut all of you down," she warned, but her heart wasn't in the threat.

"Sounds like a standoff, then. It's just the two of us, 'Bel. Come on out and dance with me."

"We all know how that ended last time," she replied, trying to hide the smile that tugged at her lips.

"Dance with Legs, then. You clipped him mighty good, but I bet he forgives you. Hell, I'll even forgive you if you just come on out."

Francis "Duke" Winchester and Legs McGraw. Notorious bounty hunters, almost as expensive as she was. Had they been any other road agents she'd have ordered the Deadbeats out in a full charge, standoff or no. But of course it was old friends that came hunting Karlowe. Crack shots, hard to kill, even if she'd wanted to. And both pretty damn good for a roll in the hay.

"I forgive you, too, Duke," she called.

Marsh leveled his rifle at her. "Sorry to interrupt the love affair, Calico, but there's no way we're opening that door."

Maribel stared down the barrel of Marsh's gun as the arc lamps failed. Marsh stared back. The growths in his eyes and the rest of his body shone with a soft blue luminescence. Was that to be her fate, as well? Would Karlowe's cure for the worms in her lungs turn her into a fungus-ridden ghost?

She shook her head. "We gotta make a deal, Marsh. He'd rather kill Karlowe than wait for the L&W troops to get here."

"You're a fool and he's a liar. He'll shoot you as soon as you open that door."

Maribel looked past the barrel of the long rifle at the door. It wasn't that far away, but neither was Marsh.

"Hell, *I'll* shoot you if you try," Marsh said.

L&W wouldn't take betrayal lightly, but they damn sure wouldn't be offering up any sort of cure after this fiasco. Her lungs itched and she knew the cough would return soon. She was almost out of tequila.

The remaining two Deadbeats brandished their rifles, taking aim at Maribel, their splotchy, rotting faces hard with fear. They were too stupid to know their rifles were next to useless in the confines of the warded car.

Maribel dropped and drew the Bowie from her boot. A quick slash laid Marsh's shins open. The *zombi* howled, spraying lightning into the sidewall. The car seemed for a moment like one of Ft. Derleth's laboratories; arcs of electricity like sizzling blue worms crawled across the warded stanchions.

She threw her shoulder against Marsh's wounded legs and sent him toppling to the floor. Ducking his rifle, she blasted the other two *zombis* with brimstone from her Hellfire gun. They collapsed, shrieking, chest cavities seared out by the burning coals.

She knelt on Marsh, pressing her knife under the *zombi*'s chin.

"L&W will kill you for this!" he snarled.

"Sorry, Marsh. I'm already dead." She leaned in on the knife until she heard the crunch of the blade against his neck bone. Severing the spinal cord wasn't the only way to stop a *zombi*, but it was the quickest. She sat back on her haunches, wiping the blade on his pants, leaving trails of sluggish blood and oily fungal ichor.

The Van Schijn car was dark again except for the eerie, green glow of the sigils on Karlowe's orichalcum drape. The reek of burning *zombi* filled her lungs and brought on another coughing spell. The worms churned in displeasure; their gnawing seared out all other thought.

She didn't notice the *zombi* with the smashed face rising up behind her until he was already at Karlowe's drape. Black worms crawled from her mouth as she turned in time to see him sawing furiously with his knife at the cords of India rubber. He tugged the warding cloth aside.

A deep voice boomed in her mind.

I WILL NOT GO BACK!

✦

Duke waited before the armoured door, sheltered in the vestibule from the sour wind that blew fitfully off the plain. Green clouds, swollen with spores, rolled in from the mountaintops. More rain. There never used to be so much out here. Legs pulsed silently in the dark. The gunfire had stopped five minutes ago, though the air still smelled burnt. In the quiet, a deep foreboding came over Duke.

Something's wrong.

Duke checked the dynamite wedged in the door and twisted the fuse to a detonator.

"Of course there is. It's Maribel."

She still loved you, even then.

Duke glared at Legs. Lightning flashed overhead.

"We're out of time, Maribel. You comin' or not?"

Clangs resounded from the other side of the armoured door and it swung open, belching smoke and the stink of prairie lightning. The dynamite, dislodged, rolled to a stop at a pair of worn black boots tooled with Mayan glyphs.

Maribel de Miedo emerged from the charred dimness of the Van Schijn car, painted black with *zombi* guts. Her sunken eyes were lambent with cloud light and shone with a lunatic glare. The entity that peered out of those baleful eyes was not Maribel.

Duke tried to shout a warning to his partner, but the beyonder, already sensing danger, staggered up on tendrils of slime. Dark things flew like ravens from his inkblot form, only to vanish in puffs of smoke as they reached the possessed Maribel.

I HAVE IMPROVED MY MIND PAST EVEN YOUR ABILITIES, BEYONDER.

Duke drew his Hexmakers and pointed them at his old beloved.

"I don't want to shoot you, 'Bel!"

SHOOT. YOU CANNOT HURT ME, Karlowe gloated, flexing his power.

Duke's fingers squeezed the triggers of their own accord, but the cursed bullets swirled in the air like brilliant horseflies before Maribel's outstretched hands. They exploded into tiny motes, each burst punctuating Karlowe's mind-words.

I WILL NOT GO BACK TO THEIR PRISON IN ZOHAR CITY.

The pronouncement resounded in Duke's skull, driving him to his knees and the revolvers from his hands. The beyonder swooped, battering Maribel/Karlowe with his own psychical energies. Even so, several slugs of brimstone burned into Legs' roiling mass. As he tumbled to the floor,

Maribel collapsed, too, worms dripping from her nose. Karlowe's black mind searched for more fertile soil than the sickly fog-lunger.

Darkness rippled across Duke's mind and he lost sight of Legs. In the last light of consciousness, he saw a dim, rosy pulsing from inside the Van Schijn car. Karlowe's brain sloshed in its jar of oil as Legs McGraw wrestled with Karlowe's loosed psychic force. If the Professor got a hold of the beyonder's mind, they were all doomed.

The detonator lay a mere foot from where his partner struggled. Duke dragged himself along the floor of the vestibule, fingernails cracking as they bit into the rough wood. His fingers closed around the plunger. Maribel, still half-mad with the sinister influence of Karlowe's brain, scooped the dynamite up before Duke could reach it.

"'Bel!"

The unearthly glow faded from her eyes, replaced by a different sort of light. Pain. The half-grin, even with the worms on her lips, was all Maribel, though.

"Dance with me?" she wheezed.

"Thought you'd never ask," Duke laughed.

Maribel hurled the dynamite into the Van Schijn car and tumbled off the vestibule.

Duke pushed the lever. The detonator clicked and the red, throbbing glow inside the car winked out of existence like a distant light at sea.

Reality twirled away with a dull roar and a spray of colours like sunset and drowning. Legs screamed and someone let the stars down from the sky.

↑

The galaxies slowed their manic race and Duke focused on just a single swirl of gaseous light below him. It felt nice to float there and watch it unfold. But the light grew brighter and the galaxy-dream receded. Maribel leaned in close, her face a rising moon.

"You awake?"

Duke felt a relief as vast as the limitless universe. It was damn good to be alive, even if the world made no sense.

He sat up, savouring each bruise and creak of his bones. They lay in the fungal scrub, a few feet from where the dynamite had blown the car off the track at a right angle. The Van Schijn car was crushed square in the middle, the centre compressed to a knot no larger than a fist. The green clouds had moved on and pure, clean starlight lit the toadstool-studded plain. Shiloh stood nearby, whickering softly.

"Nothing of Karlowe left to collect on the reward," Maribel said.

"Hey, we got you," Duke replied.

Legs lay facedown beside Duke, smelling of dead prairie dogs and burning hair. But his tentacles twitched and roiled as they always did. A man who had his friends would be all right. Duke carefully patted the ground near his partner.

"Rise and shine, McGraw. Got some riding to do."

Duke stood up, recovering his pistols. Maribel rose, wiping dead worms from her chin. Beyond the mountains, the rim of the sky paled with the first blush of morning.

"What are we going to do with you, 'Bel?"

"A three-way split?" she suggested.

She earned it, Legs mumbled, waking. *Can't leave her here for the L&W big bugs to find.*

"They'll come looking, though, that's for sure," Duke said.

Mad as spinal wasps, Legs agreed with a delicate whiff of tainted water and sickroom.

↑

While her boys debated, Maribel de Miedo stroked Shiloh's flank. Duke's professors back in Zohar City might have a cure for her, but she doubted it. Still, she reckoned she had a little time left; she might raise some hell with Duke and Legs again. The nightmare snorted with pleasure.

"Ready, girl?" she whispered to Shiloh. Duke Winchester wasn't the only one who knew how to ride her. She was a good quarter mile away before the outlaw and the beyonder noticed she was gone. She smiled as their bewildered shouts echoed across the plain. Maybe she'd even let them catch up.

Maribel rode out under the fading starlight and south to Zohar City, dreaming of distant stars.

↑

THE PILGRIMS OF PARTHEN

By Kristopher Reisz

✦

Kris Reisz lives in Alabama. Along with a handful of short stories, he's published two novels. One, *Unleashed*, is about werewolves who worship a fungal god or rot and ruin.

✦

I KNEW MACY WAS leaving, even though she wouldn't say it. She hadn't grown up here, just come up for school then stayed for me. But she'd graduated a year ago and still couldn't find a graphic design job. She had to borrow money from her mom to mail resumes to Boston and New York. Somebody would snap her up soon; her ideas and art were too striking to ignore.

When she headed somewhere new, she wouldn't want me tagging along. Why should she? I hadn't had steady work since the Cherokee Bluff subdivision had gone bankrupt. At first, she had been supportive, but, as summer wore on, she didn't talk much and never smiled. Her mind seemed a million miles away, already in Boston or New York. She'd stay up late, watching TV, so she didn't have to come to bed until I'd already fallen asleep.

Once, I built up the courage to ask her straight-out if she was leaving. Macy couldn't answer. She said, "I just want what's best for both of us. I'll always care for you, Austin. You know that."

I knew it. But I also knew she had bigger dreams than I could offer her. Macy was leaving and I couldn't blame her.

In wilting August, I bumped into Everest, a 400-pound drywall man who'd worked on Cherokee Bluff, too. Neither of us had heard anything about the back pay we were still owed. After Childress Development went bankrupt, nobody could reach Mr. Childress, just his shitheel lawyer and the lawyer never said anything.

Everest's eyes crinkled, asking me to let him know if I heard about any jobs. "It doesn't have to be drywall; I'll do whatever. Concrete, electrical work, whatever. And if your uncle needs another set of hands, I'm his guy. Tell him, okay? He knows I do good work."

I promised to talk to Uncle Chuck. Everest had kids. If anything, he was in worse shape than me. As he walked away, I pulled the last ten out of my wallet. "Oh, hey, remember that time you got lunch and I didn't have any cash? I can finally pay you back."

Everest shook his head. "Naw, brother. You keep it, okay?"

But I pressed the folded bill into his hand. "It's your money. I owe you."

It was a lie — we both knew it — but lies make things easier sometimes. Everest gave me a bear hug then leaned down to whisper, "Listen. If you really need some money, you know parthen? That mushroom the news keeps talking about? It's growing everywhere in the Cherokee Bluff houses. The shit's going for thirty dollars a button right now. It's risky, but you gotta do what you gotta do."

Stories about parthen had filled the news for months, usually with scowling congressmen and scramble-faced DEA agents. It was a hallucinogenic mushroom. Users dreamed of a city — always the same city — an alien ruin on the shores of a dying sea. Doctors didn't know what to make of it.

I was too chicken-shit to sling drugs, but I indulged occasionally. The news called parthen an epidemic threatening America's youth, but the news was always finding something to threaten America's youth with. Last summer, it'd been Haitian gangs and shark attacks.

When I got home, Macy sat at the computer, printing out more resumes to send to graphic design firms and textbook publishers. I made some soup, sat on the couch to eat and tried to think of something to say to make Macy smile. I told her about the parthen.

"Seriously?" She twisted up the side of her mouth. "You thinking about ... trying it?"

I shrugged. "I don't know. Mr. Childress still owes me back pay. Least he can do is give us a fun Saturday night, right? I mean, if you want to try it."

Macy glanced at the computer screen and stack of envelopes. "Yeah," she nodded. "That prick owes us a Saturday night. Let's call it karma." She grinned, making my heart trill.

Saturday, we headed out with a crowbar and bolt-cutters on the floor-board. The subdivision's LOTS STILL AVAILABLE sign was knocked into the mud. The roads were paved, but there were no streetlights. Stakes and guide-strings showed where flagstone paths and a community duck pond would have gone. Between lots filled with hip-high weeds and pallets of bricks, half-built houses sat abandoned with their silver insulation exposed. When the headlights touched them, they glowed with a luminous fragility, like foetuses in jars.

"Whoa, hey, somebody's here." Macy pointed toward a light in the window of one of the houses. It winked off almost as soon as she spoke.

A red F-250 was mostly hidden behind the house. It looked like Everest's truck. Poor guy must have been squatting in one of the empty houses. It explained how he knew about the parthen being here. "I think it's fine," I said. "Let's just try the houses on the other end."

The first neo-colonial we broke into had six inches of water standing in the basement. I slogged through, swinging my flashlight beam into the corners and between the joists. I found them on the wall below the laundry room hookups: a column of leathery, shelf-like mushrooms clinging to the mortar. They were the yellowish-white of bad teeth. Peeling them off the wall felt strangely cathartic, like peeling dead skin off your fingertips.

Back at the apartment, surrounded by the scraps and stubs of Macy's art supplies, we ate the parthen, one button apiece, then lay on the bed holding each other. The mushroom worked quickly, eager to welcome us. By the time I had swallowed the last bite, my skin tingled. Scientists said parthen created the illusion of kinesthesia, the sensation of moving, even as we lay still. Macy and I laughed, our faces buffeted by a wind that wasn't quite there. Momentum squeezed our stomachs and the blood drained from our limbs and faces. My fingers woven with hers, we hurtled forward so fast I blacked out.

When I jerked to, I lay in the sand on the edge of a dying sea.

The glaring sun ate up a quarter of the sky. The ocean had pulled back, leaving a dry plain of cracked mud stretching to the horizon. Salt and clay lingered on the air. Beside us rose a freestanding arch of smooth stone. Macy reached toward it.

More arches snaked between the dunes, leading to a city of pearlescent domes. It looked magnificent and heartbreaking in that dead, still place. There were people making their way toward it like pilgrims. They were all naked, and innocent and beautiful in their nakedness.

The city pulled at me and Macy both. We passed beneath the second, third, fourth arch, all mottled brownbluegreen. Each arch had a slightly different shape; each shape echoed the one before it.

A man touched my shoulder. "You can't reach the city going that fast. We can only reach it by going slow."

I didn't know what he meant. I wasn't sure if he was real or a hallucination. Smiling vaguely, I kept hiking across the hot sands. A few minutes later, something soft pressed against my ear. I turned and it was my pillow. I was back in the apartment. Macy sat propped on an elbow, staring around.

"Arches," I said and Macy turned, noticing me. I swallowed to moisten my throat. "In the middle of nothing — like a desert — there were arches leading to a big city."

Macy nodded. "Like Shinto gates, almost. But they were stone. I felt one. It had tiny fossilized creatures in it. I felt it, Austin. I could feel the texture of the .... " She squeezed my arm then pulled away. She jumped up then sat back on the edge of the bed. "That was another world. A whole other world."

Pulling off my t-shirt, I mopped the sweat off my neck. "You really think so? I mean, it's not just some hallucination?"

"It can't be. We saw the same thing. I felt the stone. It has to be real. A real alien planet." Leaning back against my chest, she wrapped my arms around herself like she used to. "We have to go back. You have more parthen, right?"

The mushroom's name came from a biological word, "parthenogenetic", meaning "virgin birth". Parthen reproduced asexually, so every fruiting body was a clone to every other, a precise genetic melody played over and over. The first troops had appeared along the shores of Lake Michigan and marched steadily southward through the Rust Belt. Drug task forces tried all sorts of different fungicides, but nothing could stop it. It liked pine barrens, abandoned husks of homes and shuttered factories where the soil should have been too sick for anything to grow.

The city became known as "Parthen", too. She was a virgin, a pristine place aching to be taken. We couldn't reach her, though.

There were 36 arches leading to the city. The second time we took the mushrooms, we awoke under the lowest arch, just like before. Together, we set out for the city. The drug's effect only lasted an hour or two and we weren't even halfway there when we tumbled back to Earth. The next time, I flat-out ran until my lungs burned like the sun-scorched sand. I got close enough to see there was nothing between the domes except dunes crowned with tough, tall grass and a wide ramp leading below one of the domes. The city was underground. But I still couldn't reach it. I collapsed and landed back in the apartment, panting for breath.

"Can't. We can't make it." My body shook from the drugs or exhaustion. "It's too far."

Macy chuckled and kissed me. "There's a secret. Some of the other pilgrims told me. Parthen can't be conquered. You have to love her. She can only be taken through love."

"Huh? What?"

"I'll show you; don't worry. But we need more mushrooms."

The city ached to be taken, but only by those who loved her. Pilgrims didn't always wake up at the lowest arch. You could arrive at any point you'd already been to, as long as you visualised that place while the drug flung you between the stars. You had to imagine every detail of it, though — the shape of the gate, the fall of the shadows, every detail from every angle. You had to love the place.

Macy was better at seeing than I was, better at being aware. Sometimes, she took my hand and ran my fingers across the spiral-shelled fossils or the subtle fracture of colours in the stone. I thought, This is why she's an artist. This is how she sees our world all the time.

It worked. We awoke at the second arch, then the fourth, then the seventh. There was never any breeze. The raging red sun always hung in the same position in the sky, like we were traveling through an instant frozen in time. On Earth, websites cropped up to share stories about Parthen. On the biggest, The Elsewhere, people wrote long treatises on astral travel, Eden and Shambhala. But really, nobody knew where Parthen was, or how we reached it. And mainly, we just had to know what lay within.

Sometimes, Macy pushed ahead before I was able to. She always helped me, though. On Earth, she'd whisper in my ear, "Remember the dune beside the arch? Remember how the sand falls down around your foot when you step?" Without Macy, I would have still been stuck at the lowest arch.

The day we reached the 31st arch, we dropped back to Earth and Macy had a message on her phone. It was one of the design firms, wanting to set up an interview. I felt the old terror that she would leave, but Macy erased the message and said, "Where would I go? I've got Parthen and you. What else could I want?"

I needed Macy to help me visualise my way to the city and she needed me to harvest the mushroom from Cherokee Bluff. As long as I could offer her Parthen, she would stay.

Two days later, walking hand-in-hand, we entered the closest dome. Macy gasped as the space opened before us. The Parthenians had lived underground in vast, upside-down ziggurats. Terraced levels ringed a huge atrium, an inverted mountain of light and cool air. There were workshops and living spaces but also aqueducts and broad open arenas.

The dome protected the subterranean village from the wind scouring the surface and the worst of the sun's heat, but it let in enough light to see and to grow crops. The lowest terraces were now-fallow fields.

All through fall, we explored the ziggurat. There was enough wonder there to keep Macy happy for a lifetime. So much better at visualising through the city, Macy continually pushed ahead of me; she couldn't help it. It was okay. On Earth, she filled sketchbooks with landmarks to help me catch up. She stopped filling out resumes and Parthen became our life. We discovered an avenue of bare-limbed trees. There, the light fell through the branches like fine lace onto Macy's cheeks and arms, making the tiny hairs on the back of her neck burn like filaments. It became my favourite place in two worlds.

More squatters had moved into the half-finished houses at Cherokee Bluff. I was wading through a basement when two scarecrow-thin punks appeared in the doorway above me holding pipes. Thank God Everest showed up and told them I was a friend. After that, I always brought snacks for their kids — Oreos, Twinkies — to trade for the parthen. They were okay, really. All of them were pilgrims and told me about new places to look for in the faraway city.

Following clues the squatters gave us, we found the barrel-vaulted tunnel leading to a second ziggurat, then a third. Macy posted some of her drawings on The Elsewhere and became sort of famous. Place names also emerged from The Elsewhere community — The Summer Ziggurat, the clover-shaped Four-Hearted Ziggurat, The Canal of Lethe, The Courthouse. The last was a palisade in The Summer Ziggurat surrounded by 81 columns. Eighty-one columns, four hearts, thirty-six arches — the Parthenians liked cube roots, but nobody knew why. Besides documenting what they'd left behind, discussions took place over the Internet on exactly who the Parthenians had been.

There were no images anywhere in the city. The Parthenians might have been blind; they only needed sunlight for their crops. Even without pictures, though, it was clear the Parthenians had been far from human. There were no stairs, only ramps. There were no beds or clothes and all tools had stubby handles. They'd been vegetarians — or, at least, nobody had found any animal bones or slaughterhouses.

Squiggling patterns of different metals were hammered into stone walls in some places. One theory was that they were some sort of tactile language. Maybe the Parthenians could feel the difference between the different types of metal, even detect their unique chemical signatures. However, if it was a language, nobody had been able to decipher it.

The Parthenians' principle science had been chemistry — workshops and multi-level laboratories were everywhere. And instead of being built of mortared stone like most places, they were always carved from the bedrock. One night, we went looking for the passage connecting The Summer Ziggurat to the one called "Whoville". I got separated from Macy again and spent the time exploring a workshop filled with elaborate glassware and braziers. Standing amid jars of clumped powders and oily liquids, I thought maybe the Parthenians had mastered alchemy instead of chemistry, some blend of science and magic that couldn't exist on our world.

When I slipped back to Earth, Macy was crying softly. "How can they all be gone? They must have been beautiful, peaceful people. How could they all just vanish?"

I held her, thinking about the workroom. After a long time, I said, "Maybe they knew they were dying out and made parthen so they'd be remembered. They created a drug that lets other people visit their home, sent it to Earth, somehow. So, when we explore the city, we're not just doing it for us. We're doing it for them, too."

Macy wiped her eyes. "You think, maybe, they wanted to inspire us? Maybe they wanted to show us what we could become."

"Sure." I kissed her. Our lips were chapped, a side effect of the parthen. "They had faith that we could become as amazing as them, someday."

Things were falling apart on Earth. The country's hairline cracks were widening. Politicians used reports of parthen — of the wonderful, strange city it revealed — to keep people frightened and stupid. They checked for parthen at the airport now and Congress rammed through a law that said you could go to jail just for having spores on your clothes. Local police tore down buildings where parthen had been discovered and filled basements with concrete. Macy and I watched the state attorney general defend the government's right to flatten homes. She declared, "People pretend this drug is harmless, but it's not. We have reports of users leaving their jobs, their families, just vanishing. We're raising a generation that does nothing but dream of an imaginary city."

Except Parthen wasn't imaginary, no matter how much they insisted it was. And the pilgrims weren't dreaming, anymore; we were waking up. We felt like pioneers from back before the country was sucked dry and flattened out, back when it was wild and green and full of possibility.

By February, the pilgrims had discovered eight ziggurats, forming a ring. There had to be a ninth — the Parthenites did everything in square roots. Finally, a regular on The Elsewhere posted directions to the ninth ziggurat. It wasn't in the centre of the ring like everyone had assumed. Instead, it jutted off the Birdsong Ziggurat like a spur.

After the directions, the poster wrote, "There are permanent bridges between our world and Parthen. You can find them from the last ziggurat."

"Permanent?" Macy asked, reading over my shoulder.

"That's what he says." I skimmed the replies following the main post. Most were asking if it was for real. The original poster never answered back. "It might be a joke."

"But what if it's not?" Macy squeezed my arm. "What if we could live in Parthen forever?"

What if we could start over? What if we could start a new society full of wonder and love and community, finally out from under the shitheel lawyers and fear-merchant politicians? That idea drew pilgrims like sugar drew ants. Before long, people started leaving. They reached the last ziggurat and learned some secret. When they returned to Earth, they would get in their car or on a plane and head ... somewhere. They never came back.

Macy and I worked our way toward the Birdsong Ziggurat and then, hopefully, the last ziggurat beyond it. Macy raced ahead like always. She loved Parthen more than she loved me, but at least she kept drawing landmarks to help me follow. After she reached the Birdsong Ziggurat, she showed me pictures of the great arcade circling the fields, its support beams twirled like confectionery. "And there's really water, Austin. I haven't seen it, yet, but I could hear a stream running. It's really faint, almost like I was imagining it."

Looking at her drawings, I begged Macy not to leave without me. Macy smiled and promised she would wait. At that moment, she probably meant it.

I tried to catch up, but I couldn't. A week later, I returned from Parthen as wine-red sunset flooded the apartment windows. Macy was stuffing clothes into a duffel bag. I knew what it meant.

"Macy, don't go."

She smiled at me, picked up her sketchbook from the nightstand. "You'll be okay. I've drawn every place you need to find. You'll —"

"No." I pushed the sketchbook away. "Just tell me how to get to Parthen permanently. Macy, talk to me, please."

"I can't explain it exactly. You have to talk to the Parthenites."

I stared at her stunned. "Wh-what?"

Macy grinned. "They're not dead. They're waiting in the last ziggurat. They'll show you what to do."

She left. I rushed downstairs after her, but she was already in her car, pulling out of the parking lot.

I couldn't lose Macy. I wouldn't be left behind on this miserable world with its bottom rotted out. Grabbing my stuff, I drove out to Cherokee Bluff. There were kids yelling, fighting each other across the rolls of dead turf, but I didn't see Everest or any other adults. I went through four houses, harvesting as much parthen as I could before the authorities discovered this place and tore it down. Without streetlights, the night was as thick as ink. In the darkness, a kid wailed, "But where's Momma? Where is she?"

At the apartment, Macy's phone was ringing. It was her mom, so I let it ring. It wouldn't be long until people came looking for her, asking questions I couldn't answer. They'd call the cops, then the cops would find parthen spores everywhere. There was really only one direction I could run.

Lying down, clutching Macy's notebook, I ate the parthen raw. The tough flesh would sour my stomach, but I didn't care. Sweat beaded down from my forehead like mushroom caps as I felt myself lifted off the Earth and sped toward Parthen.

It was hard to not push forward too fast, to memorise every sight intimately before moving on. It took days to reach the Songbird Ziggurat. In between times, I hid in the apartment, eating noodles and drinking water, letting my flesh sag off my bones. The withering of my body made my soul riper, nearly ready to pluck.

I knew what to listen for in the Songbird Ziggurat, but I still didn't quite believe it. The chitter of running water filled the great space. It was the only water anybody had found in Parthen. The thin stream tumbled into a natural chasm, an underground lake that had been here ages before the Parthenites carved the ziggurat around it.

The stream ran along the floor of a long tunnel flanked by stalactites and stalagmites. Standing at the mouth, I smelled a damp, fleshy smell. Not just stone and dry earth, but the smell of something alive.

People pushed past me to enter the tunnel and I followed. Clusters of shiny dark globes hung on the ceiling between the stalactites. One swayed softly, but I couldn't feel the wind moving it.

The last ziggurat might have been the first one the Parthenites inhabited. Unlike the others, it seemed mostly natural — a great sinkhole covered with a moon-pale dome. More of the globe clusters sat in niches and clung to walls. The air was damp and purple moss grew on the stones. But it didn't feel alien or exotic; it felt like home. I realised that — somehow — I had been yearning for this place long before parthen let me glimpse it. The mushroom had simply awakened an ache that had grown numb.

But where were the Parthenians? Where was the bridge between this world and ours? I started climbing up the stony slope to look around.

Below, a trembling voice said, "Hel ... ello. My name is Jake. Do you understand?" I looked down. A man who had entered the last ziggurat ahead of me was talking to one of the globe clusters as it oozed toward him. The clusters were alive, the Parthenians! They were an evolved fungus. It's why they lived underground, away from their sun's terrible heat.

Jake touched the Parthenian's slick flesh. One of its globes stretched into a flat-tipped tentacle. It felt his fingers, his arm, finally caressing his jaw. Laughing, Jake said, "You understand? Jake. My name is Ja —"

A dozen more tentacles bound Jake's limbs. They squeezed his torso and head. He twisted back — fingers dug into fungal flesh — but the Parthenian enveloped him. I screamed in Jake's place. Turning to help, I saw the other Parthenians sliding behind me, tentacles reaching out.

I didn't dare touch them. I tried dodging between them, but the tentacles sensed me. I backed up to the slope edge and was working up the courage to jump when the tentacle caught my thigh.

The thing wrapped around my face, pushing into my mind like a tongue forced into my mouth. Suddenly, I occupied two bodies. I was in my body and I was in the Parthenian's, chemical-sensing pits along its tendrils tasting my own sour hormones.

I knew its history. I knew about the dying world and brilliant alchemist who created the mushroom. How dwindling resources were spent sending clouds of spores to drift through space. It took centuries. The spores must have fallen on countless dead worlds before reaching

Earth. We had given up hope. Less than six thousand five hundred and sixty-one of us were still alive, huddled in the last ziggurat. But finally, the humans had come and we could escape. We could follow their astral projections back to their bodies waiting on Earth, a planet that wasn't dried out and used up.

The Parthenian slurped my mind down like an oyster, trapping me in its own blind, deaf body. I tried to shriek, curse, cry, but was bound in silence.

I've been here for weeks, or maybe just days. I can't imagine what's happening on Earth.

Crawling along the rocks, absorbing moss as nourishment, I sometimes brush against another human trapped in a Parthenian body. We huddle together, but we cannot speak. We can only trade chemical signals of fear and regret. I think most have gone mad. I force myself to stay sane for Macy. The thing that had kissed me goodbye wasn't her, just a Parthenite wearing her skin. So, I grope through the last ziggurat, searching for Macy, praying that if I do find her, I'll know it's her.

↑

MIDNIGHT MUSHRUMPS

By W.H. Pugmire

✦

Wilum Hopfrog Pugmire has been writing Lovecraftian weird fiction since 1972, when he was serving as a Mormon missionary in Ireland. His Lovecraftian obsession remains intense as he staggers toward senility. His most recent sale is to S. T. Joshi's *Black Wings III*, with a story written in collaboration with Jessica Amanda Salmonson. His books include *The Fungal Stain and Other Dreams, Encounters with Enoch Coffin* (with Jeffrey Thomas) and *Uncommon Places*. His best book, *Some Unknown Gulf of Night*, was entirely inspired by H. P. Lovecraft's monstrous growth, Fungi from Yuggoth.

✦

I.

HE DRIFTED, HIS SHADOW and he, beneath an arsenic moon, and as he lifted his eyes to the lunar sphere, its chalky beams fell like sediments of chilly gleam onto his face. He could feel that erosion of radiance crawl across his visage until they reached his eyes, into which they sank so as to find the brain within his skull. Thus, he beheld the frigid night in a different way and tasted its enchantment newly. He had never known starlight to be so intimate and coaxing, as if he could step from the solid ground and walk between the spaces of cold stars until he reached the moon, where he would dance upon its dust. Until such time, he would gambol beneath the satellite's glowing husk and shut his eyes, and dream a sculptor's dream. Thus, he capered along the desolate roadway of a forgotten town, past dwellings that sagged with age, not opening his eyes until he tripped over bricks that had fallen from some dislodged chimney. His fall was like some rude awakening and he clawed at earth as he lifted himself up on his knees. He glanced beside him and then his limbs crawled to the planks of wood that served as sidewalk, toward the crooked window that was illuminated by dancing light. The black beast watched him from that window, its wet tongue extended. Frowning, he crawled through the window, brushing against the beast as his eyes feasted on the moving flames within the hearth. The outside chill had not permeated the room and for that he was glad. Having no appetite, he did not look with longing at the aristocratic young woman who sat in her ratty armchair with a plate upon her lap, knife and fork in hand. He took in her lush red hair, her acidic-green skirt, her porcelain complexion. Her pale lips smiled, faintly, as she took the fireplace shovel and dug into a pile of ashes near the front of a hearth that was free of fire. He watched that shovel lift a pile of ashes and bring them before him. He did not move as the shovel turned so that the ashes fell upon the wooden floor. The lady patted the ashes with the shovel until they were a smooth flat surface.

"Write your name," she commanded. He hesitated one moment, holding his hand over the ashes to sense if they were hot and then he placed one moving finger into their cool, fuliginous surface, watched in silence by his companion as her canine, still at the window, groaned. He wrote his name in the debris, as the woman stabbed at the thing on the plate with her fork and began to cut a tiny portion from it. Finally, she studied the name that had been etched into the ashes. "Well, Demetrios — what brings you to my haunt?"

"You do not exist for me," he countered, "and, in truth, I think you are nothing but an imaginative artist's dream, influenced by the ghastly light of the bloated moon; for the moon has planted strange passion in my aesthetic brain, and outré song in my poetic mouth, and I would warble of eccentric ecstasy to that globe of distant dust."

Lightly, the lady laughed. "I have another idea. Come and take a bite of this. Come, Demetrios, creep closer and gaze onto my plate. You would think this was a deformed turnip, would you not, this pale thing that wears a fleshy tint? Why, it looks almost like an infant's severed foot, doesn't it? Rather wonderful, what strange fungi one may find sprouting in one's garden. Come, partake of this little slice and then your lunar ecstasy will find its match in nebulous vision."

He allowed her to place the fork into his mouth and his teeth clamped onto the thin slice of what at first was a tasteless morsel of rather spongy substance. He peered at the thing upon her plate as it began to blur and subtly curl. His senses had been affected by the soft fleshy slice that he chewed and he suspected that it was, in fact, a kind of deformed, hallucinatory mushroom that was beginning to taint his mental astuteness. He listened and imagined that he heard a rising wind and he sensed a rush of hot air that billowed to him from the hearth. Then the hearth melted from his view, as did his entire surroundings. The fellow shivered as he knelt upon a chilly patch of lonely land. The black beast, still some distance from him, regarded him with woeful eyes and then it crept forward as a particle of that on which he still feasted fell from out his mouth. The canine snout investigated the bit of mushroom and then its tongue lapped up the morsel as the man swallowed what had remained on his tongue. He watched as the beast's dark eyes began to shimmer with queer sensation, and he shuddered as the hound raised its face to the bloated moon and bayed. And then he followed, on hands and knees, as the animal began to trot from him, toward a forest into which they wandered. He followed the beast through drear shadow formed by thick branches that assembled above them, until they came to the slight mound of earth.

He approached the beast as it rested its head upon the mound and groaned, waiting for the human to join it. Its cold nose nudged his hand, as he placed that member upon the mound, and together the two creatures began to dig into the raised earth, reaching deeply into the soil until he touched something smooth and cold. He struggled to lift the object from its filthy bed and, as he did so, a patch of moonlight pierced through the stitched branches and illuminated what he held. He considered the thing's form and marveled that a growth of matter could so resemble a slumbering human infant. He saw the stunted pale limbs, the two arms and the suggestion of small legs, and he saw that one of the legs was missing a foot. How curious, that a stream of fog issued from where an infant might have worn a mouth. How peculiar, the way the fellow fancied that the object curled its form as it rested on the spread of his wide hands.

None of that mattered, however; for he was still dizzy with delight from the opium-like ecstasy that he had experienced from feasting on a sliver of pale fungus. And so, as the mist from the fungal mouth began to cloud over them, the gentleman held the mass of misshapen growth to his drooling companion, as the beast and he bent to the fleshy thing and began to consume it.

II

I CONSUMED MY MUSHROOM pie as Demetrios etched into the back of his hand with a carving knife. The black beast at his side licked at the blood that began to spill from the design that split my brother's flesh. "What a curious word," I said as I studied the letters cut into my brother's hand.

"It's the Polish word for mushroom or fungus and it's small enough to fit precisely on the back of one's hand." Taking his dinner napkin, he placed it over the incised letters and stopped the final flow of crimson liquid. His black beast collapsed onto the floor and groaned.

"I wish you wouldn't do that at the dinner table. I doubt that you have sterilised that blade. Your implement was far better employed during the time you created your curious thing. How queer of you, after having slaved on your outlandish creation, to have buried it in the earth before anyone has had the chance to admire it."

The thing had been his most ambitious project, and he had spent weeks creating it. The bulk of the figure had been carved of balsa wood that he had imported from Brazil. The shape of the figure suggested that Demetrios had meant it to be feminine, but he had attired the four-foot figure oddly, so that that which covered it resembled shreds of growth rather than clothing. He failed to give the thing a face and attired its head with a most outlandish hat that resembled a fleshy cone opened at the top, with a growth of webbing that served as veil. Truly, it was a remarkable work of art. Thus, I was perplexed when, one moonlit midnight, he carried the object (it was quite lightweight) out of his studio and into the woodland, where I was astonished to see that this most delicate of artists had excavated a round hole that burrowed deeply into the earth. Into that filthy pit he had planted his creation, covering it with the pile of disrupted dirt that rose as a mound next to the hole.

"It is not an art project," Demetrios spoke, awakening me from reverie. "It is ritualistic, something you refuse to understand."

"Well, I hate to think of how it has been abused, dwelling in that deep pit for almost nine months, molested by worms or insects or heaven knows what. And now the raised circle of earth covering it has grown a bed of mushrooms — which I must confess you have prepared beautifully in this savory pie."

"They have a richness in taste, don't they? One could become quite addicted to such a flavour and dream about it beneath cold starlight. And the psychoactive properties of these particular mushrooms are able to usher the sensitive dreamer into a rare realm of wonder and psychological insight."

"How clever of you to know that I would have an appetite at this late hour; why, it will soon be midnight. Why do you rise and move so restlessly?"

"The time of cultivation is at an end. The time is nigh to dance and dream. Come join me if you like."

I watched him walk out of the house, followed by his black beast. After a moment, I pushed out of my chair so as to join him. I felt a sudden dizziness and experienced an eccentric display of fuzzy black-and-white spots before my eyes that I could actually *feel* in my brain. Although I had stopped eating my pie, the taste of its contents stayed with me and intensified. I stepped outside and glanced at heaven, but my eyesight was blurry so that the stars in their black blanket of night resembled the dizziness that had produced the optical display of black-and-white spots that I had experienced. I caressed my forehead with a cool hand and saw where my brother had entered the woods by way of a single pathway. I staggered after him, entered the woodland and walked beneath the still moonlit trees. The woodland was a place where its dendroid inhabitants did not crowd each other and thus, the display of lunar light seeped through. I walked until I came upon Demetrios, who moved in dance around a small circle of mushrooms and dug into his wounded hand with a sharp twig, opening again the arcane symbol that he had carved there. His crimson liquid caught a reflection of moonlight as it seeped from him and dripped onto the bed of mushrooms. He laughed in a peculiar fashion, as he dropped his hand to his beast and I did not watch as the animal lapped at the symbolic scar.

I watched that bed of fungi move as something beneath it began to rise; as I watched, I felt that I had indeed been intoxicated by the contents of the pie that I had consumed and which I could still taste, intensely, in my imagination. I gazed at the queer erection that pushed out so as to mock its aborescent neighbors and I barely recognised it as my brother's artistic work — for the sculpture had transformed into a living entity. I was captivated by its bleached flesh, the folds of eerie growth that were its attire. Strangest of all was the creature's cone-like head, which opened at the top and from which a series of vines protruded that ended in pale poisonous-looking pods. I considered the miasma that seeped upward from the opening of the dome, coils of mist that wore faint phosphorescence. The web-like growth of my brother's original sculpture, that had formed a kind of veil, was gone, replaced by a fungal mask that aped a woman's countenance. Demetrios approached his sentient creation and bowed to it, offering it his wounded hand, to which the thing lowered its dome so that the pale pods could fasten to the bloodstained insignia and suck nourishment. Unable to resist the nightmarish scene, I stepped nearer to my brother, stopping only when the creature moved its funnel-like dome so that its sparkling mist shot toward my eyes. Oh, how hot that mist was as it sank into my eyes and found my brain, which it tickled with provocative memory of the mushrooms I had devoured in my pie. Ah, how my brother's beast howled at the dead moon as its form extended, transforming into a tall, lean man of dead-black colouration that raised one hand so as to make enigmatic motions to the moon. It turned, this creature, its hound-like countenance to me and offered me its embrace, but I had no desire to slink into a realm of proffered extinction. Turning away from the black man, I watched as my brother reached for his creation's anemic mask and removed it. I watched as he pressed that fungal mask against his face and I shouted as the mask took on a semblance of my brother's feverish visage. Something in the sight of that mushroom mask filled me with an almost ribald craving, a ravenous appetite. I called his name, and Demetrios unwound from his creation's embrace and floated to me. Tilting to him, I touched my lips to his dreamy face and then I kissed him with my length of tongue. As I tasted my brother, I sensed the shadow of his creation behind me as Demetrios and I were enveloped in the thickening poisonous mist that disintegrated reality and ushered us into a dominion of rich enthralling dream. Laughing coyly, Demetrios floated from me so as to dance with his transformed beast in sallow moonlight. Turning, I faced the feminine form, the faceless thing that filled my soul with uncanny hunger. Opening my jaws, I clamped my teeth to where the thing ought to have worn a face. My feast was an eternal dream.

✝

KUM, RAÚL (THE UNKNOWN TERROR)

By Steve Berman

✦

Steve Berman thinks that mushrooms look fascinating but has no urge to taste any. He is disappointed that *Suillus bovinus* is the Jersey Cow mushroom because he thinks New Jersey should be represented by a more fearsome fungus. He has sold around a hundred articles, essays and short stories and been a finalist numerous times for the Lambda Literary Award. He hopes to finish the *Guide to Lost Gay Cinematic Characters* before the end of 2013.

✦

KUM, RAÚL (*THE UNKNOWN TERROR*) — B. 1925, D. 1957

NONE OF THE INHABITANTS of Tzapotl, a small village in the jungles of southern Mexico, would have any knowledge of English if not for two Americans: Robert Hayward Barlow and Gerald Ramsey. The first was a distinguished anthropologist who would one day chair the department at the Metropolitan College in Mexico City, the second a scientist disgraced after poisoning several female students with a meal of *Boletus satanas.*

Barlow came to Tzapotl in late 1946 on sabbatical to study the local legend of the *Cueva Muerte,* a cave where the villagers held an annual human sacrifice so as to hear the whispers of their ancestors. Though fluent in both Tzeltal and Tzotzil Mayan, so he had no trouble with the Tzapotl dialect, Barlow taught the villagers some English during the months he stayed in Tzapotl. His favourite among the locals was Raúl Kum. Barlow's tutelage drifted from the casual into the romantic when Kum expressed interest in a book that Barlow had brought with him, *El baile de los cuarenta y uno,* which covered a 1901 homosexual scandal. The affair between the two men ended once Barlow, along with Kum and another native guide, began spelunking the actual cave. The three discovered a pale froth clinging and dripping down the dank walls of the cave. This was an unknown fungal species with hyphae filaments that aggressively attached to parasitoid flesh. Barlow and Kum barely escaped with their lives and the third man perished, as portions of his body were rapidly consumed and replaced by the fungus. Barlow found the experience too reminiscent of the weird fiction of his friend and first crush, the author Howard Phillips Lovecraft (See Lovecraft's 1927 short story, "The Colour Out of Space") and he suffered a nervous breakdown, fleeing Tzapotl and the jungle for the sanctuary of a Mexico City hospital. Abandoned and fearful of the horrors of *Cueva Muerte,* Kum became withdrawn and despondent.

His wont for exposing students to dangerous fungi had Ramsey banned by the Mycological Society of America and the man became convinced that some of the MSA members had hired assassins to rid the world of his genius, so he fled south into Mexico, where he could disappear. While visiting a small bordello, Ramsey happened upon a discarded issue of *Cuentos Misteriosos,* a pulp magazine that contained a 1947 story written by Barlow while he recuperated with barbiturates in a sanitarium. "*Podredumbre innoble*" mentioned both *Cueva Muerte* and nearby Tzapotl. Ramsey ignored the whore, took the magazine, and ventured into the jungle. He arrived at the village and impressed the natives with his limited knowledge of anatomy and biology. They valued his healing skills, which became the means for him to extort his way into becoming a despot. Villagers began sacrificing to Ramsey and not *Cueva Muerte*. Thus, he obtained victims for his experiments with the fungal samples he carefully culled from the cave walls. Kum grew fearful of Ramsey's control over the village and his tampering with the fungus.

Fearful that his homosexual liaisons would become known to the university board, Barlow committed suicide in the first days of 1951. *"Podredumbre innoble"* was discovered by Donald Wandrei, translated into English as "Ignoble Rot", and published in *Memories of Leng and Other Pieces* (Arkham House, 1955). Wandrei gave a copy of that volume to his personal friend, Charles Gray, an explorer and connoisseur of the uncanny who scavenged La Proveedora and came close to discovering the Inca Ice Maiden nearly a half-century before Johan Reinhard. Gray became obsessed with finding this cave. He spent much time in southern Mexico searching for Tzapotl and, in June of 1957, reached the village. Ramsey resented the man's intrusion and attempted to poison him with fungal-contaminated canned fruit, but Gray, who suffered from fructose malabsorption, discarded the offering once he left Ramsey's villa.

Kum warned him not to venture down into *Cueva Muerte,* but Gray ignored him. By this time, Ramsey's experiments had created a number of semi-ambulatory corpses thoroughly tainted and motivated by the fungus to spread and infect any animal or unfortunate they encountered. Ramsey confined these shambling monstrosities to the cave for further study. Gray became one more victim. When the explorer did not return home at the time expected, his sister, Gina, convinced her wealthy husband, Dan Matthews, to mount an expedition to find her brother. Matthews followed Gray's route but found hostile natives refusing him entry into Tzapotl. However, before he turned back, Kum approached him and promised to explain what had happened to Gray, on the condition that he be first flown to the United States — Kum wanted nothing more than to reach American soil, defect and start a new life far from Tzapotl.

Kum claimed that Gray had perished from a tropical disease, then suggested it was a spelunking mishap, leaving both Gina and her husband to suspect there was more to the story. Matthews organised a new expedition and forced Kum to accompany him back to Mexico. Once Kum stepped foot back in his old village, the locals, under orders from Ramsey, captured him. Ramsey tried, but failed, to discourage the rest of the expedition from setting foot in the cave. Matthews did not fare better than his brother-in-law, but one man, hired help, escaped.

While prisoner at the insane mycologist's villa, Kum discovered explosives — Ramsey's contingency for enforcing his dominion over Tzapotl. Kum hoped to use the dynamite to murder Ramsey, but succeeded only in damaging the fuses before being discovered. Ramsey had Kum's tongue cut out for being a traitor and then had him thrown into the cave. His death was not in vain, though, because Ramsey used the dynamite to silence Gina and the other survivor of the expedition in the only tunnel linking the cave to the surface. The explosive detonation occurred early enough to prevent the mycologist's escape and sealed off *Cueva Muerte,* preserving the world from a terrible contagion.

— From the pages of *The Guide to Lost Gay Cinematic Characters, Vol. 3: Films of the Fantastic and Feared.*

✝

CORPSE MOUTH AND SPORE NOSE

By Jeff VanderMeer

♦

Jeff VanderMeer is a two time winner of the World Fantasy Award whose stories have been published by Tor.com, *Clarkesworld, Conjunctions, Arc, Black Clock* and several year's best anthologies. Recent books include the Nebula finalist novel *Finch* (2009) and the short story collection *The Third Bear* (2010). His *The Steampunk Bible* was featured on the CBS Morning Show and has been named a finalist for the Hugo Award for best related book. He also recently co-edited the mega-anthology *The Weird* compendium with his wife Ann. A co-founder of Shared Worlds, a teen SF/F writing camp, VanderMeer has been a guest speaker at the Library of Congress and MIT, among others. He writes book reviews for the *Los Angeles Times, New York Times Book Review* and the Washington Post. VanderMeer's latest novel, just completed, is *Annihilation*.

♦

NEAR DAWN, THE DETECTIVE pulled himself, sodden and dripping, from the River Moth. Dry land felt hard and unyielding. His muscles ached. The water had made him wrinkled and old. The stench of mud and silt clung to him. All around him, light strained to break through the darkness, found fault lines and pierced the black with threads of grey and orange. To the west, from between the twinned towers the grey caps had erected when they had reconquered the city, the sky shone an unsettling shade of blue. Strange birds flew there, winking out when they reached the boundary formed by the towers.

The detective lay against the smooth stones of the jetty and realised he had never been so tired in all his life. He would have fallen asleep right there, but it did not feel safe. With a lurch and a groan, the detective stood, stretched his legs, took off his trench coat and tried to wring the water from it. After a while, he gave up. Suddenly aware that the grey caps could already be coming for him, alerted by microscopic fungal cameras, he spun around, stared inland.

No one walked the narrow streets ahead of him. No sound broke through the crazy and up-ended buildings. A mist coated the spaces between dwellings. Everything was fuzzy, indistinct. A chill seeped through the detective's wet clothing and into his skin. In the half-light, Ambergris did not appear to be a city but, instead, a blank slate waiting for his imagination to transform it, to recreate it.

Out of the mist, as the mist withdrew and circled back like some solemn, autumnal tide, a great head loomed suddenly: a product of his dreams, the unexpected prow of a ship. But no, only a statue, when finally revealed, and the detective exhaled the breath he had held. His legs shook, for the mist's withdrawal had resembled the advance of some death-pale giant.

He recognised the features now. Who would not? Voss Bender had been dead five hundred years, but no one who had ever heard his music played could forget that face. The statue's features suffered from fissures, pocks from bullet holes, infiltrations of mold and the spurious introduction of a large purple mushroom upon its head. Yet, even this did not detract from the grace of the rendering. Even the sliver of stone missing from its left eyebrow only served to make the statue appear more imperious.

Now the detective heard the sound of breathing. A quiet sound, neither laboured nor erratic. At first, the detective fancied the sound came from the statue itself, but, after listening carefully, discarded this theory. In truth, he could not tell where it came from. Perhaps Ambergris itself breathed, the breezes and updrafts that drove the mist before them the even, comfortable breath of stone.

Automatically, the detective followed the gaze of Voss Bender's statue: down and to the left. It was an old habit of his — he always must know where people were looking, for fear they stared at something more interesting, more profound, more alive ....

And so, he came upon a most remarkable signpost, shaded by the largest mushroom he had ever seen.

It stood taller than a palm tree, its trunk of lacy white flesh six feet in circumference. Its half-moon hood was stained purple and blue, with yellow streaks. The fragile grid work underneath the hood, from which the inevitable spores would one day float forth, had a lacquered, unreal appearance. Root-like tendrils gripped the pavement, cracked and speared it.

As the detective walked toward the signpost and the mushroom, the breathing sound became louder. Could it emanate from the mushroom itself? Could the mushroom be breathing?

The signpost rose almost to his height of six feet. It had originally been composed of a grey stone, but a viscous white substance had gradually seduced the cracks and other imperfections until now the detective could hardly read the words. The sign did not include the name of the city, but simply a giant "A". Beneath the A, in letters sick with flourishes, a short inscription:

Holy city, majestic, banish your fears.
Arise, emerge from your sleeping years.
Too long have you dwelt in the valley of tears.
We shall restore you with mercy and grace.

Many elements of this inscription disturbed the detective, but certainly no more so than the quiet breathing. First, he wondered who had written the words. Second, he could not connect the words to Ambergris. Third, he had no clue who "We" were or how "We" would restore the city with mercy and grace.

The detective left off such questions in favour of solving the more perplexing problem of the breather. He took out his gun, then stood motionless for a long moment, listening.

Finally, he decided the sound must be coming from *behind* the mushroom. Nimbly, he walked around the mushroom's left flank, disgusted by the stickiness under his feet.

On the opposite side, he discovered a tendril that was not a tendril. And a statue that was not a statue. Such conclusions would have been neat, safe, rational. Unfortunately, the mystery to the breathing, the detective now knew, had no rational solution. A man lay beneath the mushroom. If he had not seen that the feet merged with the root-tendril, the detective might have thought the man was just taking a nap.

The man's paleness astounded the detective — he glowed in the shadowy dawn light. His head had been stripped of all hair, including eyebrows, and so had the rest of his body. His eyes were closed. His genitals had been replaced by some frozen-blue bulb of a fungus. Tiny tentacles had sprouted from his fingernails and now searched the earth around them restlessly. From the sudden, fibrous hardness around the man's kneecaps, the detective could tell that the man became mushroom much farther up the leg than the foot, but, despite this intrusion, this invasion, he saw by the gently-rising chest and, yes, the quiet, steady breathing, that the man was alive.

The detective stood over the sleeping man, this living corpse, his gun hanging from the end of his arm, dangling from one finger. He had come to Ambergris to solve a case, *the* Case, and he had come to Ambergris to find a missing person. But not this person. And not this mystery. He began to see, with a frisson of dread, that to solve the Case, he might have to solve a dozen other cases before it. Or else they might conspire to obscure the True Case. The True Crime.

He considered the man's face. The thickness of the white mask reminded him of rubber. Everywhere, any delicacies of cheekbone, of nose, of ear, had given way to an over-ripe fullness. The breath issued from the slightest gap between the thick lips. The bulbous eyelids fluttered, the eyelashes miniatures of the tentacles that had colonised the man's fingers.

Against his own better judgment, the detective knelt beside the man. He had room for neither disgust nor fascination within him. He was simply tired and eager to explode this lesser mystery by any means possible. He tapped the side of the man's head with his gun. No response. He tapped again — harder.

The man's eyes shot open. The detective caught a swift glimpse of limitless black, across which tiny insects glided and fell, an entire world trapped on the surface of the man's eyes. The detective rose with a cry of horror, stood back, gun aimed at the man.

The mushroom-man opened his mouth — and his mouth was filled with corpses. Not a tooth remained in that mouth, that it might be more thickly packed with corpses. Lean corpses. Fat corpses. Headless corpses. Corpses with gills. Corpses with wings. Corpses with single eyes. Corpses with multiple eyes. Corpses that mumbled through their dead mouths. Corpses that tried to dance in their stumbling decay. Grinning corpses. Weeping corpses. And all of them no taller than three inches high.

The man's mouth continued to open long after it should have stopped, while the detective continued to stare at this mystery he was not sure he would ever fully understand. His finger tightened on the trigger and he brought the gun up into his hand, where he held it so tight against his palm that he burned the imprint of the grip into it.

The man began to cough up the corpses—they slid up out of his mouth at odd angles, all of them coated in mucus. They spilled across his belly and out onto the ground. Hundreds of them. They reached the detective's legs and he recoiled in disgust. And fear. But he couldn't stop staring at the tiny corpses, so like naked dolls or children. And he couldn't stop staring at the man's mouth as it continued to expand. Or at the dead eyes brimming with life.

If not for the Case, the detective would have stood there for a long time. He might have let his trenchcoat fall softly to the ground. He might have taken off all of his clothes and laid down beside the mushroom man. He might have waited for the tendrils to stealthily crawl and slide and coil across his arms and legs. He might have acquired tentacles and strange dreams to keep him from thinking about what he had become ... but something in the awful complexity of the mushroom man's face made him think of Alison, the missing girl, and, with that thought, the mist began to clear, the morning light became brighter and the trance broke. He bent low, next to the mushroom man's head.

"This isn't right," he said. "This isn't right. There is no mystery here. You are as transparent as your skin. Your case is as old as this city and no older. The solution is simple. We both know this."

The detective held the gun against the mushroom man's head, the mushroom man's gaze slowly drifted to the left, to take in the gun and the gun wielder.

Through the glut of corpses, the mushroom man mouthed, "No," in as soft a whisper as its breath.

"I. Do. Not. Believe. In. You," the detective said.

He stood. He aimed. He fired. The bullet entered the mushroom man's head — which exploded into a hundred thousand snow-white spores that lifted themselves into the air like chained explorers suddenly set free. They floated down upon the hundreds of tiny corpses. They floated down upon the remains of the mushroom man's body. They floated down upon the detective, caught in the detective's hair while he waved his hands to avoid them.

Not even the mushroom man's eyes remained — just his jutting torso, his spindly legs, the feet that were not really feet.

No one came running to investigate, despite the echoing recoil of the gunshot. No one came to arrest him. The looming mushroom did not rear back in pain. The spores rose, carried by the breeze, were destined to explore the city well in advance of the detective.

As for the detective, he just stood there, surrounded by the spores and marveled at what he had wrought. He had killed a man who was not a man. Out of the shattered head had poured a hundred thousand lives, scattered by the explosion. How did one stick to just one case in this city?

Slowly, reluctantly, the detective put away his gun. The dawn had truly arrived, a second sun beginning to blaze in the space between the grey caps' two towers. He could hear voices in the city behind him. The mist had begun to evaporate. He could see clearly now. He had a Case. He had a Client. His shoulders fell, his muscles untensed. He breathed in deeply, through his nose ....

A spore entered his nose.

He felt it wriggling in his nasal cavity. He sneezed, but the spore hooked itself into the soft flesh inside his left nostril. The pain made him jerk upright and he howled.

Abandoning all pretense, he drove his left index finger up into his nostril in search of the spore — only to be stung (he could only think of it as a bee sting) by the spore, which proceeded to advance up his nostril. The detective withdrew his finger. The tip was bleeding. In desperation, he put both hands up to the bridge of his nose, cursing as he tried to prevent the spore from going any further.

To no effect — except that now he felt the spore slide down into the back of his throat and begin to crawl back up into his mouth. He did a little jig of a dance as he tried to loop his tongue back over itself to deliver a knock-out blow.

The detective was still cursing, but the words came out all garbled and blubbering.

The spore, despite the best efforts of his tongue, stuck defiantly to the roof of his mouth. He began to feel as if he were suffocating. He again tried to dislodge the spore with his tongue. His tongue became numb then, a dead weight lolling in his mouth. He put three fingers of his left hand into his mouth, pushing aside his tongue and tried to pull the spore out, but it began to burrow into his palate to get away from his hand. Hopping on one leg, the detective dropped his gun into his trenchcoat pocket. He dug into his mouth with as many fingers as he could fit. The burrowing sensation became more intense. His fingers, getting in each other's way, caught at the tail-end of the spore. Pulled, but only succeeded in breaking off a tuft.

He withdrew his fingers, panicked. As if they had been waiting for the right time, another dozen milk-white spores floated into his mouth. He made a gurgling sound. He clutched his throat. It felt as if he were choking to death on feathers. He began to feel faint. He gargled. Tried to scream. Fell to his knees. Beside the tiny corpses. There was a humming in his ears. He could sense a breath, like the breath of the world, and a tinny laughter. The spores were laughing at him. *We shall restore you with mercy and grace ....*

Anger rose within him. As he continued to be deprived of oxygen, the sensation of mocking laughter from the spores intensified. He rose to one knee, tried to insist that he would not become a home for corpses. But all that came out was a whimper. He fell back against the ground.

For a moment — a horrible, gnawing millisecond — as the detective hunched over on his knees among the corpses, there was a great Nothing in his head. Not a thought. Not a memory or even Memory. There was only the relentless squirming of the spores as they raced through his body.

Then, like a King Squid exploding to the surface, the detective wrenched himself to his feet. He muttered to himself. He leaned over and swiped at his trenchcoat. Picked it up. He cocked his head like a monkey, looking around him. He licked his lips. He stared down at the shattered head, the corpse mouth that had once been him.

"Haw haw haw." The great, looping syllables came out of the detective's mouth as if he had always spoken that way. The detective's body danced a thuggish dance around the husked-out corpse. "Haw haw haw. Odessa Bliss! I. Am. Odessa. Bliss!" bellowed the detective. And he scratched an armpit absentmindedly.

Then, with a frightening burst of speed, the detective's hijacked body ran into the city of Ambergris, legs pumping, face contorted in an expression of sheer and unrelieved stupidity, sometimes abandoning the straight arrow of its lumbering path to jump for joy at freedom.

The detective no longer heard the giggling of the spores. The detective heard only the vacuous mumbles and half-formed thoughts of Odessa Bliss. The Case had been subsumed by this new situation. He had no case now. He did not even have his own mind. A phrase curled through his proto-thoughts like a length of razor sharp wire: *"We shall restore you with mercy and grace ...."*

Soon, he had a new perspective on everything.

↑

GOATSBRIDE

By Richard Gavin

↑

Richard Gavin has authored four acclaimed collections of eldritch horror fiction: *Charnel Wine* (Rainfall Books, 2004), *Omens* (Mythos Books, 2007), *The Darkly Splendid Realm* (Dark Regions Press, 2009) and *At Fear's Altar* (Hippocampus Press, 2012). He has also published non-fiction writings on the macabre and the esoteric. Richard lives in Ontario, Canada with his beloved wife and their brood. Visit him online at www.richardgavin.net.

↑

MARIETTA CAME TO THE Fallows to wait once more for the ghost-lights. And, although they would manifest for her that day, she had no inkling that this would be the last time she would see them.

Her pilgrimage unfurled under the blaze of mid-afternoon. The ghostlights appeared in their customary manner, boiling up out of the aether itself. Tiny splatters of luxuriously-coloured light, their centres the purple-black of heart's blood, their edges wreathed in a gaudy gleam of chartreuse. They were suspended in midair like Yuletide baubles hung with spider's skeins.

The uncomfortably cold, soaked earth of the Fallows began to climb up around the holey leather that covered Marietta's feet as she stood stone-still in the field, gazing. Although only her lungs and eyelids were moving, and, even then, scarcely, Marietta nonetheless felt as though she were cart-wheeling forward, spinning through the borderless country inside herself.

After so many visitations, she was well accustomed to such sensations, but thrilled to them all the same. She pressed her eyelids closed, watching the paler suggestions of the ghostlights cascading through the fleshly veils of her eyelids.

She was straining to hear the sound of *his* leap, or his terrible bellow that had long ago inspired all the local shepherds to usher their flocks elsewhere. (Marietta was, to the best of her knowledge, the only one who still visited the Fallows.)

But these heralds of his arrival did not come.

Opening her eyes, she was puzzled by the grim vacancy of both the field and the woods that framed it.

All at once, the landscape felt altered. Even the ghostlights shifted their pattern. They began to manically twirl and flex.

Then they began to drift, leaving thin trails of putrid fog in their wake.

Marietta followed them to the far end of the field.

The ghostlights seemed to swarm together to create a kind of constellation. The atmosphere thickened with a rare new gravity, which pulled Marietta's gaze to a mud patch that stretched drably beneath the brightly churning orbs.

The ground here drooped in a lazy slope; forging a ditch that distinguished the Fallows from the copse that grew dense and wild alongside it.

There, heaped upon the dirt like a flung bale of hay, was a nightmare in flesh and fur. Marietta's senses were so offended by the sight that she reflexively turned away, counting off enough heartbeats to melt the phantasm back into nothing more than the twisted boughs that had been made to breathe only by her own imagination.

But, when Marietta opened her eyes, she discovered that her attempt to banish it had been in vain.

The leaping one was still lying broken in the mud. The shock of discovery tainted the atmosphere with a numbness as cold and grey as a stone marker.

Talons of sorrow pushed deeply, deeply into Marietta until, punctured, she could only collapse at the side of her great love.

The crooked one's jaws were moving, but no sound escaped his mouth. When Marietta's sobs softened at last, the only noise she could discern was the delicate plash of ichor against stone.

She could but watch as the vital fluid emptied itself from the various wounds that brightened the leathery skin of his trunk, mottled the blackish wool on the wayward contours of his grand legs. Emerging from the tangles of fur was his great livid serpent of muscle, its skin the hue of an overripe plum. Marietta found herself staring at it in a shameful-yet-unbreakable trance. As this snake flexed, the black pit of its eye widened, releasing a reedy sine, a sound not unlike a song. The vivid ichor even spilled from this throbbing hole, mingling with the oh-so-mortal drabness of the earth.

Marietta believed that the thing was beseeching her with its unworldly eyes. Their irises were the blue of a frozen sea; their pupils vertical slit-like things, cauldron-black and omniscient. A filmy membrane winked across them in rapid sweeps, pushing the grit and sludge to the rim of the reddened sockets.

She wanted so much to question him, to learn what had happened and how. But Marietta knew that, although her lover's plump tongue had many uses, speech was not among them.

Had the others found him? Had they traced him to the great ruddy cave where he slumbered and then beaten him, cut him with blades, pierced him with arrows?

The grove suddenly dimmed. At first Marietta, wondered if time had disappeared (hours always melted much more swiftly when she was with him), but she realised that the darkening was the result of the ghostlights winking out in tedious succession.

Now their colours existed only in the vital ichor that bled out of the dying god and seeped into the earth around his gnarled hands and the scuffed lustre of his cloven feet.

New forms began to halo the failing old one: flies who had come not to crown him, but to sup on the outpouring streams of his lifeblood. Marietta swatted away as many as she could, but, soon, they were legion. They swarmed in swiftly. After lapping up the vivid ichor, the bugs came away intoxicated. Their flight paths were visibly meandering, their pace logy. Never had they suckled a blood so rarefied.

Marietta traced her hand along the sharply jutting bone structure of his face. Through the filthy moss of his beard, a deep, silent oval of agony widened.

I'll come back, Marietta sent to him. *I'll come back with help or with wine, or a song. I'll come back with something to cure you. They'll come looking for me if I don't get back to the village, but I* will *come back to you. Please stay with me. Please.*

⬆

The girl knew no sleep that night. When, upon sunrise, she returned to the Fallows, she discovered that even the gory remnant of her great love had vanished.

She shirked her chores in order to spend the lion's share of the day scouring the meadows and the dim groves and the shadow-moistened caves. In her pouch she had a small ration of wine and some salt to titillate a waning palate. But he was nowhere to be found.

Even the lurid pond of his blood had been subsumed by the soil.

Marietta lowered herself onto the site of his expiration, too gutted to even weep.

✝

The invasion commenced the very next morning. Great ships appeared, carrying people with ghost-pale flesh and a faith that was alien to these ancient woods.

The imprint-free villages of pitched canvas were razed, as swiftly as fired bullets, as inexorably as the descending blade. What swelled in their stead were structures forged from gutted forests. The ruddy contours of his great organic temple were smothered by chapels of chastity, of symmetry. His sighs and shrieks were bridled by a faith that wrestled to keep all ecstasies infuriatingly aloof until after one's flesh had turned respectably cold.

The Fallows were upturned and transmuted into a golden carpet of wheat. Harvests sprouted and were soon sown as the interlopers put down deeper roots.

Marietta lingered, not for family ties, but to keep vigil in the place that had been his, been theirs.

She earned her keep by carrying out the meagre toils of one of the prominent families in the village. She slept on a cot in the barn and prepared their meals to their unique specifications. She scrubbed the smoothed wood of their floors and washed their dishes of clay. When their stiff clothing looked too lived-in, Marietta mended them with a silver needle and thread.

But, at night, when the austere ones were slumbering, she would bear a lantern back to the former Fallows and would call his name into the darkness.

Did these people even know the name of the one who had called these rustic hills his own? Had they any hint of the forces that churned beneath their pathways and their churches and their snug homes?

Surely, some among them would ache for it, could they but discover the Source ….

Marietta wished and, ultimately, the ghostlights returned … but in a changed state.

In the early harvest of the year, during one of Marietta's rare afternoon visits to her paramour's landmark, she discovered that the ghost-lights were now colouring the wheat itself.

It had been a rainy season and the crops that had sprouted were not golden, but whitish and blotchy with a peculiar fungus: blue and green and flecked with a black that made Marietta think of the vault that held the stars; the darkness that had been the nativity of her great love, whose birth had heralded the primal dawn. And now his sovereign blood was flowering once more, chthonic and musty and raw.

The people were so desperate to maintain their comfort that they chanced the possibility of toxicity rather than deny themselves a bountiful table.

They cut the grotesque shoots and ground them. Though the resultant grist was pasty and smelled of unturned roots, they baked it into their loaves, which were devoured with thanksgiving to their Maker. Such were the gifts bestowed to the true.

♠

Fittingly, it was a young woman who first felt the ichor burning within her. She would awaken with strange stories of nocturnal flights through eerie woodlands and of the touch of an inhuman lover.

Marietta would often comfort the daughter, encouraging her to keep such fancies to herself, to rest, and to, of course, eat heartily of the bread and wheat gruel she prepared for the girl daily.

The keepers of the stringent faith soon learned of similar night-rides from other girls in the village. Superstition grew rampant as reports of a great horned form emerging from the woods to hold congress caused great alarm, then persecution, and finally executions.

Twenty girls found death at the end of a rope. Men of reason pleaded with the authorities that the true problem was a blend of superstition, adolescent fancy and a tainted crop from the previous autumn. *Ergot* was the name some gave it: a strange mould that had infected the girls with sickness, with vivid nightmares.

But by then the ghostlights had ignited the blood of the chaste. This sanguinary pyre heralded the long awaited Return ....

✦

The clan who had conspired to put an end to the diabolism was small but among the most fanatical. They went out to the Fallows, now stripped, where the girls had claimed they had seen *It*.

There they waited, without benefit of fire or food. In a blackness as cold as the deep sea, they waited.

The ghostlights were the first manifestation they witnessed and, even then, with unbelieving eyes.

Then, seized with panic, they saw the goatish shape as it came bounding from an ugly patch of woods and into the clearing.

Nothing, they thought, could be more ineffable than the awesome bent giant who was now lumbering toward them, reeking of dread-sweat and olde lust.

But, one by one, they glanced upward to see the face of the unclad woman who rode upon the creature's back.

More dreadful than the appearance of the Beast was the face of its Bride. Her aspect, the living emblem of unbridled Rapture.

✦

TUBBY MCMUNGUS, FAT FROM FUNGUS

By Molly Tanzer and Jesse Bullington

✝

Molly Tanzer burst onto the international scene of haute couture merkin making with her independent NetherFresh line, a bold fusion of classical lines, modern textures and a decidedly post-modern sensibility. Following a meteoric rise to the upper echelons of naughty bits high fashion, she quickly solidified her reputation as a mons pubis perruquier par excellence with her frankly challenging Cuttlefish Nightmare exhibition. Rather than deigning to address the baseless rumors of rampant catmint abuse that have dogged both the designer and her models, Tanzer has instead turned her attention toward a writing career, publishing short fiction in venues such as *The Book of Cthulhu, Running with the Pack* and Innsmouth Free Press' previous anthologies *Historical Lovecraft* and *Future Lovecraft.* In September of 2012, her debut tome *A Pretty Mouth* was published by Lazy Fascist Press, and while it is brimming with historical weirdness, unchecked degeneracy, bizarre transmogrifications, unexpected allusions, ribald humor, and copious puberty horror, it does not have any talking animals or merkins in it. Unfortunately.

Jesse Bullington is the author of *The Sad Tale of the Brothers Grossbart*, *The Enterprise of Death* and the forthcoming *The Folly of the World*, as well as assorted other fictions. A truly dedicated Brony, he could never pick his favorite My Little Pony, but he admires Pinkie Pie's pluck, vim, and spirit. He also enjoys hoppy IPAs, Korean crime cinema and playing with ferrets. His longtime rivalry with Molly Tanzer's cat Lemmy provided the authors substantial inspiration for this piece. He lives in Boulder CO, but you can find him online at www.jessebullington. com

✦

THOUGH THE TIME OF the Great Itching is but a memory, if you venture into the Cheapside slums on a warm summer's eve you can still hear the little rat-pups singing this skipping-song as they jump-rope:

> Tubby McMungus, fat from fungus,
> Spread the patch-plague all among us!
> Fake-fur-bedecked,
> Bald patches unchecked,
> How many beasts did he infect?
> One, Two, Three ….

And so on.

But there are few creatures outside our colonies who still remember that this rhyme shares a subject with another popular ditty:

> Do you know the Merkin-Maker
> The Merkin-Maker
> The Merkin-Maker?
> Do you know the Merkin-Maker
> Who sells on St. James's Street?

But they surely are about the same bad puss.

In the days following the Restoration, when the merrie monarch Chester II revived the glorious Cat Court, there lived a merkin-maker by the name of Tabby McMungus. McMungus was the proprietor of an exclusive boutique on St. James's Street, where the *noblesse* would go to groom themselves sweet. His shop, Grimalkin's Merkins, sat between Furcombe's Perfumerie and Cattray's, a high-end tobacconist, and on every day of the week, you could see gentlecats in their high boots and ruffs nimble-footing over to McMungus'.

McMungus was a smart businesscat and, thus, knew his clientele for the fickle creatures that they were. To that end, he crafted the greatest assortment of luxury merkins to be had in all of London-Town using scales and supple leathers, exotic furs and rarer feathers. He even crafted a merkin of living catnip for King Chester II himself when the monarch wished to seduce Lady Widdershins, Duchess of Portsmouth, who did indeed become his mistress. It was made of fertile earth held in place with mesh, sown with seeds; all the King had to do was water it regularly to keep it fresh and potent. With that sort of talent to be had for a price, none of the Court would *ever* be caught wearing any of the merkins to be had at the shops of Mrs. Mews or even the Bond Street Wig-Weavers.

Now, given the demands and diversity of his clientele, McMungus could hardly be expected to manage the work on his own! Nay, he employed an apprentice, an emigrant doe-rat called Miss Mousha. Underpaid, unappreciated and overworked, she did her best — but McMungus was as difficult a master as any in a fairy tale, or tract on the tribulations of the working classes.

"Oh, Miss Mousha," we heard McMungus growl as he sat smoking his pipe and drinking a postprandial glass of sherry the afternoon it all began. "My belly is full and so is my pipe" (he pronounced it *peep*, a peculiarity of speech it had taken Miss Mousha some time to comprehend), "yet you're still hard at work. While I dine on exotic mushrooms and smoke rare toback, you labour until your paws bleed. Is that fair, Mousha? Is it *just?*"

"I couldn't say, sir," Miss Mousha squeaked, her brow damp with sweat as she punched needle-hole after needle-hole in a patch of leather nearly as big as herself.

"Before you came, Mousha, my claws would cramp doing that sort of work," said McMungus, flexing one paw as he puffed. "It is a great help, what you do."

"Thank you, Mr. McMungus," said Miss Mousha. Compliments from her master were rare and his unexpected kindness made her workload seem much more bearable.

"But sometimes," he said, narrowing his orange eyes, "I do not know if employing you is worth it, for I am forever plagued by *your ratty stench!*"

"Oh, sir. I *am* sorry, sir," said Miss Mousha. Sadly, that was more like it. She tried not to feel sorry for herself; she knew she was lucky to have a job. There were many rats who could not find any employment, so even though she had already developed acute rheumatism in her short tenure as Mr. McMungus's apprentice, she tried to find the bright side of things. It was hard, though, especially when —

"Mousha, you dumb bitch!" McMungus yowled, startling the rat from her reverie. "I said *crème* leather for the backing, *crème*, damn your eyes!"

"*Crème?*" Miss Mousha blinked down at the leather. "But, sir, this is *crème*. I —"

"Balderdash!" McMungus cast his clay pipe into the hearth, where it exploded. Miss Mousha cowered as the tom stormed around his shop until he located a swatch of leather and, shaking it in her face, exclaimed, "*This* is *crème!* What you've got there is cream! *Cream!* Don't you know the difference?"

Miss Mousha *did* know the difference and, so, she knew that what she was working on was *crème* in colour. It was just that the candlelight made it look paler … Not that Miss Mousha would correct him, of course. It was not wise to correct McMungus, not when he had been into his pipe and his sherry.

"Cream!" McMungus raged, casting the swatch at her feet and stalking to the door. Pulling his high boots on, he snarled, "You've ruined my mood — how shall I woo any new commissions at the Mad Menagerie tonight? If I look like a grumble-puss, no one will want to talk to me about my merkin-making!"

"You're always so jocular and pleasant, sir. I'm sure —"

"Be sure of nothing! I warn you, Mousha," he waggled a claw at her. "If I don't secure enough orders tonight, I shall need to reconsider if I can afford an apprentice. And if I fall upon hard enough times, little Mousha, I might just use *you* for a merkin!"

And then he whirled his cape around his shoulders and stormed out, slamming the door behind him. Miss Mousha buried her face in the half-punched *crème* leather.

After this dramatic exit, we saw McMungus pause and listen at his door, just so he could be sure Miss Mousha's tears were flowing. Perceiving a pathetic sob, he sallied forth to the Mangelwurzel, his favourite public house, where he restored his spirits with two pints of bitter and a nuzzle at the tuzzy-wuzzy of Calico Annabelle, a molly whose time was usually for sale. Though McMungus was not profligate — what good shopkeeper is? — he had not lied about needing to be in top form that night for the Mad Menagerie and, so, considered his coin that afternoon well-spent.

The Mad Menagerie, you see, was an annual entertainment, sponsored by King Chester himself, much anticipated by every member of the Cat Court. It was really more a high-stakes competition than an entertainment, we should clarify, as the Mad Menagerie has, like so much, passed into history.

Every year for the Mad Menagerie, wealthy noblecats would attempt to outdo one another by paying game-hunters to capture the rarest, most unusual creatures. They would hire handlers to parade them before a panel of judges — and then take all the credit themselves, of course! The winner was awarded a gold-handled whip and given the appointment of Master of the Menagerie for the following year. So, you can see why everypuss who was anypuss would be at Whitehall to witness the spectacle.

Now, for those well-to-do merchants like McMungus, the Mad Menagerie was also an opportunity to showcase their wares and attract new clients. To that end, he hurried home so he would have plenty of time to make himself smart. He donned a short velvet cape, his best boots, his most impressive capotain, and — of course — a merkin he had manufactured especially for the event. Spring was coming and, so, he had sought to recall the colours of that season. The backing was a gold-green field woven of wool and hummingbird-wings, studded with lacquered holly-berries painted with black spots, and it was trimmed all around with blue feathers. The effect was that of looking upon a meadow thick with ladybugs on a cloudless day, and he knew it to be the finest merkin he had yet created.

It was with supreme confidence that McMungus jumped down from his coach that night and strutted up to the palace … only to be waylaid by his comrade, Captain Edwin, a sable ferret who had made a name for himself during the Second Battle of Newbury. Quite the fop these days, he was dressed elegantly in a stiff pink ruff and lace gloves, low buckled shoes, clocked stockings and — Mr. McMungus was pleased to note — a merkin of fine seal-leather that he had purchased barely a fortnight ago from McMungus' shop.

"Ah, Tabby!" cried Captain Edwin. "You're looking well — perhaps a little too well!" He poked McMungus in his wobbly midsection.

"Business has been good, Eddie," replied McMungus, rubbing his tummy, "but tonight is about pleasure. I am *so* looking forward to the majestic display of nature's curiosities."

"Hogshit," said Captain Edwin. "You're here to peddle your dick-wigs by flattering the peerage. And why shouldn't you? Got to stay current, or they'll soon forget all about you and your merkins; move on to the next craze, what? Blast, there's Lady Du Peltier's father. I'd better scoot!"

As Captain Edwin bounded away, McMungus went in search of refreshment; after snagging a bowl of syllabub from the buffet, he wandered in among the gentlecats, noting who was wearing his merkins — and who was not. He was pleased to see his wares girding many an important loin and was feeling pretty good about his prospects. But then, just as he saw the major domo appear bearing the golden bell that would announce the start of the Mad Menagerie, he overheard a clowder of fops chattering about a certain "Seignior Chiazza".

This stopped McMungus in his tracks. He knew this noble Italian was a manufacturer of merkins, but always felt them to be rather gaudy and pretentious ... at least, by English standards. It was difficult to speak for Continentals. So, you can imagine his surprise when he heard these local gallants declaring how they would never be seen in anyone else's merkins ever again!

"He's the best; that's all there is to it," said Lord Delon. This wounded McMungus — over the years, Lord Delon had spent twice as many guineas at Grimalkin's Merkins than any other noblecat, yet, tonight, he sported a merkin in the Italian style, all tinkling silver bells and crimson satin! "I can't believe I used to settle for the merkins at that dive on St. James's Street — I can't recall was it called!"

"It is a lovely piece," admitted Count Hubert. "But satin is so delicate. How does it support the weight of the bells?"

"This *isn't* satin," said Delon. "It's the leather of an elusive creature from the Orient. *That* is why Seignior Chiazza is the *best* merkin-maker. His materials are always so luxurious! He would never consider anything so common as *satin*. This is Rumble-Bump skin."

"Rumble-Bump? Rare?" McMungus interrupted, before he had thought what next to say. To buy himself time he faked a laugh. It sounded like he was passing a hairball — no, wait, we suddenly remember, he *did* pass a hairball, a large calico one. It landed on the carpet with a soft *plap*.

"Ah, McMungus," said Lord Delon, his face contorting as he attempted to raise an eyebrow and wrinkle his pink nose at the same time. McMungus smiled back at him — he'd known the gentlecat had not really forgotten his name and took this acknowledgement as a small coup. "We were just —"

"Decrying the deplorable state of Italian merkin-making; yes, I heard," said McMungus quickly. "Someone mentioned Rumble-Bump skin, which gave me quite the start — I cannot imagine even an *Italian* stooping to the use of such a common hide."

This elicited quite the sniggering from the other gentlepusses, but Lord Delon dismissed them with a wave of his paw. "Rumble-Bump is anything *but* common. It is the rarest beast —"

"Poppycock!" sneered McMungus. "Rumble-Bump is thought to be rare in these parts, but only because most Englishtoms don't realise it is cant for Crimson River-Eel. Pity the gib caught out in society with a peasant's dinner framing his loins!"

The tittering of the nobles in Delon's entourage was drowned out by the hiss of the lord himself as he said, "Tossssh! I wonder what exotic materials *you're* making your merkins from these days, you shabby tabby, that you should slander real mastercrafters? Hen-feathers from exceptional Essex? Whelk shells from distant Dover?"

McMungus blushed red as a Rumble-Bump under his orange fur, for the mercurial nobles were once again laughing at him, but he quickly silenced them with a boast he regretted as soon as it left his lips: "My spring line, Lord Delon, is made of such luxurious, unique, priceless pelts, that were you to make me a reasonable offer for *one* of them, you should require *a loan from a bank!*"

Lord Delon's green eyes widened and he growled, furious, but, before a glove could be thrown down, the golden bell rang across the hall. McMungus bade Delon a hasty farewell and nimbly scurried away; Lord Delon snorted a pinch of nip from his bejeweled nipbox and pretended not to care. None of the other nobles dared laugh, given the viciousness of McMungus's insult, but very few failed to hold a handkerchief up to cover their wicked grins. Whatever sport the Mad Menagerie offered this year, it would be hard-pressed to compete with the display they had just beheld.

Unsurprisingly, McMungus had a devil of a time enjoying his evening. As strange and wonderful as the Cerulean Sea-Beast or the Plumed Wumpus surely were, during the whole of the spectacle, he could feel the baleful gaze of Lord Delon burning into him from across the hall. What on earth had possessed him to make such an enemy of his former patron? Bad a prospect as that surely was, a much grimmer one presented itself in the form of a message Captain Edwin delivered midway through the Menagerie.

"Is it true, Tabby? Say it is!"

"Only if it's not," said McMungus distractedly. "For God's sake, be still. I can't see the Pippletrix!"

"What?" Captain Edwin continued to duke in front of his friend. "Listen! Word's out on your wager with Delon! The King's to be the judge! Once and for all, we'll show those oily spaghetti-slurpers what we think of their Papist merkins!"

"What?" gasped McMungus. "What wager?"

"Whether you or Seignior Chiazza can make the finer merkin before the Easter Ball. I should be the one to model it for you, don't you think, especially with King Chester judging? He once —"

But McMungus had stopped listening, as his heart seemed to have seized in his chest. Delon, that villain! Gazing across where the Pippletrix was being led back behind the curtain, Delon met the merkin-maker's eyes and waved his handkerchief in salute. Making matters even worse, King Chester noticed the exchange and raised a fuzzy eyebrow at McMungus. So, it really was true.

McMungus knew if he were bested by an Italian in front of the entire court, he might as well retire — no gentlecat would ever set foot in his shop again! He may have been proud, but he was no fool, and with Lord Delon financing the most ostentatious commission money could buy, the Italian merkin-maker held a devastating advantage. Might as well sack Miss Mousha, pack up the shop and run away to Holland, where his cousin made periwigs. Better to be an anonymous Dutch merchant than to face a courtly humiliation. All hope was lost; his life was in shambles. Nothing could save him, save —

"— tonight's final exhibition," the major domo announced as the saffron curtain parted, "thought to be last of its kind. Lady Widdershins presents a creature now unique on the whole of the face of the earth. For his majesty's pleasure, here we have ... the *last living Truffalo*."

Even McMungus' internal caterwauling could not compete with the sight before him and he went as silent as the rest of the normally cacophonous court. Even Captain Edwin stopped bouncing around, turning to gawp at the animal being led down the runway.

The Truffalo's upturned snout tested the air; its hooves clip-clopped daintily along the floor; its beady eyes seemed to stare into McMungus' own. His heart thrilled when it hooted a song, and if he had been able to tear his eyes from the beast, he would have seen he was not alone. All were transfixed by the Truffalo's grace and beauty. But McMungus found himself bewitched by a very particular copse of hair beneath its chin — a shimmering rainbow-beard that sang to the merkin-maker in a way no other patch nor thatch ever had. It was the most beautiful creature he had ever seen ....

And, if he could but obtain it, the solution to his most vexing problem!

"Just you wait, Eddie," said McMungus, leaning into Captain Edwin. "Maybe you'll model this merkin and maybe you won't — but I'll win this wager; you see if I don't!"

We may be the only ones who know what really happened later that night, in the stables where the attractions from the Mad Menagerie were housed. And though we know you may judge us for it, we confess we did not interfere in any way, helping neither Mr. McMungus nor the Truffalo. It is not our way. We watch from our perches in the rafters and lofts, listen from our dwellings in your attics. We observe from belfries, too: a cliché, perhaps, but they are well-suited to our needs. Suffice it to say we were there, blink-eyed and leather-winged — shuffling keening licking snuffling grooming — but not *too* occupied to see, after every stable-kitten had gone yawning to bed, the outer door open a crack — and a lone figure squeeze through with, admittedly, some difficulty.

McMungus held his paw in front of his candle, but the flame still guttered; he was trembling with nervousness. He wanted, nay, *needed* to hurry — but though he looked carefully into every stall or pen for his quarry, the Truffalo was nowhere to be seen!

He kicked the straw with his boot, spat in disgust — and very nearly fled when his ruckus disturbed a napping stable-catling into a prodigious snore. Yet, when he turned, his candle-flame flared and he spied a door at the back of the stables. Investigating further, he discovered the king's mews, where his falcons and hunting-hawks were housed.

And that night, it also housed the Truffalo.

Who would have guessed that, despite those hooves and a thorough lack of wings, the beast would still prefer to roost on a perch than sleep in a stall? But the natural world is full of marvels, is it not?

"There you are," murmured McMungus, his excitement mounting as the Truffalo's beard-hairs glimmered in the candlelight. "Let's play barber, shall we?"

He grabbed one of the knives the falconers used for cutting jesses and advanced on the Truffalo. It whinnied at him, but McMungus softly cooed to it and the creature settled down, accepting his presence. Good thing, too, for McMungus needed to get very close, indeed.

Though dazzled by the creature's fur, as McMungus drew closer, he saw its hide was gorgeous, as well. In between the patchy tufts of the beast's shining pelt, phosphorescent whorls pulsed all over its skin, shimmering greenish blotches that, when McMungus touched one, left behind a powdery residue on his paw-pads.

Unsure if he should be amazed or disgusted, McMungus wiped the dust on his haunch, where it left a blue-green streak on his orange fur. Curious as to how long the glow would last, he used his knife to shave some of the powder off of the skin-whorls. Having nowhere else to deposit it, he scraped the edge of the blade into the bowl of his filigreed meerschaum pipe, which he only ever smoked at court. The residue illuminated the interior of the bowl with a spectral light.

Collecting the residue had unsettled the Truffalo, so McMungus stroked the creature's back to soothe it before setting to denuding it of its beard. Using his knife, he tried to cut quietly and quickly, not wanting to tug on any of the hairs, but the fur was coarse and resisted his blade. He had to saw at it to sever the strands, and so, to keep himself focused and the Truffalo at ease, he murmured a jolly song as he worked:

Do you know the Merkin-Maker
The Merkin-Maker
The Merkin-Maker?
Do you know the Merkin-Maker
Who sells on St. James's Street?

Once he had collected a hefty pawful of the shiny strands, McMungus lowered his knife — only to see, just behind where he had trimmed, a throat-tuft of the most brilliant peacock-green he had ever beheld. Entranced, the cat hefted his blade once more ....

McMungus had not thought these hairs would be so difficult to trim, but they were. The angle was all wrong, so he took his time and made sure to be quite careful — but then, entirely by accident, he yanked a little too hard.

The creature screeched and pulled its head away from McMungus; McMungus, in a panic to pacify the beast, jerked his paw away. Alas! With the cat's frantic movement, the knife-blade shone brighter than the creature's patchy skin and, *quelle horreur*, violet blood spurted out from the Truffalo's throat, spilling over McMungus' paws and arms and cape and face! He was absolutely covered in the hot, sticky liquid and, when the Truffalo fell off its perch and began to thrash and shit itself upon the sawdust-covered floor, McMungus knew his life was over. Surely, he would be heard; surely, someone would come; surely, surely. ...

McMungus returned to his senses in a dark alley several streets away from Whitehall — clutching the knife, the small pipe full of glowing powder and the hairs he had trimmed from the Truffalo.

He had escaped!

With a mew of triumph, he scampered back to his shop. He may have killed a unique and beautiful creature, the last of its kind, but he had achieved his own purpose in the doing of it. *Not such a shabby tabby after all,* he chuckled, tucking the hairs into his boot so he could open the door to Grimalkin's Merkins.

"Mr. McMungus, whatever has happened?"

"What?!" McMungus swung 'round. He had not expected to find Miss Mousha still working — but there she was, staring at his blood-caked fur.

"N - nothing!" snarled McMungus. "Never you mind! You, ah, go on home, Mousha — but be here early anon! We have a new commission — a big job. You see here I'm covered in dye, already, ah, and I shall need you *alert*." He fumbled with his belt-pouch and threw a handful of coins at Miss Mousha, more than she had earned in working for him for a whole year. "Go and buy yourself some cheese and go to sleep, Mousha — then, tomorrow! Tomorrow!"

"Yes, sir, Mr. McMungus," said Miss Mousha, as she gathered up the coins — and fled.

Given that several of our number made their beds in the loft above Grimalkin's Merkins, we were able to watch Mr. McMungus as he worked over the next few weeks — and work hard he certainly did. The merkin-maker threw the whole of himself into the endeavour, labouring over the new merkin day and night, sometimes beginning even before Miss Mousha arrived — and, every day, that poor doe came an hour before sunrise; well, every day except Caturday, of course.

At first, McMungus refused to let his apprentice lend any help whatsoever, bidding her merely clean up after him and keep the candles lit for fear she would spoil his Great Work, but, as the days passed, a curious development forced his increasingly pudgy paw: The merkin-maker took ill. Unable to keep his claws steady, he had no recourse but to accept her assistance.

You might think a pupil would be delighted to aid her teacher in his masterpiece, but we saw all too clearly Miss Mousha's trepidation at handling the strangely luminescent powder, her nervousness over touching the shimmering beard. We suspect — for she did not share her thoughts with us — that her anxiety was partly her concern for

McMungus and partly that she, not being stupid, realised his strange malady had begun hot upon his bringing home those odd materials. The latter we surmise because she used gloves while working, which was not her custom.

Her caution was justified; McMungus's illness was terrible. It began with an intermittent itching a day or two after he began work on the merkin. As the tabby was prone to odd complaints — itches, sneezes, night-hoss, and something he called "hot nostril" — Miss Mousha thought little of it … until she noticed he had licked himself raw in places, so dire was the irritation!

It made Miss Mousha blush to see her employer's bare skin shining through the ever-widening breaks in his fur — and yet, she could not help but look. It was a curious thing: Rather than being smooth and pasty, as she had expected, McMungus's epidermis was mottled with the most lovely pale-blue whorls, as though seashells pressed up through his skin. At first, she thought it must be the candlelight playing merry hell with her overtaxed eyes, but, when he absent-mindedly scratched one of these spots, it pulsed with the dim light of a distant star. We saw her looking back and forth betwixt the thimbleful of "dried firefly spit" Mr. McMungus had so recently acquired for this new project and the almost-glowing spirals speckling his patchy hide; perhaps she noticed some similarity, but we did not ask her ….

In the final days before the Easter Ball, Miss Mousha was obliged to take over more and more of the project, as a frightful new development took place. Though Miss Mousha whispered to herself that she was imagining things, after McMungus demanded she take a break one morning for a few hours to let out the seams of his favourite waistcoat, she could no longer deny it: Mr. McMungus was as bloated as a drowned toad. Swollen and increasingly immobile, her employer was now constantly scratching at himself — and not with his tongue or toes like any noblecat should. Instead, he fixed a merkin-punch to a yardstick, as his girth was now such that he could not reach any of the worst tickles.

Crabby a feline as he could often be, Miss Mousha's heart went out to her master as she redoubled her efforts to ensure the merkin in her work-hardened paws was the finest ever made by cat or rat — and even as she felt a strange itching begin under her own fur, as well. She went to an apothecary and purchased a tincture for it, but she did not tell her master she had done so. He had grown strangely paranoid and suspicious and seemed to suspect everyone of plotting against him, herself included.

Despite her resolve, Miss Mousha's complaints began to hinder her pace and, so, it was only the night before the Easter Ball that the merkin was, at last, finished. The rat's poor paws had been rubbed completely free of fur from all the extra hours she had volunteered, but she did not care, for what a triumph the merkin was!

She brought it for McMungus to admire and admire he did. So, imagine her shock when, at that late hour, he insisted that she craft a dozen more! Her disbelief at this impossible order was somewhat mitigated when her master clarified that these twelve additional merkins were to be simple affairs, made from nothing more exotic than kidskin and cat-hair, but still. She was weary to her very bones, so, when, at last, she laid the last orange merkin on the worktable and rose to her shaky feet, she began to weep from exhaustion.

McMungus, startled into kindness, put an almost fatherly paw on her shoulder — but then withdrew it quickly, grimacing in disgust when he saw the strap of her apron had worn her fur clean away to her blue skin. He was doubly revolted when he saw, too, that the belly beneath that apron was twice as round as it had been a fortnight ago! How shameful — of course she was tired if she'd been out getting herself pregnant when she should have been sleeping! The thought of all the pinkies wriggling in her guts turned his own; still, her merkin-work was magnificent and McMungus felt he owed her a compliment.

"Excellent job," he said. "Take a holiday tomorrow — but be here the day after! You shall return to quite the increased workload, I should think! When those prissy pusses see this piece, they'll be breaking down my door!"

"Yes, sir," said Miss Mousha, her eyes brimming with tears as she looked down at her ruined paws.

"Oh — and you won't tell anyone about those last pieces you made — will you, Mousha?" growled McMungus.

"Of course not, sir!" she squeaked. "I'd never tell a soul!"

"Supurrrrb," he purred. "Because if you did, Mousha —"

"No one will know. I *promise*," interrupted Miss Mousha, too tired for manners. "I've been so mum about it I don't think even the attic-bats suspect what we've been up to!"

Alas! We know she never meant to cause mischief, but, nevertheless, alas!

"Indeed," said McMungus. We should have known from how pale his patches went that something was amiss! "In*deed*, Mousha. Well, good night."

"Good night, sir," she said and departed.

"Yes, a very good night," McMungus said under his breath and then, too loudly we know now, he added, "I shall have to ask my upstairs tenants if they know of another potential apprentice. Mousha's so fat she'll spill her pups any moment and I'll really be in trouble if I don't have a replacement at the ready. I *do* hope some of them are in …. "

We heard him rummaging around, but who would be wary of a tradesman picking up his flensing tools? We heard him on the stair, but we were expecting him after what he'd said to his quiet shop and had already put the kettle on. We saw his ruff-wreathed head poke through the trap, eyes aglow and then Tabby McMungus squeezed through the trap-door and into our attic.

"Let me just close that window to the street," said McMungus, as he waddled across the garret. "I know your kind like the dark, so let's not have that pesky moon shining in on us …. "

And we could hear him all too well as he muttered, "Never worked in *bat* before. Something for the summer line, mayhap …. "

Now, those of us *not* being murdered by a bad tabby over the perceived crime of possessing keen ears heard much that night. All the Cat Court was abuzz with rumour and speculation. Between bites of *canapés* and sips of champagne, every puss was speaking of the same thing: Would Mr. McMungus win the wager, or would Seignior Chiazza, the

Italian master? Bets were placed on the bet, as nobles are wont to do, but the odds were all in Seignior Chiazza's favour. Captain Edwin alone entertained even the slightest hope of a victory for McMungus, but who in all the Isles of Manx would back a weasel's favourite?

It was Seignior Chiazza who entered the king's hall first that night, revealing his merkin to the sound of ringing trumpets. Even Captain Edwin went quiet at the sight, for a finer piece of wiggery had never before been seen at the Cat Court. Even those skeptical of Continental fashion could not dispute the glory of the Seignior's merkin, a Rococo piece of such delicate beauty that more than one molly swooned at the sight of it and more than one tom wept to know his own loins would never be valanced as finely as this upstart Italian's. We saw King Chester himself bow upon seeing it — and heard him make a tasteful enquiry after its asking price.

The wager — nay, that Tabby McMungus was even expected to *attend*, fell from the minds of the Court as all jostled closer to get a better look at the feather-and-shell mortis, the butterfly-antenna threading, the precision of the needlework. The already-enraptured audience issued a collective sigh as the lanky, spot-hided Seignior, after winking at his patron Lord Delon, triggered the music-box component of his masterpiece, filling the silent hall with a haunting aria.

The entire Cat Court was entranced — awestruck — bewitched! The wager seemed so decided in the Seignior's favour that the clowder jumped as one when — just as the merkin's tune completed itself — three sharp raps came from the entrance to the hall. All eyes turned to the open double doors; King Chester deigned to glance up, half-annoyed at the intrusion, half-curious so see who would have the cheek to bang his swagger stick on the floor like a solicitor calling on a country squire.

There, silhouetted in the wide doorway, was none other than Tabby McMungus himself!

He waddled into the hall as if he owned the palace and, to the Cat Court's credit, the first thing we heard them commenting upon was neither how handsome was his fur (it shone from what must have been hours of grooming) nor the unexpected girth McMungus had acquired during the last month (though it was startling), but, rather, the magnificence of the merkin he had crafted. It was a thing of rare beauty and, though subtler than Seignior Chiazza's, no less marvelous for it. The gentlecats immediately began to argue in whispers: Was it pale-blue, or pale-green, or the pale purple-pink of wampum from the Colonies? Did it shimmer or glow? Was it woven or knotted?

Hearing the hubbub, Seignior Chiazza looked around at the captivated Court and, dismayed, realised he had all but lost — and lost to *whom?* Mr. McMungus of Grimalkin's Merkins? It was not to be borne! Why — just look at him! Fat, gross, low and staggering under the weight of his own bloated stomach!

The Seignior desperately glanced back at King Chester, whose covetous eyes were transfixed upon McMungus' magnificence. With the sovereign so obviously enchanted, all seemed lost, but then Seignior Chiazza noticed the molly by the King's side: Lady Widdershins, the Duchess of Portsmouth. She alone seemed unimpressed by McMungus's merkin — nay, she seemed … dismayed! Revolted, even!

Seignior Chiazza saw the way to win back the crowd's favour and, yes, the bet itself. Everyone knew Lady Widdershins had King Chester tied around her dewclaw; perhaps, if he won her over, she could influence the mangy monarch? He knew that sort of behaviour was dishonourable, but he couldn't lose! Lord Delon's continued — and necessary — patronage rested on Chiazza's winning and he had poured a not-insubstantial portion of his own savings into the construction of his contest entry!

The Seignior made his decision. Striding up to McMungus and sniffing in disdain, he said loudly:

"I see nothing remarkable in this merkin — or, for that matter, its maker! Why, it is so commonplace that to present it here is nothing less than an insult to this court!"

"Indeed, sir?" McMungus slurred. His lips were as swollen as the rest of him. "Are you calling me out?"

"Calling you out?" Seignior Chiazza tittered behind his paw. "To call you out, I would need to know what you are *called*! It has escaped me — was it … Tabby McMungus? Because, if so, I think you ought to change it to *Tubby* McMungus!" And then he poked McMungus in his pendulous gut.

"Oouf," said McMungus, feeling a bit funny in his tummy.

"This is an outrage!" cried Colonel Edwin, loyal to the last.

"I want that merkin!" yowled the King, pointing rudely at McMungus's crotch.

"For Bastet's sake, don't touch it!" exclaimed Lady Widdershins.

Now, if you have ever observed a cat, *any* cat, noble-littered or not, around an object he or she desires, you know it is not possible for that species to resist their thieving impulses — *especially* when that cat knows the object in question is beloved by another. Leave your delicious sandwich on a table for the briefest of moments and, if a queen takes a fancy to it, she will eat it; leave your ball of worsted on your floor and if a gib is in a playful mood, he will do what he will with it.

So, you can well imagine how the next few minutes played out: King Chester II darted forward, running on all fours like a common dog in the street and attempted to wrest the merkin from McMungus. The *noblesse*, seeing their king in such a state, scooted after him (One must, after all, follow the mode!) and, soon, the entire Cat Court had fallen upon McMungus. There was a great ruckus of howling and spitting and scratching and biting —

Then the sound of rending material —

A heavenward puff of sparkly dust —

And the riot of noblecats broke up, each clutching his or her own scrap of merkin!

"Oouf," said McMungus again, trampled, battered and denuded of his life's work. He could not hoist his tumescent body off the flagstones of the hall without assistance — but the worst was yet to come!

"Stop!" screeched Lady Widdershins at the top of her lungs.

All the cats of the Cat Court, including King Chester, looked up from admiring their beautiful merkin-scraps and saw the molly hovering, curiously, in the entryway, her handkerchief held up over her nose. She looked desperate, ready to fly to pieces — or, at least, out of the room.

"What is it, my Lady?" asked the King, somewhat calmed from having seized the finest piece of the wig for himself.

"That merkin …. " she shook her head. "I daresay it was made from —" She gasped. "— *Truffalo hair!*"

"But the Truffalo has already departed, returned to its home along the Silk Road!" protested the King.

"No, it has not," said Lady Widdershins, still not lowering her handkerchief. "It was buried in a lime-lined grave *weeks* ago. It … died. Hemorrhaged to death from the pain of his ailment, ah, we think? It wasn't really … oh, the shame! But all of you, put down that merkin! The Truffalo wasn't really … a Truffalo. It was a common Yorkshire Tree-Tapir." She hung her head. "It contracted some sort of — well, we don't really know. The farrier suspected a fungal infection from eating rotten grain. It causes sores and hair loss and bloating — and it spreads like *wildfire*, I'm afraid, which is why the handlers at the Menagerie wore those long gloves. The sores get all … powdery. If it gets on you …. "

And then she fled the hall.

As one, the cats turned to look at McMungus, where he still lay on the floor, prone as a flipped tortoise and wide-eyed in horror. He writhed a little under their accusatory stares.

"Have you experienced any of these symptoms, Mr. McMungus?" asked the King, very quietly, indeed.

"No!" protested McMungus. "The long hours … eating poorly. You know how it goes! Don't you? Look at me — do I look … *infected* to you? Where, then, are these sores? What hair-loss can you see?"

It was then — at that very moment — that we exacted our revenge.

"Liar!" we squeaked, descending *en masse* from the rafters. "Murderer! Will you cause *more* deaths this night?"

Our cousins who had escaped the massacre in the garret at Grimalkin's had told us all, of course — there are no secrets among our people — and thus, we knew not only of McMungus's crime, but also his deception. We swooped down upon him and tore from his arms and legs and belly and back the dozen or so small, plain merkins Miss Mousha had crafted from leather and orange fur. Under them, as you already know, McMungus was riddled with the same telltale whorls that had so impressed at the Mad Menagerie, but now horrified the Cat Court!

"You risked all of us ... for the sake of a wager?" King Chester looked appalled, the Cat Court furious.

"Er," said McMungus, wishing, we are sure, that he had the power to get up and run for his life.

"Seize him!" cried King Chester. "To the dungeons with him! Hold him until we confirm Lady Widdershins's allegations. And if we are all subjected to this *plague* ... well, your fate will be decided then, *Tubby McMungus!*"

Over the next month, the Cat Court experienced some significant life changes. Merkins, perhaps not unexpectedly, fell out of fashion ... among the surviving members of the court, that is. More than one noblecat, we are sad to say, succumbed to dropsy, and some to blood loss from scratching too hard at the fungal whorls that affected most everyone who had attended the Ball.

But the *noblesse* were hardly the only ones claimed by the patch-plague, or the Great Itching, as the unfortunate *faux*-Truffalo's malady came to be called by Londoners. It did indeed spread like wildfire and the noblecats, heedless of anyone but themselves, infected their servants, who spread it further afield: to the apothecaries, grocers, prostitutes and other merchant-types who satisfied the needs of the wealthy. Those merchants, of course, spread it to their errand-kittens and under-housemaids, their suppliers and, of course, prostitutes, and when those unfortunate souls went home, they spread it to their brothers and sisters and parents and uncles ....

Thankfully, before *too* many had died, a Dutch physick by the name of Dr. Poes discovered an easy and inexpensive remedy made from grated garlic and lavender essence. Yet, being cured was not enough to satisfy unhappy London-Town. They had been sorely troubled by the patch-plague, after all — but, as is always the case, no one thought to blame the aristocracy. Thus, it was not Lady Widdershins who was punished for bringing the Truffalo to court in the first place: It was, of course, Mr. McMungus.

The merkin-maker had languished, untreated, in the dungeons for the duration of the Great Itching, increasingly swollen, increasingly hairless. He did not know those of his profession had become *persona non grata*; he did not know a cure had been found. He did not even know what had become of his apprentice, Miss Mousha (We do; she died). All he knew was that one day, when he was idly batting at dust motes in the meager sunshine that came in through the high window of his cell, he was seized by palace guards, had each of his four paws tied to a hungry carriage-hog, and, though he screamed for mercy, was drawn and quartered for his crimes against cat and country.

And so ends the ignominious tale of Tubby McMungus. His name has passed into legend; his crimes have been largely forgotten; and all that is left of him are two silly songs. None remember the glory of his merkins, save us — but history is written by the victors.

↑

WILD MUSHROOMS

By Jane Hertenstein

↑

Jane Hertenstein is the author of over 30 published stories both macro and micro: fiction, creative non-fiction and blurred genre. In addition she has published a YA novel, *Beyond Paradise* and a non-fiction project, *Orphan Girl: The Memoir of a Chicago Bag Lady*, which garnered national reviews. Jane is the recipient of a grant from the Illinois Arts Council. Her work has appeared or is forthcoming in: *Hunger Mountain, Rosebud, Word Riot, Flashquake, Fiction Fix, Frostwriting* and several themed anthologies. She teaches a workshop on Flash Memoir and can be contacted through her blog http://memoirouswrite.blogspot.com/

↑

WE ONCE HAD AN infestation of oyster mushrooms sprouting in the corner of our unfinished basement after a heavy July downpour. Mother used straight bleach to kill them, but they came back, again and again, a persistent, pervasive fruit. A blight impossible to get rid of.

Hunting for mushrooms wasn't simply recreational for my family; it was how my parents put me through college, made the down payments on the living room carpeting and eventually paid for Tata's treatments. In the early years, it was mushrooms that sustained us. My mother would freeze a Chicken of the Woods like one would a whole fryer, adding slivers of it to stews or flavouring soup throughout the winter.

My parents came to the States from Czechoslovakia (when it was Czechoslovakia), where it was a tradition to forage. One generation taught the next what to look for. Very rarely did someone die from eating a "bad" mushroom. Once you know the difference between a cep and a Death Cap, it is difficult to confuse the two. Mom and Tata came to America in 1969 after "Prague Spring". (My mother remembered the morels as being particularly abundant that year.) They simply walked out. I was skeptical; how was that possible? People didn't just walk out of a Communist country. "You mean *you escaped*," I corrected her.

I've always had doubts about my ability to fully understand them. I grew up hearing Czech spoken in the house, but, as soon as I entered kindergarten, I forgot the language, left it far behind. I often found myself correcting my parents' floundering English in an incriminating tone of voice.

"We just walked out," she repeated. "We say, 'Okay, today the day.' We put on layers of cloths." (Mother always mixed her words up. I blame her — I frequently have trouble remembering the difference between 'breath' and 'breathe'.) "Pretty hot outside, we sweat. We walk through forest with basket. No one see us. Just look like peasants. Mushroom pickers. Cross border; make our way to Austria."

I was embarrassed by their thick Slavic accent. During a time of Cold War, kids were always asking if we were Russian. I especially hated Mom and Tata's combination of clothes (cloths?). From October to April, my father liked to wear over his shirts a thick wool vest that smelled heavily of human perspiration, much like an overripe toadstool, and Mother lived in floral housedresses, the kind that, when you bend over, reveals the lardy part of the upper thigh. For her, it was either the housedress or an all-over apron paired with rubber mackintoshes for slogging about in

132

the fields. When you're 13, the worst thing you can think of is running into a classmate while at the IGA in town, with your mother pushing the grocery cart dressed like a babushka mushroom hunter.

I suspect that the difficult relationship I had with my parents stemmed, not so much from language confusion, as from a gap, a failure to grasp all that they'd been through. We were worlds apart, like the difference between an emerging nation and a developed country. It's hard for me to believe I might have once dreamed in Czech.

↑

It was always my job to clean the mushrooms. Saturdays and Sundays were reserved for *houba* hunting. I'd bring homework with me and sit in the car, or else read in the backseat while they walked off into the woods. It was bad enough to have immigrant parents, but I was petrified of having to explain to my friends why I couldn't spend the night or come to their birthday party or simply hang out on the weekend.

Mom and Tata would haul their harvest back to the car, where they'd unload the basket onto a moth-eaten Hudson Bay blanket. Immediately, my sinuses were attacked, a fusty odour on the order of old gym shoes, mildewed crawl spaces, fermented yard waste. Basic. Organic. Rusty pine needles and black, mulchy earth clung to the thick stems or thread roots. I used an old hand towel to brush them off. "No water!" my father hysterically warned. Mushrooms, when wet, seem to melt, perhaps because they are 90% water, a fact I learned in biology class. Dirt ringed my fingernails, embedding beneath them, and stained the calluses on the outside of my index finger. It took successive washings ("Too much water!" my father would complain, tsking. "You waste.") before my hands came clean. The smell, though, lingered in my nose as if imprinted on that part of the brain.

↑

FUNGI

My first year at college, I met a boy. I was so surprised; it felt like luck, which is why I suspected it was love. I hadn't been on the look-out, going to bars or floor parties. We met outside the movie theater on Court Street when I ran into his car on my bike. He had pulled up and flung open his door, just as I was riding by. I was thrown over my handlebars and landed on my head in the middle of the sidewalk. Good thing I was wearing a helmet. I never lost consciousness or suffered a concussion. He stayed with me the whole time until an ambulance arrived. I was actually more worried about my bike, which got even more mangled when a passing truck scooped it up and dragged it down the street. The boy and I stayed in touch over the Christmas holiday. At first, he felt guilty. The police cited him in their report as being the one at fault. So, Matt had to pay for my hospital bill — or, rather, his insurance, actually, *his parent's* insurance, paid — but it was only one night and just for observation because I complained of a stiff neck.

We dated for three years off and on, and not always exclusively, and then, in my senior year, we got into a big fight, broke up, and immediately got back together in a way that convinced me he was serious. With graduation looming and our future staring us coldly in the face, it was time to make post-collegiate plans. We both wanted to be in a big city and, since I didn't have a car, it made sense to apply for jobs in Chicago — he in sales and me in PR and/or communications. He suggested that we live together. Over spring break, I brought Matt home to my parents' house in downstate Illinois.

Mom made a glazed puff pastry wreath with a dyed egg in the centre and slow-cooked pork tenderloin in the oven. She garnished the baking dish with carrots and potatoes, and, of course, mushrooms. Matt took a bite and groaned as if in ecstasy. "Oh my God!"

"Yeah," I agreed, "the meat melts in your mouth. Good job, Mom!"

"No, no, something else. A rich, nutty flavour. What is it?"

Chanterelles and bay boletes dried from last season and reconstituted with the other vegetables. When I told him, he was immediately

134

intrigued. "Wild mushrooms. Wow, how do you know where to find them?"

My father tapped his temple as if insinuating inside his head. "We hunters have our secrets," he said, smiling cryptically.

Matt had to check it out for himself, so he and I drove out to a nature preserve. Snow had only recently receded. In the shadows was honeycombed ice as intricate as lace, easily crushed underfoot. The spongy ground was perfect for spawning mushrooms. We parked by the roadside and I retrieved out of the trunk of his car the old Hudson Bay blanket I'd thrown in at the last minute. "Don't be surprised if we don't find anything," I cautioned him. "It's a bit early." Though I was hoping we'd get lucky and find a morel. Morels were fetching $10 a pound at the time. Maybe we could put a deposit down on an apartment. After walking around for about an hour, we threw the blanket on the ground and made out, the aroma of warmed earth beneath us.

Things, though, didn't work out. He took a job in Phoenix and I ended up renting a studio. Later, I revisited the spot of our lovemaking and discovered a fairy ring, like eggs nestled in the short grass. I crouched down to inspect the tops, just to be sure, because there is a poisonous look-alike, not lethal but enough to make one sick.

↑

After two decades of living on the rural edge, my parents suddenly found themselves in the suburbs. Bridal Path Estates, Stonehenge Terrace, mini mansions on what used to be soybean fields. The three-car garages were bigger than our two-bedroom bungalow. Run-off from the chemically treated lawns caused the mushroom mortality rate to spike. Mom and Tata had to drive farther and farther away for their mushrooming forays.

A lot of people think mushrooms can grow anywhere, like rodents and other kinds of common pests. Indeed, in the most unlikely of places, Antarctica, there is a mushroom which grows at the rate of one inch for every five years. In the Chilean desert, there is a variety that survives on a diet of fog. Aside from those two extreme examples, conditions for mushrooms have to be just right. One degree hotter or colder affects them, the amount of rainfall or moisture in the soil, their tentative relationship to surrounding vegetation. Some mushrooms can only be found growing in tandem, or under a certain kind of tree, ergo the hedgehog fungus' reliance on the old fir tree. It's a mystery, a wonder. I can still see my father standing in dusty, forest-filtered light, giant puffballs at his feet like alien pod people. Unaware of me, he was in the presence of something much greater.

↑

Tata left the house in the middle of the night in order to get an early start at daybreak. It'd been a hard winter, made harder by the chemo. The doctor said he was in remission. The cancer was still there, but under control, manageable. Tata had lost a lot of weight. He resembled a photograph taken of him and Mom in Czechoslovakia before they escaped, *walked out*. High cheekbones hung on a lean face surrounded by a bounty of hair, a blond pompadour. Only now, his cheeks were grizzled and the hair was thinned, dull, with blue veins showing through. He left Mom asleep on the couch, no note. Likely, he was in too big of a hurry to get going. It was the prime season for black morels.

A veteran hunter can go his whole life without ever seeing one. They are like the golden egg of mushroom hunting, a hole-in-one, the big pay-off. Like a truffle pig, my Tata had a nose for morels, an intuition for where to find them, such as beneath an elm log or under a layer of rotting apples in an abandoned orchard.

The typical morel is about four inches tall, with the texture of a sponge, all wrinkled and hollow, phallic-shaped. It tastes like no other, a combination of surprising flavours like pineapple and filet mignon. And unexplainable, like hope and love, longing and regret. To eat one is to experience transcendence on par with a religious conversion.

He never came back. It was the end of March and nights were cold, below freezing. A search party was formed, but, without a definite idea of his whereabouts, it was like searching for a needle in a haystack, or a black trumpet, tough to spot because of its colour, which tends to blend in with the ground cover. Then, in the beginning of April, it snowed and the rescue teams switched to recovery efforts. Tata had kept his secret patches secret, even from Mom. She suspected he had gone into the woods to die. She reverted to talking to me in Czech, though I understood very little.

Finally, the following fall, a father and son came upon skeletal remains. When the county came out, sheriff deputies and forensics, they took snapshots, just in case there had been foul play. Mom insisted on viewing the pictures. The coroner was concerned that they might be too gruesome. A positive identification wasn't dependent upon her recognising the faded and broken clothing — though the vest would have been evidence enough. She took the half-dozen photos closer to a window, away from the glare of the fluorescent lights, and, one by one, studied them. At one point, she exclaimed — I believe I got her meaning, although some specific words can't be translated — "Look! There! A morel growing next to the foot."

We buried what was left of him in the National Bohemian Cemetery off of Peterson Road.

♦

The last wild mushroom I ate was in 1999. Mom sold the house, designated a teardown. The property it sat on was worth more than the wood and stone and seeping basement with its fungal matter. She went back to Czechoslovakia or, rather, the Czech Republic to live comfortably in a small house next to a forest where she hunts routinely, when she isn't too busy playing games on the Internet. Mom is addicted to the computer. She e-mailed me a photo of a cluster of leopard mushrooms, no good to eat, but beautiful, nevertheless.

I live alone in Chicago and shop at Whole Foods, where a package of buttons costs about $3.60. I throw them into scrambled eggs, not so much for flavour but for the aesthetics. There is no more taste to them than the Styrofoam carton they come in and the texture is disgraceful — limp, without body. There is no *there* there.

Last Saturday, I was driving back into town after a conference and, off to the side of the congested Dan Ryan in that toxic netherland between the berm and guardrail, I spied a shaggy ink cap, distinct even from a distance, next to a discarded Starbuck's cup. The traffic was bumper-to-bumper. It would have been nothing to stop, open the car door and jump out and pluck it. I was so tempted; I actually put the car into PARK. I couldn't think of why I wanted it so much and the more I pondered, the more I lost my nerve. Maybe it was the tears, blinding me. It was hard to breath (breathe?).

Since then, I haven't been able to get mushrooms out of my head. I see them everywhere. Cropping up in dark cracks. I am haunted by them. They are in my blood, running through my veins, feeding off the detritus inside of me.

↑

OUR STORIES WILL LIVE FOREVER

By Paul Tremblay

✦

Paul Tremblay is the author of the novels *The Little Sleep, No Sleep Till Wonderland* and *Swallowing a Donkey's Eye,* and the short story collection *In The Mean Time.* His essays and short fiction have appeared in *The Los Angeles Times,* FiveChapters.com and *Best American Fantasy 3.* He is the co-editor of four anthologies including *Creatures: Thirty Years of Monster Stories* (with John Langan). Paul is currently on the board of directors for the Shirley Jackson Awards. He fears many things, including the return of his banished uvula.

✦

12C. THE INK SMUDGES on my hastily printed out ticket evince my personal demise, which may or may not be Icarian. Clearly, the fickle process of evolution has left our DNA an amino acid or two lacking that we would choose to pay for the following privilege: to accept the temporary cattle branding of regimented seat assignment letters and numbers, to guzzle three-dollar diet sodas with ingredients found to be lethal to rats, all the while hurtling through the stratosphere at five-hundred-plus miles an hour.

All of which is to say: I hate flying.

As the tin can with wings lumbers down the tarmac, I try to ignore the in-the-unlikely-event-of-an-emergency instructions the attendant mimes through with all of the enthusiasm of a proctologist. Instead, I focus my anxiety into a singularity of hate for two passengers: One is the loathsome man across the aisle who does not believe that the pre-flight instructions to power off and unplug his electronic device for thirty nanoseconds apply to him.

The other passenger is in the seat to my right. He is a blond, short-haired young man, likely only in his early twenties (hints of post-pubescent acne ring his hairline), and he wears a brown sports coat with suede patches, as dark as commas, on the elbows. As one of the last passengers to board the airplane, his attire was what I first noticed. More noticeable was how he poured himself into the seat next to mine, followed by his awkwardly pommel-horsing into a fetal position with a near perfect face-in-hands landing. I assume he suffers from some form of illness. I do hope that it is of the self-inflicted kind rather than the result of an exotic contagion. I have yet to get a waft of alcohol emanating from his prone form, but, to be honest, I generally make it my business to avoid wafts when possible. Reaching above my seat, I adjust the oscillating blasts of circulated air accordingly.

During takeoff, the noises of structural stress, my alarmingly increasing angle of elevation and the contemplation of the physics of flight send the frightened rabbit in my chest scurrying for safety within the tightening warren. I make silent and embarrassing offers to propitiate the new gods of flight.

Oh, please, oh, please, oh, please ….

With some secret state of collective horizontal finally achieved, the pilot turns off the "buckle seat belts" sign and I exhale for the first time in thirty-five thousand feet. My blond neighbour puts down the grey, flimsy, plastic seat-back tray and leans forward on it; his head burrows deep inside his crossed arms, as if the tray is a desktop and he is a recalcitrant student brazenly napping in front of the teacher. I resist saying, "Excuse me, sir, but I do not think that is a load-bearing tray. Not that I'm implying you're a fathead." I vow to use my imagined quip in an as-of-yet unwritten story, which elicits a coy smile and an air-leaking-out-of-a-tire giggle. My compactly prostrate neighbour has the final, checkmate laugh, however, as I spy a politely discrete vomit bag on the floor under his shaking tray. With nowhere to go, I sidle in place (Does this count as in-flight exercise? One must worry about being still too long at these altitudes, as clots will form in the legs, then douse their merry way through the circulatory system to the lungs, heart, or brain …). If I could move into the next longitude away from his, I would.

The captain's garbled voice transmits through static-filled speakers, which does not reflect well on the aging electrical system of our intrepid airbus. Whether or not he's employing a two-wave radio or tin cans and string, the captain gets his message across: a forewarning of turbulence ahead. His syllables and syntax lilt in a practiced manner, one likely honed and focus-grouped to project a Zen vibe quite the opposite of what one associates with impending fiery obliteration. I confess to my ignorance concerning the science of flight, as I do not understand why, if the pilot knows there will be turbulence, that it simply cannot be avoided, like a car (a traditionally proper mode of transport) avoiding a pothole. Well, the plane rumbles through that first pothole and the next. As we dip and dance our merry way through the bumpy air, I imagine the overhead compartments straining against their overweight carry-on cargo, never mind the accumulated weight of us chattel sitting politely in our seats. Each jarring disturbance vibrates in a chain reaction of terror through the plane's floor, shaking and twisting my seat, tilting and torquing the entire cabin, and, please, there's no chance of my looking out the portside window to see the impossibly thin wings vibrate like tuning forks. My hands ball into impotent fists and I begin to sweat, to be blunt, in places that I didn't think I could sweat.

I slowly lie back against the headrest — slowly, because I'm afraid a hasty, too-quick movement might be the tipping point in our catastrophic equilibrium and, yes, it's utterly irrational and narcissistic to believe that my smallest movements and panicked thoughts would have any effect on the chaotic environment around me, however, under these circumstances, I *do* believe, which makes everything worse. My fear breaks down the very core of my inner self, id and ego with their knees comically clacking together. The next turbulent bump is particularly forceful and I'm convinced I can see into the future, that the next jolt will lift us from our seats, crack the cabin. The fault line will be in the section ahead of me, the lights will go out, there'll be a terrible bright light, then a sucking coldness and a plummeting, and I won't even be able to scream before the blackness.

I close my eyes and catalog the millions of people who have flown successfully. I focus on individuals and the secret lives of airline pilots and attendants for whom flying is a quaintly quotidian occurrence. I remind myself of the unblinking statistics: that even if one plane per day were to dart into the *terra firma*, it still would be safer to fly than to drive. However, like most Westerners, I'm functionally illiterate when it comes to mathematics and statistics; the numbers bring no comfort to my fearful lizard brain.

What feels like years later, the captain announces that we're safe to move about the cabin, as if we are aboard a luxury liner and the decks drip in golden sunlight. Preferring to lead my fellow passengers by example, I remain seated and make busy with my lecture notes, my *raison* for placing my own bacteria into this flying Petri dish of death.

I'm a minor author, much to my constant consternation, but a proud autodidact. Tomorrow morning, I'm to give a lecture on a collection of long-dead minor authors at a minor literary conference. At least, I'm assured, the hotel will feature adequate amenities, if I ever get there and this trip affords me four days away from my day job: an IT gig that is barely worth mentioning, so I won't. My lecture is an elegiac lament concerning literary heroes forgotten by history and a rant aimed squarely at the innately ethereal, impermanent nature of postmodernism, particularly as how it relates to our eroding Gothic fiction tradition, postmodernism being antithetical to timelessness in literature, to the nature of narrative itself, with its proclivity to promote the motifs of the mass popular culture and media of the 'frivolous now'. I hope the irony of my using PowerPoint during my lecture will not be lost on the students.

I'm not so adamantine as to realize that the war against postmodernism is long lost; we are all fated to reside within its blurry boundaries. To wit: I've placed myself in the belly of this aerial torture chamber with the hope that my lecture will get me *seen*, that my *network* will have expanded, that perhaps some of the students in attendance will sum up my ninety-minute lecture as a perky Facebook status update, or a one-hundred-forty character tweet including the phrase, "*It rocked!*," which would then, if I'm fortunate, result in my Amazon sales rank ticking up a few notches, like the doomsday clock. It doesn't get more hellishly postmodern than that.

Another announcement over the intercom breaks my reverie. Regimented by time and tradition, the attendant is making his first run with the drink cart: a cumbersome metal beast that renders the aisle impassable. How is that not a breach of safety, a breach of in-the-unlikely-event-of? I'd continue, however, superstition precludes me from using the word *breach* again.

My blond neighbour unexpectedly animates at the enticing offer of overpriced beverages. He breaks etiquette by demanding two cups of water. The attendant reluctantly obliges, passing two wide-mouthed plastic cups. The blond man inhales the first cup of water then re-assumes his head-on-desk position, cradling the still-full second cup. Perhaps the blond man deserves pity. Perhaps he's not hungover or virus-riddled, but, instead, like myself, suffers at the knotted, white-knuckled hands of aviatophobia. Regardless, remaining in my seat to obsessively watch his second cup of water slide and sway in the not-so-gentle, unseen, gale-force breezes through which we rocket has edged me beyond my limit, particularly when (after drinking my own cup of water) the pressure in my bladder has surpassed undeniability.

The sloth-esque drink cart finally finishes its labourious passage. I unbuckle my safety belt (a laughably flimsy and frayed strip of nylon), which brings its own twinge of warning within my system that I should not be doing this, that now will be when *the bad* happens. Walking down the aisle, I grip seat backs and rappel toward to the plane's tail. One attendant sits in a compact bench seat that has folded out of the plane's rear panel. Doesn't she realise she's sitting on a flimsy, manufactured ledge, one that leaves her permanently dangling above a precipice? She reads a gossip magazine and does not watch me origami myself inside the phone booth-sized restroom. If only there were an "S" on my chest to reveal; of course, the flying issue would remain. I slide the accordion door closed and engage the lock and its *Occupied* signage.

The roar of engines and violently parted air is amplified here, inside this weakly lit metal box. What if it's all gone when I open the door, and it's just me and this restroom, an elevator with a cut cable, forever descending? The now-familiar tremours of turbulence rumble through the plane. I teeter and bump into the shrinking walls and ceiling of the restroom. After urinating while precariously balanced above the metal toilet (I've never felt more vulnerable or ridiculous), I wash my fogged glasses and splash cold water on my face and beard. The second of two staccato jolts launches me into the sink and mirror. A red light above the restroom door blinks and the captain announces that we are to return to our seats, lift our trays and buckle our safety belts. I clutch the edges of the sink and stare into the mirror at the hunched, ascetic, dripping, terrified me, Quasimodo without his bell and belle and I ask myself why I agreed to do this, why I've ever agreed to do anything, as it's now painfully clear there is no point: I wrote a ninety-minute lecture on authors and books someone read once upon a time while arrogantly promulgating an ideal of deathless, timeless prose. I, myself, write penny dreadfuls of varying levels of monetary and personal success and failure. That I ever existed in the first place will not matter and I will be forgotten in a blink, as we all will be, and this, this is all an infinite jest, and it's here in the bouncing ball of the airplane restroom that I'm staring at the truth of our human condition, and it's one of existential, nihilistic, and cosmic aloneness.

Perhaps I should simply return to my seat.

I spill out of the restroom as I attempt to gain equilibrium, the plane lurching and tilting along with my frantic corrective movements, as though I am the fulcrum of the plane's lever. The cabin lights flicker and the atmosphere ionises with my thick worry and the whimper of mortality. My traitorous feet fail me now; they won't take me down the dark and treacherous aisle; they deny the folly that returning to my seat would result in safety and salvation. There's a stomach-shriveling dip and a teeth-rattling bang, a bang implies impact with something. Can there be a bang if there's no solid mass with which to impact? The groans of steel, alloy and plastic are the death throes of our technocratic civilization!

Then the plane stills. The resulting silence within the cabin is as uncanny as it is unexpected. I stagger toward my seat and past scores of passengers who have taken a posture identical to my blond neighbour: leaned forward, arms and heads down on their trays despite the captain's clear instruction to fold them into their upright positions. I dare a look back to the plane's rear and do not see the attendant in her seat. Perhaps she is hunkered with the other attendant at the front, behind the velvet blue curtain of First Class. Am I missing something? Am I flying with inveterate rule breakers or is there a new crash position that is blissfully unknown to me?

Almost to my seat and the plane is again buffeted by turbulence: an unrelenting, almost-tidal attack. A plummeting drop followed by a sudden overcorrection in our upward trajectory that lifts me off my feet. My loose lecture notes, which I left on the seat, explode into the pressurised air; the effluvium of my literary life's mission statement billows and spreads throughout the haunted cabin. I cannot collect those notes now and I briefly mourn the slipping away of ideas, those soon-to-be forgotten dreams, as I scramble into my seat and fasten my belt with the shakiest of hands. The next body blow cuts the main cabin lights and translucent oxygen masks drop from hidden ceiling compartments. In the odd under-glow of the aisle's emergency lighting, the masks are jellyfish divining the deep.

As I desperately fumble with the tentacled mask, an arm reaches across my lap, fiddles with the latch and gently unfolds my service tray. The blond man without sitting up, without lifting his head, places his vomit bag on my tray and says, "Take this if you want to live." His cliché line, one uttered by many a steroid-fueled American action hero, notwithstanding, I open the crinkly bag and empty its contents onto the tray: a dark lump, the size of my thumb, with an exterior that appears to be oily or moist, but is, instead, flaky and dry to the touch. Thick-stemmed and capped off at the top, it looks like a mushroom.

I turn to say something to my neighbour and, in the dim lighting, with his brown tweed sports coat, he looks like a mound of soil, of peat, of earth itself. I ask, "What is this?" There is no answer and perhaps there is an answer. Perhaps there's the tip of a brown tendril peeking out between his lips or it might be a shadow. Cupping the mushroom in my hands as if it is a robin's egg I wish to return to its nest, I briefly survey the cabin and see my still fluttering, dying-bird notes and the sway of the oxygen masks, none of which have found their intended purchase upon the gentle faces of passengers. My other neighbours are motionless, moldering, indistinct lumps.

The plane swoons and powers into a nosedive. Something breaks somewhere inside of me and outside of me. Without forethought, driven by hardwired instinct, I put the mushroom in my mouth. It disintegrates into mulch shards. Its earthy taste and smell, that of wood, soil, plant, and something else I can't quite identify, but which strikes me as anciently familiar, fills my mouth: immiscible with my saliva while, at the same time, deeply soothing, and sinking beyond tongue, palate, esophagus, membrane and directly into my bones. I lean forward, falling like an aged — but dignified — conifer, and come to rest with my head and arms on the tray, which is as comforting as a bed of moss, and I close my eyes.

Somewhere beyond the physical realm, I can see the never-ending future: The plane will, in moments and in *memoriae*, lose all power and it will crash. There will be no survivors, but, as promised, I will survive. I will not scream and I will not be alone. Everything onboard the plane will be incinerated in chemically enhanced fires that will burn beyond temperatures of contemplation and cleanse us of our old bodies. Scores of investigators and inspection teams will then overlook us, us underneath our new soil: the ash of the wreckage, the ash of our everlasting rebirth. We will all become one. Our filaments will twine together, forming our network of hyphae, our mycelium with a reach that will extend for miles and for centuries; you will not be able to determine our method of growth, or how we grow, or how we communicate. We will not be anthropomorphised, as we will be, simply, *beyond*. Our fruiting bodies will confound, belying our true size, which will be measured in hectares. Our language will be time itself. We will communicate and we will commune in the tongues of geological age. We will extend rhizomorphs deeper into the earth and we will grow to be as big and as old as the world. Our reach will be as unlimited as our appetite.

It won't be long before everything changes for you. But for us, there will be no change. There will only be us, beyond shape, time and space. We will never be alone. We will always be a mosaic of many. Unlike your impermanent dusty tomes of old and your digitally pixilated ephemera, our stories will live forever.

↑

WHERE DEAD MEN GO TO DREAM

By A.C. Wise

↑

A. C. Wise was born and raised in Montreal and currently lives in the
Philadelphia area. Her work has appeared in publications such as *Future
Lovecraft*, ChiZine, Clarkesworld and *The Best Horror of the Year Vol.
4*. In addition to her fiction, she co-edits the online 'zine, the *Journal
of Unlikely Entomology*, along with Bernie Mojzes. The author can be
found online at www.acwise.net

↑

SHE WAS THE REAL deal.

Jonah had watched her long enough to know and long enough to
know better, too. He should turn around and walk away. A woman
selling dreams; it was madness. He crushed out the last of his cigarette,
but didn't take a single step to leave the crowded train station.

No. Madness was a razor against his skin every night, trying to
recapture the feeling of a hundred shards of mirrored glass slicing into

his flesh. Love was madness, an infection deep in his bones. Madness was further down the road, *this* road full of not knowing and no answers.

"Shit." He flicked the butt of his cigarette away and made his way toward the woman who sold dreams.

Merrin was gone, probably dead. Probably. But he didn't know for sure. All he knew was that she'd disappeared into the night and it was his fault. None of the usual avenues had turned up any trace of her. If he wanted answers ... *if* ... then madness or not, it had to be dreams and the woman who sold them.

The woman sat among the roots of the vast iron tree in the centre of the station, legs tucked beneath a red skirt spread on the mosaic tile floor like pooling blood. At her back, the trunk twisted up and up, and overhead branches held up the station's glass ceiling. From each branch, globes — strange, moon-coloured fruit — hung, ready to light the station at twilight.

A cloth holding bones, coins, stones and leaves — every possible tool of scrying — lay spread before her. She looked up as Jonah approached, tilting her head.

"You smell of loss." Her eyes were white, frosted with a delicate pattern of mold, like lace over irises that had once been green. Jonah crouched.

"I ... I'm looking for someone. I heard you sell true dreams." Jonah's voice emerged hoarse, from a throat gone parchment-dry.

The woman said nothing, filament-veiled eyes looking through his skin to sort his bones, weigh his soul.

"Sorry. I've made a mistake. Sorry."

He rose to leave, but the woman's hand shot out, catching his wrist. Off-balance, he nearly tumbled into her lap. He stared at the hand gripping his arm. A skirling pattern of white, blue and green covered the back of her hand, spiraling up beneath her sleeve. Not a tattoo, not ink: mold.

"You're looking for a dream?" She leaned close, flashing teeth as evidence of her pleasure at his discomfort.

They were stained dark and Jonah doubted the stains came from tobacco. He couldn't begin to guess the woman's age. Anger — or something like it — hardened the lines around her mouth and put a bitter light in her eyes. She might have been ten years younger than him, or ten years older.

"How much?"

"Let's see." The woman laid a hand against his cheek.

Where her fingertips touched, Jonah felt tacky strands, like a spider-gossamer, pulled from beneath his skin. The woman drew back, unraveling the strands, only to wind them, cat's-cradle-wise, around her fingers. Jonah couldn't see the web, but he could feel it and he knew exactly what the dream-seller would see, taste, smell, hear.

Merrin. And the imprint of his fingers blurring the mirrors covering her skin. The scent of his blood, drawn every time they made love, mingled with her sweat. Murmured words and tiny sounds of pleasure; the beating of his heart, too loud inside his skin. Love.

"The coins in your pocket. All of them." The dream-seller leaned back.

Jonah filled her palm. She weighed silver and gold, before vanishing the coins too quickly for Jonah to see where they'd gone.

"Not here." The woman lifted the hem of her skirt, drawing a card from the top of her boot. It bore an address on Bergamon Street, in the Old Quarter. "Come late tonight. I have what you're looking for."

↑

Light skittered across the blade. He couldn't quell the shaking, not completely. Never could, not since Merrin had disappeared.

Jonah gripped the handle and drew a long, shallow cut along his thigh. He sucked in a breath, flicked drops of red from the razor's thin edge. His pulse steadied; the pain centred him.

Still, memories unfurled.

Merrin's tongue gathered sweat and blood from his skin. She raised her head long enough to smile at him. "I'm sorry. I didn't mean to hurt you."

"I know." Jonah stroked her hair, breathing her in.

She smelled like glass, which smelled like nothing except her. She smelled like Merrin — the scent only intensified by sex, heightening her *herness* as her skin slicked bright under his touch.

Jonah liked to believe Merrin was most herself after they made love. As if she came more sharply into focus when they touched, her essence clarified in the afterglow of sex.

Another shallow cut, matching the first.

The pain faded, too fast. But in the blood-sting, the razor slice, he could almost reach her. He could unwind time and hold her again.

Merrin's eyes were the same shade as the mirrors covering her skin, no colour and every colour, catching the light reflecting whatever was around them. They became sunset and starlight, moonglow and new leaves; they encompassed his world.

"Come on. Let's get you cleaned up." He took her hand, leading her from the bed to the bathroom.

He filled the claw-footed tub, the one luxury in his cramped apartment. Steam billowed, clouding her glass. The water swirled pink as she lowered herself into the tub.

"Don't you want to wash, too?" She trailed her fingers in the water.

"I'm in no rush." Jonah wrung excess water from a sponge. "I'll clean up later."

Another cut — lazy, quick. He barely felt the pain.

Merrin leaned forward, arms wrapped around her legs. Jonah sponged her mirror-studded skin. Water-dark tendrils of hair curled against her neck and shoulders. He breathed steam, breathed her.

Cut. Jagged. Hard.

He'd promised not to, but he looked. Below the surface, which merely reflected the room around them, lay the true essence of Merrin's mirrors. Fractured light and possible futures sliding across her skin.

Children they'd have one day — a boy, a girl, or both, and both with Merrin's dark red hair. Their house — a cottage by the sea, an apartment with a balcony overlooking the city, a stone bungalow surrounded by a rambling garden. Their future scattered mosaic-wise on her skin — Jonah and Merrin making love, a thousand repetitions in a thousand fragments of glass, each iteration taking his breath away.

A cut, deeper this time.

Then. *Then -*

Jonah sucked in a breath. Merrin shivered, the bathwater suddenly grown cold. The image changed, their perfect future replaced by a starkness that mocked Jonah with its implacability.

In every fragment of glass, Merrin lay dead.

Pale skin cradled shards of mirror — cracked, broken, emptied of every possible future.

"What's wrong?" She stiffened.

"Nothing." Jonah tried to back away, to unsee. His legs wouldn't straighten, keeping him crouched beside the tub, gripping its edge so hard his bones ached against his skin.

Merrin's eyes widened, reflecting the horror of his expression. She reached past him, dripping, to pull a towel around her as she stood.

"I told you not to look." Goose-bumps prickled between her glass.

Merrin stepped out of the tub. Water pooled at her feet.

Her fear — he'd put it there. Her anger, too. She'd seen what he'd seen, just by looking at his face, and it left her lips pressed thin, her expression closed and grim.

"Merrin …." He reached for her and she twisted away.

Jonah's fingers brushed the edge of the towel, but she kept going, bare feet slapping tile then the wood in the hall. His memory always quickened the footsteps, turning them into a run.

The razor, jagged, went deep. Jonah hissed pain and dropped the blade, shaking hard.

He let out a breath and gathered a wadded sheet to press against the wound and staunch the blood. It soaked red in an instant.

Merrin. If she was dead, did he really want to know? If she'd run away, if she was still alive and wanted nothing to do with him, would that be better?

She'd told him once her mirrors could lie. They showed possibility, not truth.

Jonah rose, dropping the bloodied sheet in a heap next to the door. He'd go to the dream-seller. Even if he didn't like the answer, he *had* to know.

↑

A green stink rose from the canals, wrapping Jonah's nose and mouth as he crossed one of the myriad stone bridges stitching the city together. His clothes snagged at his wounds, threatening to reopen them with every step. Brass numbers set into the bricks beside each door gleamed in sickly light from the globes hanging like overripe fruit from the twisted, iron trees lining Bergamon Street. Each light dragged his shadow away, fraying it and bleeding it into the city's greater dark.

He stopped at the address matching the dream-seller's card, a narrow brownstone joined to identical houses on either side. The woman opened the door before he knocked, light from the hallway framing her. She'd shed the headscarf, revealing a head bald save for the mold, delicate as lace, spiraling across her scalp and trailing down her neck.

"Come in."

Jonah followed her to a room crowded with a couch and low chairs, all patterned in faded red and gold. A cup of tea waited on a table in front of the couch, just the right temperature, as if she'd timed its making to his arrival.

"Orange pekoe." She smiled. She'd even added exactly the right amount of honey.

Despite the over-abundance of chairs, she didn't sit. The dream-seller leaned in the doorway, watching him as she sipped from a cup smelling faintly of jasmine.

"What use is it, knowing the future, if you can't change it, if your lover ends up dead anyway?"

Her words cut, almost as sharp as the razor. Jonah's cup rattled as he set it down, the desire to run overwhelming. But the dream-seller stood in the doorway, blocking him.

"Why did you come here, really?"

"I have to know what happened to her." Jonah hated how small his voice sounded.

"Dreams don't tell the truth any more than mirrors do. They're fickle."

Behind the bloom of mold covering her eyes, she watched him — intent as though the white filaments only sharpened her vision.

"What do you *really* want?"

Jonah's teeth hurt. His whole body hurt. He couldn't look the dream-seller in the eye. He looked at his hands, instead, shaking, pressed flat against his thighs.

"I want Merrin to forgive me."

"Ah." She nodded. "As long as you're clear." A smile shadowed her lips as she turned. "Come with me."

Jonah hesitated, but honesty had left him exhausted. He abandoned his tea and followed the dream-seller.

"Amaryllis." The woman's voice trailed back to him. It took Jonah a moment to realise the word was her name.

She opened a door in her tiny kitchen, leading him down a wooden staircase. The basement was cold; it smelled of cobwebs and the canals. Jonah imagined thick water pressed against the walls on the other side.

"I'll respect you enough not to ask you if you want to change your mind," Amaryllis said.

The dream-seller pulled a string dangling from the ceiling, flooding the room with uncompromising light. Their shadows stretched across the brushed concrete, stopping short of a dense, metal door set in the far wall.

Amaryllis crossed the room and pulled the door wide. It released with a faint hiss, a sound matched by the catch of Jonah's breath. Amaryllis stepped aside; the sight inside the cold storage room gut-punched him.

A dead man hung from a dozen thin ropes. His bare, blue-grey feet pointed down; his head lolled as though, at any moment, he would wake. Mushrooms — as thin as breath, as grey as moth wings — covered every inch of his skin. Only his face was clear, save one delicate blossom, just below his right eye.

"They didn't fruit until he died." Amaryllis' voice pulled Jonah back.

He closed his mouth, turning to stare at her instead of the dead man. She looked past him to the corpse, so Jonah couldn't tell which one she addressed.

"There's an imbalance in every relationship, one person who loves more than the other."

Jonah opened his mouth to protest, but she went on. "I loved more and he loved equally, everyone, just the same. It got him killed.

"He was shot. A jealous husband, a jealous wife — it doesn't matter. Everyone wanted something from him, more than he had to give.

"But I was the one they brought his body to in the end. I took care of him when he was alive, dream-drunk; why shouldn't I watch over him once he was dead? Nothing changes. After a week, two officials from the city came and told me I had to burn or bury him. They said I couldn't let him lie there and rot. It wasn't safe, wasn't sanitary.

"But I knew and I kept waiting. And I was right. He didn't rot; he bloomed."

Amaryllis plucked the mushroom from the dead man's cheek. She held it up to the harsh light, letting it shine through to show the delicate gills underneath. The mushroom's cap was so thin a breath might melt it. Jonah held his.

She twirled the stalk, pensive, eyes fixed on the mushroom now, and still not on Jonah.

"When he was alive, his skin grew with poppies the colour of blood." Amaryllis' mouth shaped a wistful smile.

Her lover hung — dead not dreaming, or dreaming not dead, ready to wake at any moment and stop Jonah's breath by opening his eyes. Had he felt it when she plucked the mushroom from his skin? Did it hurt?

A patch of mold curled across Amaryllis' cheek, gentle as a lover's touch. She put a hand to it, the hard line of her lips softening further.

Amaryllis held the mushroom out to him. "Let it melt on your tongue and you'll find your way to where dead men go to dream."

↑

In the glow shed from the iron trees lining the canal, the mushroom looked even more ephemeral. Jonah brushed the cap with one finger, wondering why it didn't bruise. He leaned against the low wall of the bridge crossing the canal.

The night smelled green and black.

What was better as a last image — Merrin running away from him, angry and frightened, or Merrin dead, her mirrors cracked and empty? It wasn't too late. He could still change his mind.

Jonah set the mushroom on his tongue. It melted the instant he closed his mouth, tasting of dust-turned wine, butter and deep cold — not earth but the worms moving through it; not the worms but their dreams. The last taste hit the back of his throat and Jonah gagged. He turned, gripping the bridge, fighting to keep the insubstantial slickness down. He sucked in a breath, the sick smell of the canal refreshing against the thickness coating his tongue, crawling down his throat and up his nose.

The world tilted. Sweat popped out cold all over his body. He stared fixedly at his wavering reflection in the dark water, focusing on it, focusing on not falling in. The image split, doubled, and a face beside his that wasn't his turned toward him.

Jonah whirled, backing against the bridge wall. The dead man wore loose black trousers and a black shirt hanging open. Beneath the shirt, covering his skin, poppies bloomed dense.

"Amaryllis sent you." It wasn't a question.

Jonah gripped the stone behind him. The man tilted his head, a curious and patient gesture. Dark hair brushed his collar and curled soft against his cheeks. His black eyes were tinged red, as if his entire being was soaked in subtle blood.

He took a step forward, reaching as if to soothe a frightened animal. Beneath the dead man's bare feet, the cobblestones cracked. Bright petals unfurled in the cracks, filling the air with a sickly-sweet smell, just on the edge of rot. Poppies ran riot, racing out from beneath his soles to swallow the stones.

The dead man took another step and the sky flickered. The night flipped from black to white. The dead man's skin turned grey, the blooms on his skin withering and falling away. He opened his mouth and black river water spilled down his chin.

Jonah reeled back; his only thought was escape. A hand covered in petals caught Jonah before he fell, pulling him back from the bridge's edge. The dead man eyes were black-red once more, his skin whole and blooming with flowers.

His gaze searched Jonah the way Amaryllis' had, sorting his bones.

"Are you sure you want this?" the dead man asked. "I could make you forget, instead." His breath smelled like poppies, too.

The grey-dead fingers plucked a flower from an equally grey chest and held it out. The corpse's eyes were black coffee, edged in dried blood. They were the colour of midnight and crimson dawn. He was the most beautiful man Jonah had ever seen, and the most terrifying.

Jonah opened his mouth, closed it on silence, then shook his head. "I need to know."

He couldn't look directly at the dead man as he gave his answer, but he glanced at him from beneath half-lowered lids.

The dead man's smile was crooked. "Too bad."

He tossed the poppy over the bridge and the canal caught it. It floated for a moment, incongruous against the slick green-black before sinking. The sky flickered again; the bridge trembled. The stone split and pale mushrooms fruited in place of red petals. Eyes white, skin blue, the dead man pointed to the water.

"There."

Dread swelled in Jonah's throat, stopping his breath. It stiffened the muscles of his neck so he couldn't turn his head. He knew what he would see and he didn't want it anymore. But it was too late to change his mind.

After an eternity, he turned.

Merrin rose, dripping, from the water. It ran black on her skin, like ink, fat drops tracing the flesh between the mirrors. Between floating and walking, swimming and drowning, she moved to the edge of the canal and clambered up the slick stone.

Jonah's pulse hammered, fear rooting him to the spot. Merrin crossed the bridge and stopped inches from him, her eyes the dull, shattered colour of broken glass. When she blinked blood ran from her lids. All over her skin, her mirrors were broken. Jonah couldn't see anything in them at all.

"I'm sorry." He reached for her.

She flinched away. "You shouldn't have looked so deep."

Jonah clenched his jaw, his fingers. "You shouldn't have run. I could have helped you. We could have figured something out, together."

Merrin blinked. More blood ran from her eyes. She shivered.

"No." Her voice blew — a cold wind coming from far away.

Jonah reached for her again, and again, she pulled away.

"I wasn't scared of death." Merrin's tone and gaze were steady. She met Jonah's eyes. "Every time you looked in my mirrors, all those possible futures narrowed the world. They piled up against me until I couldn't breathe. You saw what you wanted to see and you never once asked me what *I* wanted."

"That's not true! I never ...."

Jonah shook his head. He knew what he'd seen in her skin — all the houses they might live in, the children they would have had, different iterations, but always together, always happy. He reached for her shoulder. He caught her this time, digging his fingers in when she tried to twist away.

He gripped harder, desperate to hold her. His hands slipped, moved, squeezed. His thumbs pressed against her windpipe, crushing.

Her mirrored eyes widened, truth and lies tumbling through them; Jonah couldn't tell them apart.

His love had terrified her. She'd run away seeking her death. Her death was a tragic accident. She wasn't dead at all. She had a secret lover, a life of crime. He'd never really known her. She was a stranger and her mirrors had only shown him what he wanted to see.

"Stop." It wasn't Merrin's voice but the dead man's.

He put a hand on Jonah's wrist. Grey poppies, moth-wing-thin, covered his skin. His eyes were white, tinged with red.

Jonah let go, startled. His palms were lacerated a dozen times, slick with blood.

He whirled back to Merrin, but the space where she'd stood was empty, the only evidence of her the black water pooled on the stone. Everything had gone wrong. He'd meant to say he was sorry. He'd meant to fix everything. And now it was too late. Again.

"You should have taken forgetting." The dead man fingered the edge of one of poppies growing out of his skin, a delicate mushroom flower.

"Is it too late?"

"Probably. For you." The dead man's smile flickered like the world, the sky shivering back from white to black. The air smelled like poppies; his smile tasted like oblivion. "But then again, dreams are strange and fickle things."

Jonah blinked. He stood on the bridge alone, the thick haze of the canal rising around him. The iron trees shed haunted light. There were no flowers, no mushrooms blooming between the cracks in the stones.

The stars hadn't shifted an inch. The night went on, just as it had been before, as though he'd never dreamed.

Jonah ran a hand over his scarred flesh, the latest cuts just beginning to heal. They itched and he rolled back his sleeve. It might have been a shadow, a trick of the light, but he thought he saw a faint tracery of mold between the red and white lines.

The scent of crushed flowers mingled with the chill scent of a room beneath a small, furniture crowded house. He thought of eyes frosted white and eyes the colour of black earth, soaked in blood.

Maybe it wasn't too late.

Dreams were strange and fickle things, after all.

↑

DUST FROM A DARK FLOWER

By Daniel Mills

✦

Daniel Mills is the author of *Revenants: A Dream of New England* (Chomu Press, 2011), selected by Booklist as one of the Top 10 Historical Novels of 2011. His short fiction has appeared or is forthcoming in a variety of venues, including *Delicate Toxins* (Side Real Press, 2011), *Supernatural Tales 20* (Supernatural Tales Press, 2011), *Dadaoism* (Chomu Press, 2012), *A Season in Carcosa* (Miskatonic River Press, 2012), *The Grimscribe's Puppets* (Miskatonic River Press, 2012) and *The Mammoth Book of Best New Horror 23* (Robinson, 2012). He lives in Vermont.

✦

Being a true account of the recent happenings
at the burying ground in Falmouth Village
as related by the murderer Hosea Edwards
on the night before his death

I

I AM HOSEA EDWARDS, physician to the Village of Falmouth in the New Hampshire Grants and Deacon to the congregation thereof. Sentenced to hang for the murders of the Verger Samuel Crabb and the Reverend Judah Stone, and the subsequent destruction, by fire, of the Falmouth meetinghouse, I leave behind these pages, that they might be found by my jailers after my death.

Tomorrow evening, I will be ashes, my body burned on my instructions; and though I die a criminal, my conscience is clear. At my trial, I offered no plea or protest of innocence, for I hoped yet to spare you the knowledge of these events. But the time is short: The White child is dead and buried these two days and the long night nearly spent.

There can be no more hesitation. A full accounting must be made.

II

Last winter, the Reverend Ambrose Cooper, who first ordained me to the Deaconate, and with whom I had traveled from the town of Marshfield in Massachusetts to Falmouth on the west bank of the Connecticut River in the year 1767, returned to the Lord at the age of one-and-sixty. The ground being well-frozen, his body was transferred to the vault following the funeral to be buried in the spring.

The season soon passed; the grave was prepared; and, on the second of April, we lowered him into the ground. Our church's request for a minister had not yet been fulfilled and, so, the Reverend Crane from neighbouring Putney presided over the burial and erection of the slate headstone, upon which Samuel Crabb, the Church Verger, had laboured all winter.

'Twas a thing of singular elegance and beauty: fully four feet high and so heavy it required the village's five stoutest men to lower it into the sod. The stone was further distinguished by some of Crabb's finest work, including an inset likeness of the minister in his vestments, followed by some words of tribute that I had myself prepared. At the base of the stone was an epitaph that the minister had chosen when he sensed his time was upon him:

And he carried me away in the spirit to a great and a high mountain, and he shewed me the great city, Holy Jerusalem, descending out of heaven from God (Rev. 21:10).

They were sanguine words, perfectly befitting a man of his character, but on that dim April morning, with a soft rain falling and the wet earth yielding before us like the opening of a throat, I found I could not share in their hope; and afterward, when I returned home to my cottage, I fell to my knees before the fire and wept.

While the Reverend Cooper was in all respects irreplaceable, the Church soon dispatched a new minister to Falmouth. The Reverend Judah Stone, formerly of Norfolk in the British Isles, arrived in town on the 22nd of April and immediately assumed residence in the parsonage, which was sited outside the village proper at the base of Meetinghouse Hill.

A man of thirty, Reverend Stone seemed possessed of an imperturbable mildness and good humour. Many was the morning I saw him pass before the windows of my cottage with his hat tugged down to his brow, waving to all he encountered and greeting them with his usual cheer. His fondness of children was well-known, as was the patience he exercised in all aspects of his ministry, from the pulpit to the sickbed.

That is not to say that he was without eccentricity: His abhorrence of human contact quickly became apparent to us (and to me, personally, when he refused to take my hand on the occasion of our first meeting) and he was regularly attended by the aroma of the rose-water in which he washed. Furthermore, he was said to suffer from some obscure ailment of the joints, which pained him constantly, though he never consented to be examined.

But these were minor matters and inconsequential to us, given the depth of his knowledge and the strength of his faith; indeed, there were times that he seemed to us more spirit than flesh. In short, we soon came to believe that the Reverend Stone had been delivered unto us in answer to our oft-repeated prayers — but that was before the strange events at Meetinghouse Hill.

III

The Verger Crabb was the first to take notice. He raised the matter with the Reverend Stone, who dismissed the Verger's concerns with his customary solicitude and urged him to think no more of it. But Crabb could not push the matter from his mind and passed an uneasy night in his one-room cottage by the burying ground. The next morning he yoked his ox and readied his cart, and traveled to the village to seek my advice. When I learned of his discovery, I wasted no time in insisting that I accompany him to the churchyard that very day.

The sun was nearing the meridian when we arrived at the hill. We chained the ox at the base of the drumlin and completed the climb on foot. Crabb led me to one corner of the graveyard, northwest of the meetinghouse, to the grave of the Mead child, a girl stillborn three years before. The low slate had sunk halfway into the ground and now listed to one side at a sharp angle, as though to indicate the nearby grave of her unmarried mother, who had followed the infant in death, despite the Reverend Cooper's tender ministrations.

"You must watch me," quoth Crabb, "and closely."

Kneeling beside the infant's grave, he ran his index finger along the stone. 'Twas a gentle gesture, of exceeding delicateness, and yet the slate itself seemed to crumble upon contact with his skin. The stone flaked away in a cloud of black dust, finer in consistency than gunpowder, but of much the same colour. The Verger shewed me his finger, the tip of which was beaded with granules of the strange material. I noticed then, for the first time, that the man himself appeared pallid and gaunt, as in the throes of illness.

"For how long has it been like this?" I inquired of him, thinking, perhaps, that the stone's position on the outskirts of the churchyard had left it vulnerable to the influence of weather; but Crabb's answer made this impossible:

"Since yesterday morning."

I waved the Verger away and placed my satchel on the ground beside the headstone. Extracting a scalpel from my bag, I moved the sharp edge along the top of the slate and observed, once more, the curious manner in which it yielded to the faintest contact; first, in brittle shavings like a hardened cheese, and again, as a black powder. The latter form clung to the blade, but was wiped away with ease, leaving behind a stain. In this, I was reminded of nothing so much as the dust from a dark flower.

Next, I applied myself to an inspection of the marker's face, which I found to be in a similarly delicate condition. My scalpel stripped away the stone with ease, exposing a layer of black, ash-like sediment below the surface. Of this I collected a sample and secreted it away in my bag for further study. My initial observations had already led me to suspect that the substance was organic in nature; I hoped subsequent tests might lend further credence to this theory.

Afterward, Crabb and I descended the hill together and rode back into the village, where he left me off with a solemn promise to inform me of any further developments. Then he turned round the cart and clomped back toward the meetinghouse.

IV

Though I am not a man of science, my years at Philadelphia College bestowed on me a robust appreciation for, and passable knowledge of, Descartes' Method. Upon returning home, I set about preparing an appropriate framework by which to analyse the chemical properties of the black powder.

Having first divided my sample into three parts, I sifted the first third into a pewter bowl, which I left exposed to the air, while adding the second third into a glass dish containing water, retaining the final third for additional tests, as necessary.

On the following morning, the first sample appeared no different. However, the second sample, which had steeped in water, had undergone a singular transformation. By some obscure agency, the powder had congealed overnight and extruded itself into a series of black hairs, fibrous and delicate, all of which were fastened by unknown means to the bottom of the dish, as though seeking for purchase there.

The stench was indescribable; I can only say that it reminded me of the fluid from a lanced boil. Dark specks leapt into my vision and I turned swiftly away, lest I succumb to a spell of fainting.

That evening, I lighted a tallow candle and subjected the substance to one final test. With the aid of my steel forceps, often employed by me during so-called "breach" birthings, I gathered a small quantity of the remaining powder and held it to the flame. To my surprise, the sample ignited with startling swiftness and burned down to the forceps in the span of a heartbeat, releasing a plume of acrid smoke that caught like bile in my throat.

Afterward, when I went to wipe the instrument clean, I was surprised to find it devoid of char or ash. Whatever its nature, the substance in question had evidently burned through completely, leaving no trace of itself behind.

V

The following day, a Wednesday, I received a second visit from Crabb. He sought me out at the White farm four miles from the village, whereunto I had been called to perform an amputation on the eldest White child, Ethan, whose right leg had begun to exhibit signs of gangrene.

The procedure was performed with assistance from the boy's mother, who provided rum and a leather strap while the younger boys, Martin and John, watched from the doorway. The dressings in place, I made my farewells and exited the house.

Crabb waited for me outside with the ox and cart. As before, the Verger appeared sickly, his eyes hooded as if he had not slept in days. "The matter has become serious," intoned he with his typical solemnity. "I came for you at once."

We arrived at Meetinghouse Hill early in the afternoon and scaled the steep hillside. Our steps brought us to within ten paces of the parsonage windows, behind which the Reverend Stone was just visible to us, his sharp edges softened by the distortive effects of Crown Glass.

I inquired of the Verger whether Stone knew of these new developments, but Crabb shook his head. "It seemed of little use," he said. "His pain has been worse, of late, and he does not wish for me to disturb him."

The northwest corner of the burying ground had, it seemed, been subject to some queer manner of flooding or subsidence. The infant Mead's stone was now completely black and featureless, with shards of broken slate littering the ground before it.

Each of the stones around it, including that of the child's mother, was likewise speckled with the same black dust, which loosed in whirling clouds whenever the wind swept down from the meetinghouse and shook the *arbor vitae*. A faint odour hung over that dreary scene, not dissimilar to the pus-smell produced by my earlier experiments.

A cursory inspection of the child's stone confirmed that it was no longer slate at all; instead, it seemed wholly composed of a porous organic material. I turned my attention to the base of the stone and cleared away the wet earth with one hand, only to learn that the growth reached deep into the ground, as though rooted somewhere below our feet.

The conclusion to which I came was, admittedly, fanciful, but also undeniable, for surely this black thing had come out of the ground and then, penetrating upward, proceeded to replace the slate from *inside*. Eventually, the outermost layer of stone cracked open like an acorn, leaving a faceless duplicate in its place.

Our course of action seemed clear. If this were some manner of sickness particular to the earth — a "gangrene of the soil," as I described it to Crabb — then we had no choice but to seek out the source of the infection and cut it away.

"But first, we must put the matter to the Reverend," said I, "and let him be the judge. Though I am not desirous of disturbing this consecrated ground, it may yet prove necessary."

VI

Sometime later, we rapped upon the door of the parsonage and were received into the parlour by the Reverend Stone, who invited us to sit by the hearth. The minister was attired in his usual austere robes, with a high collar that reached to the throat. The scent of rose-water was, as ever, evident. He offered us ale, which we refused, and settled himself in a chair opposite us, wincing as he did so for the pain of his ailment. "'Tis a distinct pleasure," said he, with a forced smile, "but I sense you have not come merely to visit."

We admitted this was so and Crabb proceeded to summarise the strange happenings of the last three days. He made rather a neat account of it, pausing, from time to time, only to cough into his kerchief. When he had finished, I offered my own conclusions and advised in favour of delving beneath the graveyard so as to find the source of the infestation. At this suggestion, Stone raised his hand and addressed us in tones of tired admonishment.

"We must not be overly hasty," said he. "Your findings are strange and, undoubtedly, they are suggestive. However, they are, as yet, little more than that."

He stood and shewed us out of the parlour. "And now I fear you must excuse me, for young Martin White will be here shortly. Please be assured that I shall pray upon the matter, as you have described it, and that you shall soon have my decision."

Outside the parsonage, the Verger and I bade each other farewell, but the other man lingered purposefully beside his cart, so that I knew he had more to tell me.

"There is something else," said he, after a moment's consideration. "I did not like to say, at first, for I know the esteem in which you hold his memory, but the rot has spread to the new section of the burying ground, southeast of the meetinghouse, where the Reverend Cooper lies."

"Show me," said I, attempting an air of authority, though my words came out strangled and faint. And so it was that we climbed the hill to the churchyard once more and made our way to the Reverend Cooper's stone. Dread beset me as we entered the new section, followed in turn by a surge of terror at my first glimpse of the Reverend's monument. Although every grave-marker bore a dusting of black powder, Reverend Cooper's stone appeared most sorely affected.

The rot had pushed out from behind his carved likeness and rendered him faceless: as grim and terrible as the specter of Death. My words of tribute had been erased entirely, blotted out by the spreading stain, so that only the final words of his epitaph were visible:

Out of heaven from God.

'Twas a dire omen, suggesting, as it did, that this strange infestation was visited upon us as a judgment from the Almighty; yet, I knew this could not be the case, for there was no man alive or dead more saintly than the departed minister. Our town deserved no such punishment, I was sure, but I was likewise certain this was no deed of man or nature. That left only Lucifer, the Father of Lies. But is it not true that even the work of the Devil glorifies His Holy Name?

Much shaken, I returned to my horse, mounted and kicked the beast toward home. After forty paces, I encountered Martin White, a boy of twelve, who was evidently en route to his appointment with the new minister. He walked with slate and hornbook beneath one arm and with face downcast, as though immersed in a reverie. He did not lift his head, nor display recognition of any kind, but merely passed by me without speaking and, thusly, into the shadow of Meetinghouse Hill.

VII

For the next two days, I strove to push the matter from my mind and see to my duties about the village. But when Friday came with yet no word from the Verger, I decided, myself, to call on him at once. I readied my bag and the instruments of my profession, and rode to the meetinghouse, where I found the man at work on the edge of the churchyard.

His illness had worsened and he was plainly quite weak — too weak, I thought, to manage the ox and cart on his own, thereby explaining his prolonged absence. Nonetheless, he refused an examination. "It is not yet so bad as that," said he, "nor is it a physick I require."

I did not understand his meaning, for the man's illness was clearly of a deteriorative nature: His collar was soaked through with sweat, while his breast was flecked with bits of black spittle. Crabb shook his head. "You must not think me a fool, Doctor. I am unwell, aye, but such sickness as I may have lies not only here" (he pointed to his breast with his thumb) "but all round us. In the graveyard. In the earth itself."

He coughed noisily into one cupped hand, then turned over the palm to shew me. There was spittle there, and blood, but also present in suspension were fine strands of a black material identical to those produced by my experiment.

Crabb smiled horribly, baring his teeth. "The rot is far-progressed," said he. "The Mead girl's stone is crumbling, shedding itself like the skin of a leper, while the Reverend Cooper's grave is blackening more each day. To-morrow, 'twill be naught but dust and ashes."

"We must tell the Reverend Stone. Has he rendered his decision?"

"He has not. Nor will he welcome the interruption."

"Perhaps not, but I see no other recourse."

"Aye," the Verger agreed. "I have kept the folk of the village away, but they shall learn of it in time — by the Sabbath morn, if not before. What then?"

He was right, of course; I could well imagine the ensuing panic, the fear that takes hold in small towns like Falmouth and soon breeds itself into hysteria, as in Salem Village or in the days of the last war. We needed to act, and quickly.

The door to the parsonage was opened by the Reverend Stone, who wore his customary robes and perfume. By the grimness of his bearing, 'twas plain that he was ill-pleased by our presence there, while his features were pale and contorted as in pain.

He did not invite us inside, but heard us out from the doorway, careful to maintain a courteous manner throughout our relation, despite his clear displeasure. After we had finished, he remained silent for a long time before addressing us with a voice like spring's last ice.

"Yesterday, you sought my counsel and today, you tell me what must be done? In all likelihood, this 'rot' you speak of is merely another natural phenomenon that Men of Science," (and here, he looked directly at me) "for of all their claims to erudition, are helpless to explain. Under no circumstances will the Lord permit us delvings in this graveyard. I would implore you both, as your pastor and as shepherd to this community, to trouble yourselves no more. Good day."

With that, he shut the door on us. The sound echoed from the hill with the finality of a musket's shot. Crabb turned to look at me. His canines appeared startlingly white against the black depths of his throat and his breath, too, was foetid.

By instinct or intuition, I knew he would not live to see another Sabbath, but we were not, as yet, helpless to save him. What is more, I could not countenance his death, any more than I could allow for the final profanation of the Reverend Cooper, a man unblemished in all things, who had gone to his grave with humble dignity to await the Day of Resurrection.

The time was short. I detailed my plan to the Verger, who gave his assent and arranged for me to meet him in the dark of the midnight. Then I mounted and returned home.

VIII

Four hours after twilight, I readied my saddlebags with spade and mattock, set a fresh candle within my lanthorn and stole behind the house to the stable, where the horse stood sleeping. I woke him with a gentle pat and laid my saddlebags across him. Then I climbed into the saddle and nudged him to a walk.

Soon, we were outside the village and amidst the woods, where the trees were budding, though not yet in blossom. Black and cancerous, their branches rattled with the wind, bending themselves to the cries of the owls and the calls of wolves from the north, so that they formed a kind of music, an eerie cacophony that followed me from the village and trailed me like the moonlight to the base of Meetinghouse Hill.

Fifty paces from the parsonage, I dismounted and ascended the hill on foot, with the saddlebags over my arm. There were no lights visible inside, not even the faint glow of a fire, but I waited until summiting the drumlin before lighting my lanthorn.

Crabb lingered near the gate of the churchyard. He was attired in heavy furs and woollens, with cold sweat shining on his face. With both hands, he held an unlit torch, the end of which trembled visibly, though with fright or fever I could not tell.

We did not speak, nor had we need of it. Crabb ignited his torch and, lifting high the light, shuffled toward the northwest corner of the burying ground. He was unsteady on his feet, dangerously so, and I made certain to walk beside him, so that I might catch him if he fell.

As Crabb had indicated, a profound change had taken place in the days since my last visit to the graveyard. All of the stones in the northwest corner had succumbed to the rot, including that of the Mead girl's mother. Around her marker lay strewn innumerable shards of slate, which had cracked and fallen away, leaving behind a stone-shaped duplicate composed of that queer material: dark and spongy, not unlike the inside of a bone.

I handed to Crabb the mattock and took the spade in hand. Together, we began our diggings, confining our efforts to the vicinity of the infant's grave. We soon learned that what had formerly been her stone — and was now a monstrous outgrowth — reached all the way down to the small coffin. Indeed, upon closer inspection, this black column seemed to grow *from* the box itself, narrowing to a rough circle, no wider than a man's closed fist, where it breached the lid.

"More light," I urged Crabb, who leant forward to direct his torch's glow into the grave itself. In that flickering illumination, I observed clearly that the black thing had, in fact, grown up from *inside* the coffin. In appearance, it resembled a kind of hideous, ropy cord that had been braided and twisted several times over. As I watched, it quivered faintly along its muscled length, pulsing rhythmically, as with the beating of a heart.

My stomach turned; the fever-stench was overwhelming.

With a prayer for courage, I raised the spade and brought its edge down hard upon the unnatural growth. I directed the blow toward the narrowest point of the rope, only to find that its essential substance was as dense as granite: The spade cut no deeper than half-an-inch before being repulsed. I employed my bone-saw but to no better result, for the teeth, despite their sharpness, failed to find their grip. Crabb offered his assistance, but was likewise unable to sever the ropy fibers with the mattock. We had little choice, then, but to prise open the already-ruptured coffin, though we were both affrighted of what might lie within.

Crabb removed the nails with the blade of the mattock, but could not lift the lid on account of the obtruding growth. We dared not risk breaking open the box, as the resulting din would surely lead to our being discovered in our ghastly work, but I contrived a solution with the use of the bone-saw and successfully removed the bottom two-thirds of the lid, thus allowing us to shine a light inside.

After three years in the ground, the child's flesh had been eaten away, leaving a rough jumble of bones and joints. I glimpsed her feet first of all, then discerned the shape of the ribs and pelvis. What I saw next chilled the very breath in my lungs.

The babe's skull was shattered, burst open like a bird's egg. The black growth sprouted up from the remnants of her jaw, eruptive, in the manner of a seed that has nourished itself on the earth before exploding into flower. Reeling, I staggered back and dropped to my knees, as in weary supplication to whatever dread power had loosed itself upon the village.

The child was dead these three years. Naught remained save bones; on what, then, had the black rot fed itself? I thought of Paul's first letter to the Corinthians: *There is a natural body and there is a spiritual body.* In the absence of the former, had this creature, whether of God or the

Devil, found sustenance on the latter; and then, finding it to its taste, proceeded to *feast*?

I trembled to think of the departed minister, who had gone to the grave with the promise of resurrection, only to find waiting his own annihilation: a patient, noisome darkness like the fires of Gehenna.

Crabb stooped down beside me, breathing hard through lungs half-choked with dust or fluid. "We have uncovered the root," said he and pointed down into the coffin, indicating a position immediately below the broken skull. "Do you see?"

A thin cable, one inch round and similar to an umbilicus, had entered the infant's skull via the trachea, having first penetrated the box from below. Arising, I stooped to shift the weight of the coffin, moving it just enough to expose the tail of the umbilicus underneath.

From the coffin, the cord led southeast toward the meetinghouse. I dared not touch it and could scarcely breathe for weight of the realisation, but Crabb hesitated not at all. He hefted the mattock behind his head, and then, with one deft stroke, split the root in two.

We breathed easier, then, and the moon shone bright upon us as we filled the grave with wet sod. I suggested we conceal the disturbed ground with weeds and brown grasses, to which task the Verger attended ably, but our labours for that night were not yet at an end. Crabb sensed this as well as I did and I motioned to him to collect our tools and follow me to the new section, hiding our lights when we passed within view of the parsonage.

IX

We arrived at the Reverend Cooper's stone, which the lanthorn revealed to be completely featureless, the last of the chiselled epitaph having been erased by the creeping rot. I nodded to Crabb and took from him the spade; and though it pained me worse than grief, I knew we had no choice but to disturb my dear friend's grave.

After the Gale of Sixty-Eight, in which the larches came down, we had uprooted the stumps out of the earth, where, to our surprise, we found the trees were not in themselves separate, but grew from a single root. Much in the same way, I thought that if we were to trace the roots from every fibrous branch, every dark and crumbling flower, then we might yet pinpoint the source of the infestation and cut it away.

Crabb broke the earth with his mattock, the blade biting deep. From out of the ground steamed that familiar odour that was at once sweet and bitter, like that of moulding apples. Together, we worked at unburying the minister's coffin. The labour wore hard upon the Verger, I could tell, for he rested often and coughed and shook, but always returned to the task with the listless focus of a somnambulant, or of a man long dead.

At last, the outline of the minister's box revealed itself, whereupon I turned away, aghast, and could not stir myself to continue. I covered my face with my hands, but could not tamp my ears, which heard first the shriek of the dislodged nails as they were removed, followed by the distinctive squeal-and-bite of the saw-blade and the groan of the shifted lid.

The Verger inhaled sharply. Silence ensued, stretching for a minute or more before the spade descended and struck the inside of the coffin with a hollow *thunk*. I heard the coffin lid replaced, the mournful sound of sod on coffin-wood, and then — nothing.

I opened my eyes. Crabb had perched himself upon the edge of the grave with the spade-handle resting betwixt his legs. On his face he wore an expression of utter shock and bewilderment. I lowered myself beside him. His head swiveled. He looked at me directly, but his expression was curiously placid, almost vacant.

"'Twas horrible," said he. "He looked the same as on the day we laid him down, no different save for the rot. It had grown out of his throat, the black thing, wide enough for to crack the jawbone. His mouth was open, as if he were crying out in agony, and the expression on his face — I have never seen such despair."

"It is done?" I asked, not wishing to consider the implications of his discovery. "The root, it has been severed?"

"Aye," he affirmed. "It is done. Though I fear we may have tarried too long."

"Where did it lead?"

"Northwest."

"Toward the meetinghouse?"

He turned his eyes upon me again, the moon glimmering like foxfire upon his pale visage. "Not toward it," said he, shaking his head. "Not 'toward' it at all. But *to* it. There can be no question but that it began there."

X

Scarcely an hour of darkness remained by the time I reached the village. Exhausted and unsettled, I resolved myself on sleep, only to be roused from slumber after no more than a quarter of an hour by a frantic pounding at the door.

'Twas John White, the youngest member of his family. The sun hung low in the eastern sky, violet at this early hour and I realised upon seeing him that John must have left his home, on foot and unaccompanied, in the darkest hour of the night.

I wasted no time in extracting the tale from him. Earlier that evening, his younger brother Martin, who had been ill these last three days, had taken a turn for the worse and slipped into unconsciousness. With Ethan unrecovered, and his mother occupied in tending to Martin, she had sent her youngest child to fetch help. And so, he had come to me.

I dressed myself and readied the horse. Then, taking John behind me in the saddle, I rode hard for the White farm. The road was empty before us, the maples green and flowering, and I knew, by the warmth of the light on my back, that the day would be humid in the extreme.

At the White Farm, we dismounted in the yard. I handed John the lead and bade him stable the horse while I flew into the house and climbed the narrow staircase to the loft space, adjacent the chimney, wherein the family customarily slept.

But upon that morning, not one member of that household lay slumbering: Ethan, aged 16, tossed restlessly on one side of the bed and cried out piteously, pained by the itch of his missing limb, while Martin lay quietly beside him with his face upturned, soaked through with fever, his underclothes hanging from him like wet rags. Their mother occupied a chair by the bedside, one hand resting on Martin's brow, holding in place a scrap of white cloth. She acknowledged me with the slightest of nods, but I knew she did not intend for rudeness. In widowhood, she had grown strong, but these latest trials had nearly defeated her.

Immediately, I made haste to examine the unconscious lad. By inclining my ear to his chest, I ascertained that the heart was still beating, though its rhythm was uneven. His breathing was likewise staggered and shallow, so that I suspected the presence of some obstruction in the lungs. I rolled back the fabric of his shirt, exposing his chest to the light of my candle. At this, his mother gasped. I fear that I, too, may have recoiled in shock.

For the boy's chest was obscured by a mass of tumourous black growths, domed in the manner of warts and sprouting from the flesh to either side of the sternum. They must have seeded in his lungs and thenceforth expanded until breaching the skin like mushrooms after a rain. I touched my finger to the top of one such growth and observed its porous consistency; the tumour depressed at contact before springing back to resume its earlier shape. This recalled to my mind certain facts: not only the infestation in the churchyard, but the Verger's sickness and the visit that Martin himself had made but recently to Meetinghouse Hill.

I rolled the lad onto his right side, so that I might better view the pale flesh of his back. Here, my candle picked out the same dark growths, presented in rough alignment with the position of his lungs in his breast. 'Twas a miracle, surely, that Martin yet lived, but I knew his chances of recovery to be slim. Nonetheless, I could not allow this illness to claim him uncontested.

I opened my bag, removing first the cups, then the curettes. By this time, John had joined us in the loft and I asked him to heat the glass cups in the fire downstairs. He returned shortly, at which time I took the cups from him and applied them directly to Martin's back.

The skin swelled and blistered, and his mother winced at the sizzle of charred flesh. Incredible though it appeared, the sickness itself seemed to retreat from the outer edges of the cups, and even flamed up under the dome of the glass, where the heat was most intense. Slowly, boils took shape beneath the cups, drawing the ill-humours out of the body and concentrating them in a single place, so that they might be easily lanced and drawn away.

Removing the cups, I placed each of them twice more, so that a total of six boils had formed, three to either side of the spinal column. Selecting the slimmest and sharpest of the curettes, I lanced the fluid from each of these boils in turn, collecting the bloody runoff in a pewter dish, which I directed John to empty into the fire downstairs.

This being speedily accomplished, I bandaged the open wounds. Calling next for water, I scrubbed clean the cups of char and pus. Then I uttered a quick prayer for the boy's recovery and wished his family farewell.

I was halfway home when the cough overtook me. My chest heaved with every painful hack, as though attempting to expel, by force, some foreign body that had lodged itself inside of me. I reined in the horse and gasped for air, lest I collapse, unconscious. At length, the fit passed, and when I wiped clean my mouth, my hand came away smeared and flecked with dark matter.

XI

The remainder of the day was spent in prayer and fevered meditation. I had already correlated the illness of the White child with that of the Verger Crabb; the onset of my own cough with my recent proximity to the aforementioned persons; the location of the infested graves with the site of the meetinghouse; and, perhaps most alarmingly, the onset of the rotting sickness with the arrival in Falmouth of the Reverend Stone. Confronted with such evidence, I knew not in which way I should proceed, but knew only that I could not stand idle.

And so, I rode for Meetinghouse Hill. Arriving at dusk, I climbed the hill to the Verger's cottage, careful to avoid the windows of the parsonage, and rapped peremptorily at his door. No answering cry came within, no din of footsteps. I waited; knocked again. Receiving no response, I admitted myself to the common room.

Crabb lay sprawled, face-up, on the dirt floor. His mouth was wide, his cheeks so blue and swollen that I scarcely recognised him. 'Twas likely he had died of suffocation, which was, I believe, a small mercy, as it spared him the sight with which I found myself confronted.

From his throat there protruded an erect black coil, three inches across and hooked at its end, terminating more than a yard above his mouth. Knotted, rope-like, it rippled and twitched in place, moving like a leech, clawing upward, as though to seek the light.

I turned and fled. I dared not halt until the door was shut behind me and I was well clear of the cottage. I thought of the Verger's soul, on which the thing had fed itself, and forced myself to leave him, making for the graveyard, certain, as I was, that I could do nothing further for him.

By this time, the sun was all but gone, leaving behind a fragrant darkness, scented with the musk of spring shoots and the aroma of contagion. In less than a week, the sickness had germinated, rooted and given flower. The Reverend Cooper's stone was crumbling into powder, as were the graves all around and there was not a single stone in that churchyard that did not carry the signs of infestation and decay. Only one place remained for me to explore.

I crossed the graveyard to the meetinghouse and unfastened the door to the sanctuary. The air inside was at once stale and damp and nauseating. The sweet stench of putrescence lay upon that place, as strong here as in the minister's opened grave, but, even in the gloom, the interior appeared to me unaltered.

Lighting my lanthorn, I stepped through the doorway. The windows were dark and the shadows, layered thickly, unravelled in the lanthorn's beam to reveal the same unpainted trusses, the familiar pews. I proceeded midway down the aisle and turned to scrutinise the balcony overhead. All was as it should have been and yet, the churchyard infestation had begun here; of that, there could be no doubt.

Then to my ears came the rustle of fabric, like a broom being dragged over the floor. I spun round, terrified, and directed my light toward the pulpit, beneath which stood the Reverend Stone.

His bearing was stiff, as from hours knelt in prayer, and he stood before me shirtless with a Cat O' Nine Tails in hand. The barbed rope-ends shewed crimson in the lanthorn's glow, beaded with blood where they had scourged his back. Worse still was the sight of his chest, which was covered with dark tumours in such thick profusion that I nearly mistook them for hair.

But it was his expression which froze me with horror, at the same time that I was moved, somehow, to pity. For never before had I seen such anguish in a human face, nor would I have dreamed it possible to bear such agony and live — if he were truly living.

The whip dropped from his hands. His eyes bulged, the whites shining and he stumbled toward me with arms outstretched, as though to catch me in an embrace.

Sickened and fearful, I forced myself to step backward, nearly tripping over the aisle's skirting as I did so, but unable to turn around, unwilling to show my back, even for a moment, to this man — this thing — that continued to advance on me, not with menace but with pathetic desperation, murmuring his prayers all the while.

"O God, as You are my judge, You know I never meant for it to happen. You alone know what it is like to bear this burden, to be cursed with this affliction for the greater glory of Your Name. I ask only that You help me, for I cannot help myself."

He lunged toward me. His bare arms, like his chest, were covered in black growths, and I understood at once the reasons for his habitual manner of dress. I threw myself backward, but caught my foot on the skirting so that I dropped heavily onto my back. The lanthorn went sailing through the dark, striking the low balcony overhead, where it shattered.

The wooden beams ignited. Fire raced up the tresses to the ceiling, traversing the sanctuary with shocking speed, as though the building were not merely infested with the black rot, but verily *made of it*, formulated entirely of the selfsame sickness as the minister possessed, the same corruptive influence of which Martin, Crabb and I, too, had been made a victim.

Stone paid the flames no heed, but fell upon me like a crying child, moaning as he fastened his arms round me. "Hold me," said he. "Hold me."

I smelled the sickness on him for the first time, the odour that lurked beneath the rose-water in which he regularly washed. I gagged, lost my breath and nearly fainted, but, by some supreme effort born out of terror, succeeded in dislodging the diseased minister and throwing him wide so that he landed in the aisle.

The ceiling dripped overhead. Coals fell, burning, from the balcony, igniting where they landed amidst the pews. The windows exploded outward, causing an in-rush of cool air that fanned the blaze ever-higher, sweeping toward us like a rolling wave. The heat was unbearable, the stench even more so, but I forced open the door and threw myself beneath the flames, which erupted at this new incursion of air, and rolled until I reached what I judged to be a safe distance.

I looked back toward the meetinghouse. Through the doorway, I glimpsed the minister, who continued to gaze at me through the flames, his face a mask of the uttermost anguish, watching me even as the fires broke over him and consumed him from the inside-out.

Shortly thereafter, the roof fell with a splitting crash, causing sparks to fly loose in great clouds. I lurched to my feet once more, ignoring the pain of my many burns, and staggered down the slope of the drumlin, turning round one final time to watch the Reverend Cooper's grave go up like a torch, followed by the whole of the northwest corner and the Verger's cottage. I fell to the ground before the parsonage and there lay insensible until the villagers found me.

XII

I awoke in the custody of the law, accused of lighting the fire and of the two deaths that resulted. On the following morning, I was taken in chains to the courthouse in Westminster and detained until my trial. There, it emerged that the Falmouth meetinghouse had burned through in minutes, resulting in no ashes; only a greasy stain upon the ground. My lanthorn was recovered, though no traces of the man of whose murder I stand convicted, while Crabb's cottage was likewise consumed with his body inside, leaving me as the final witness to the strange events on Meetinghouse Hill — or so, for a time, I allowed myself to believe.

This evening, I learned of the fate of Martin White, who died three nights past of a "sickness like the pox," and was buried quickly, for fear of spreading contagion. I hesitate to write this, for I am acquainted, intimately, with the hardships his family has endured during these latter days, but the lad's body *must* be exhumed, and speedily, and burned as I am to be. He shall have neither corpus nor stone, but the Lord will not forget him, even as He has not forsaken me throughout these latest trials.

My illness has worsened in the days since the fire. The black tumours, now present in abundance, grow from my chest and back so that I scarcely sleep at night, and even then, I dream. In the mornings, I wake to this filthy cell, my shirtfront dirtied with blood and spittle, but I remain untroubled, knowing myself fortunate, for these sufferings will end — and soon.

Only with the most acute grief do I think of the Verger Crabb, who died in agony on the floor of his cottage, and of my dear friend the Reverend Cooper, the greatest man I have known, and of the black thing that fed upon them both, denying them, in this way, the promise to which Election made them heir. For them, there is only darkness, as there was for the Reverend Stone, and I can but mourn them as the unbeliever mourns all life, all loss, and the final passing of this world into a night unending.

Thus concludes my account.
May the peace of Our Lord Jesus Christ be upon your spirit —

H. Edwards
Westminster, 1773

✝

A MONSTER IN THE MIDST

By Julio Toro San Martin

✦

Julio Toro San Martin resides and grew up in Toronto, Canada and has had short stories published online in *Innsmouth Magazine* and *The Lovecraft Ezine*, and also in the print anthologies *Historical Lovecraft* and *Future Lovecraft*.

✦

LE VICOMTE TRISTE TO *LE GRAND DUC*

NOW THAT THE WORLD is going to hell, I think of how I should have shot you with my gun and not my wit, oh, so long ago over our game of *ecarte*. But, oh well, what's a Vicomte to do, *monsieur*?

You do remember my faithful clockwork man? Of course you must. He lies now how the world will soon lie, dead and undone by his master, oozing mucous and fungal matter. They will say: It was the glorious 158th year of our glorious mushroom age, when it all came to nothing.

Or, hopefully, someone will say it. Hopefully, it will not be you. I will not, henceforth, address you as you so like, by the title of *Monsieur le Grand Duc*, but simply as *monsieur*, as I deem more appropriate, and as is still good etiquette, despite the diminishment of title.

Eight months ago, I remember watching my man grab great handfuls of fungal matter and fill my steam carriage and himself with the lumpy fuel. I winced, as you no doubt remember my disgust at the filthy growths and their smell, so sweet to most, so putrid to *moi*. It was with even greater trepidation that I witnessed how ravenously he stuffed himself with the new toxic outgrowths of the fungus. The stupid automaton had practically filled his head with some of the slimier and more liquescent green transmutations of the substance, so that it oozed over him and hung off his chin in flabby waves of solid jelly.

Then I noted how one of my valet's eyes glowed with a lust and yearning unsettling to behold. He walked toward the clockwork man and dipped a greedy, jerking finger like a great plowing oar into the massy substance of my man's egg-like head and then proceeded to hungrily lick the loathsome substance off his own finger, like a slobbering animal. His eyes took on a glossy, idiotic cast and he fell over.

I knew, of course, that he was now under the hypnotic fatal sleep of the green fungus and its slime. It had but recently manifested itself and I was closely studying it, to make a scientific treatise for *L'École Mycologique*, which I was readying to present at our next meeting.

I observed how, almost instantaneously, my valet's lower jaw began to putrefy and turn into mush. In seconds, his jaw was a fetid liquid. Soon, *monsieur*, the man was liquid himself. I was alarmed to find this new anomalous metamorphic by-product of the green fungus. Up until then, it had only worked as a sort of opiate that led to death in about ninety-five percent of its consumers. The other five percent, who awoke, described its effects as hallucinatory, a shamanistic type of experience, which involved travelling to strange, exotic locales ... or perhaps other worlds ... seeing queer dark beings and culminating in an encounter with a strange, green star-shaped or jellyfish-like entity that imparted (as far as I am aware) no wisdom, but merely *was*, and pulsated at the centre of a gigantic mushroom world. This was the first observation which I made and which was later observed and confirmed by all of Europe, including yourself. Later (as you know), I also documented how a strong compulsion affected some innocents to eat of the substance: how only some takers were liquefied; how, of those who awoke from its effects, a small percentage were transformed into a new aesthetic of the grotesque; and how the survivors of the opiate soon started their own cult, centred around the green godling (May God in Heaven have mercy on their souls). The frighteningly deformed members are held in high esteem, now. The most monstrous are high priests, of which there are some whispers ... dare I say it ... that there are even some who are unnameable in their horror, and who are considered demi-gods, the highest masters of earth's great chain of being.

But that is all too far in the past.

You are aware, *monsieur*, how, 19 days ago, I presented myself before *L'École Mycologique*, with a petition to seek out the source, if there was one, for the green fungal menace. I only asked for a vast, steampowered airship, from the King's royal navy, and permission to leave early to attend a *mecanique* performance of both Moliere's *Les Precieuses Ridicules* and Beaumarchais' *Le Mariage de Figaro*, at the Theatre-Francais. I was nearly denied all three requests, by you. But thankfully (or not, as it would seem), your dissenting vote, and that of your colleagues in your absences, was annulled by our esteemed secretary of L'Academie des Sciences, the Marquis de Condorcet.

In two days' time, I was ready to leave on my mission, *monsieur*.

I dressed for the occasion in a wine-dark, silk-velvet suit of the highest courtly fashion, the richly embroidered coat high-collared, and the waistcoat opulently decorated with diamonds for buttons. I also wore shoes and breech buckles, and a jewelled scabbard at my side, a white flounced frill at the neck and sleeves and, atop my head, an auburn, small-yet-stylish, lightly powered wig with, of course (since I was, in a sense, going to war), a military cocked hat of fine fabric atop the wig. My clockwork man and valets were also dressed impeccably.

At our farewell, damsels wept to see me go and Mademoiselle Tussaud fainted horribly. Do tell the poor creature not to wait for me.

I stood at the stern of the ship, a chambered cannongun slung over my left shoulder. After saluting the officers, the pageantry and science members, and our King Louis and Queen Marie Antoinette, who had both come especially from Versailles to see me go, I asked the helmsman to circle Paris once and then to head off into the bright, cerulean sky.

Cheering crowds followed us, trumpeters trumpeted gaily below and French flags waved proudly. We flew over large buildings, streets, cabs, coaches, parks, vendors, the Louvre, the districts, the filthy populace — in short, over everything. I saw street urchins and city-workers picking and cleaning the membranous film of fungi which grew on the walls and on the ground, on trees everywhere, and threatened to engulf the city, if it were left to spread unchecked. Here and there, I noted drooling supine bodies, no doubt victims of their own uncontrollable urges for the deadly green slime mold.

In no time, our steamship and attached aerostat, with its three accompanying smaller dirigibles, flew over the naval harbour. We cruised calmly onto the Seine and followed the course of the river. I read alarm and fear in some of the men, but that was of no great concern to me, since I reasoned my adventurous spirit was enough joy for everyone.

↑

"*Vive la France! Vive la liberté!*" I yelled, as I stood courageously at the bow of the ship, a good, strong breeze blowing through my wig. A young boy, a sullen naval student named 'Napoleon', was so touched by my enthusiasm for this liberty and patriotism that I now felt that he also joined me in hollering passionately at the sky.

It was a clear day, with only a few clouds not far above us and a hot sun flaring down. We travelled at a good nautical pace, the sailors keeping the coals and fungus burning. The combined steam allowed the overhead large aerostat to easily bear the burden of our heavily ironclad warship.

In no time, we flew onto the Atlantic Ocean and I marvelled nauseatedly to behold, outstretched before me in all directions, a vast, viscous, bobbing desert of slime and mushroom. Indeed, here it was impressed on me nakedly and powerfully, how much of our earth the organism was truly lord of!

By day, as we travelled, all I could see was the mold and, faraway through my spyglass, almost as if purposely keeping a distance, barely discernable seagulls, that to my scientific mind did not look or fly quite like seagulls should. By night, the green, intrusive slime glowed eerily and cast a greenish light on the silent world.

When everyone else was asleep, I would look through my spyglass, alone and hidden, at the gruesome film that covered the ocean, which, in places, was elevated and more compacted into solid islands of sponge or smaller iceberg-like mounds. As I looked at the fungus in the dark, I could discern in places, either beneath it in the water or, more horribly, of the stuff itself, amorphous shapes that, to my mind, seemed to be following our fast-moving ship. I liked it not.

Because of this, one day, I said to the captain, "*Capitaine*, I command you to change course immediately. I believe we are being followed. By changing course, it might confuse our pursuers and cause them, or it, either to lose interest in us or lose track of us. We shall reach our destination from another direction."

To which he answered, flushed, "Monsieur le Vicomte! To do so we would have to recalibrate our computational astrolabe and also more than likely extend our journey! This will not sit well with our helmsman in the former, nor with our men in the latter. How sure are you that we are being followed?"

"I am not sure at all. But I command it."

After this brief exchange, he quickly changed to an indirect route, and I am sure that it was because of this caution on my part that the first leg of my journey was saved.

↑

My second leg began one morning when we arrived near our destination. An officer of the watch spotted a column of black smoke ascending from the horizon of our port side. Cautiously we neared the source of the smoke, the helmsman causing the steam from the aerostat balloon to lower us so we could have a better view, once we realised the site was of no danger.

Below us were three navy warships, ironclads like our own, still smouldering from a recent tragedy, and all black and burnt and devoid of crew. Their bulks were enmeshed and floating on a great plateau of gruesome jelly. Their aerostats were burnt to ashes. These three ships were the titanic hulls of empires, namely, England's, Spain's and Russia's. No doubt, ours would have made a fourth.

Later in the day, the captain said to me, "It is certain they did not destroy each other. Their cannons never fired a shot, from what our investigations can tell. Apparently, two ships are old and the Russian ship more recent. It must have fallen or crashed into the other two."

Not wishing to put the crew into any more danger, nor finding myself with time to fully delve into this mystery, I decided to disembark.

The captain asked me if I had any suspicions as to what had happened to the Russian ship.

I said, with certainty, "Sabotage."

✦

And so, the third and last leg of my journey began.

Call it madness or an egocentric wish to be thought a hero, or perhaps a too-great love for my fellow man, but, that very day, I left, accompanied only by my clockwork man. We left inside a metal machine that I had transported onto the ship, one of my own new experimental inventions, which I called a 'submarine'.

The fungus near the ship was compact and solid, so that my submarine, walking and resembling a half-monkey, half-octopus creature, took us on a vast journey atop that pustulous landscape.

My *mecanique* man told me where to go. You ask why, perhaps? Because, *monsieur*, in my skill with automata, I had installed in my man a means by which he could, like a hound, track the source of our predicament. He merely had to fill his head with the vile substance and, instantly, he felt the source, like a beacon. Do not be surprised at this, since you yourself are aware of my prodigious scientific skill with the construction of servile robots.

Sometime during mid-day, I looked behind me and, through the glass dome atop the submersible, which housed us and the control panels, I saw shadows following us at a far distance. I could not make out their shapes exactly, but something in how they moved made me shiver. I sped up my construct.

It was not long before my man told me to stop and dive into the mushroom island. I looked up at the hot sun and bade it farewell, before I plunged my ironcast into the flesh of the slime.

It dug into the substance, shredding the organism's tissues with its many arms as we travelled, until the submarine broke into clear water below the mass. It swam at top speed, like an octopus, beneath the Atlantic; schools of shiny and lightning-fast fish passing by it. I marvelled.

Following thick filaments of fungi down, eventually, we reached a hole. Falling into it, after a few hours, we emerged in a cave, hundreds of feet under the ocean.

I was surprised to find readings which told me there was oxygen here. After a curious exploration of my surroundings, my automaton pointed out our new direction. It was a tunnel, but the tunnel's entrance was too small to fit our vehicle, so, climbing out of the walking cephalopod, we continued the journey on foot.

↑

While in the tunnel, we were illumed by the glowing green slime. I despised being so close to the disgusting stuff. We passed, to my shock, a hideously smelling, decomposing corpse, which I quickly surmised was a Yankee — no doubt, I morbidly joked, unaware of his recent triumph over England in his revolutionary war. As I wondered what new surprises were in store for me, we neared the end of the tunnel and, *monsieur*, surprised I was, indeed, to behold what next I saw.

✝

Exiting the tunnel, we beheld a monstrously massive cavern, undulating and alive with the slime — at its centre, vibrating horribly, a cyclopean green-wheeled or starfish-shaped mushroom. It was attached to the rest of the fungus and slime, like a many-tentacled thing, and I was sure it was the fruiting source of the green ooze. There it hung, like a pulsing, grotesque spider in its own web. It was the brain of the world-conquering membranous scum. The deity of the hallucinators' mushroom world, which was our own world! God-like, indeed, it was!

Suddenly, I felt a powerful blow to my head. I collapsed — weak, bleeding and dizzy — onto the goo. Before I fainted, I saw a thick grey and yeasty slop of a leg step into my line of vision.

✝

I awoke to a strange chanting directed towards that contamination at the centre of our world. Beside me I saw, lying also, my clockwork man.

I was, no doubt, in the clutches of the green godling's insane cult. I was forgotten for the moment as they praised it.

Never have you seen, *monsieur*, such a depraved motley of diseased humanity. They stood like stunted sponge things, for "human" I dare not term them, comprised of growths and deformities too hideous to enumerate and covered with green goo of an unclean corruption. They stepped towards the fungoid entity. With each step, their bodies quaked, so much so that I feared their cellular integrity might collapse. Then a marvellous thing happened.

They began to disintegrate!

The huge cavern was filled with their moans as they putrefied and turned to slop. The stoutest, I saw turn and try to escape. I knew then this was not part of their plan. The god was incomprehensibly destroying its own worshippers!

What was happening? Bravely, I stepped toward the malevolent thing. Nothing happened.

I surmised that the mushroom-mind had evolved consciousness from the parent mindless fungus over years in isolation and had then, instinctively for survival, spread its green slime and tissue, like a cancer, over the parent species and even through it, taking it over, compromising the parent species' own integrity, transforming the parent's flesh in places into itself. All this while, it possessed nothing more than a simple, primitive brain, being defensively instinctual and unthinking like an animal and unaware of anything except its own kind.

Realising this, I picked up my cannongun, which one of the mushroom beings had carried and walked towards the pulsating tumour. Though suspended, it seemed to squat before me like a malicious imp, spokes of fungal rays radiating from it in all directions. I touched its gob-smooth and slippery flesh. It glowed green. In places, a muck of impurity dripped unsettlingly from it. Everything about it aroused deep disgust in my being. Surely, this was life antithetical to man. And yet, oh yet, it was an awe-inspiring sight. Here was a baby, a new-born life-form, lush with fecundity, first of its kind, the earth-circling lord of this world. I petted it, imagining its thought processes to be like those of a dog. Then, taking aim for humanity, I blasted it out of the animal kingdom.

I will not lie, I will not say it wept or screamed or thrashed and hurled about in agony, as it burnt mightily on fire. It merely burnt, soundlessly, pulsing erratically, though once, I think I did detect, for a second, the faintest outline of a distorted, anguished, semi-human face appear and then disappear on its surface. Perhaps it did this for my benefit. Once it was a charred husk, it burst, releasing smoke, and then it flattened out like an airless bag.

I rejoiced at how easy it was to destroy! Then the cellular deterioration of the fungus around me started.

↑

My clockwork man and I ran in fear. The fertile, luxuriantly tropical mushroom vibrancy around us was disintegrating, as if the vital life of the fungal body, with the centre no longer there to pump life through its veins, was dying. And, so I learned the dead entity was not only the fungus' mind, but also its heart.

I felt as if rich oxygen and warmth, the very humidity of the air, were being sucked out of the cavern.

When we reached my submersible, I saw it was damaged — no doubt by those cultists who had followed us and who were now dead.

We managed to make it back to the mushroom island before the machine completely broke down. I saw then how the island was also slowly deteriorating. I noted how thin filaments of fungus, resembling seaweed, and also thin slime, interconnected to other excremental fungal islands. These islands, too, were falling apart. What an immense arterial network the god had a hold of on this earth! And now it was all dying!

Was I hero or villain?

As I sat contemplating all this new information, I could hear my clockwork man's gears beside me, whirring and clattering. Then, for the first time in ages, I heard through the gramophone embedded in his chest, a small artificial laugh, which grew louder and louder.

"What are you laughing at?" I yelled at him, disgusted.

He struggled to use speech tubes long in disuse. Slowly, a sentence began to emerge. "Master is blind," he said.

I was incensed at his statement and yet, afraid. "How so?" I asked, secretly dreading his answer.

He spasmed. I could hear his computational box clunking in his chest.

Then he answered me. "*Monsieur* has not taken into consideration all the tools available to him from the current sciences. When the fungus first appeared, it rapidly spread and destroyed most of the greenery and trees of the earth, while also becoming an important source of fuel and food, among other things, for your species, which greatly changed your world. Those green plants I previously mentioned, it is thought they originally supplied earth with oxygen, which your species breathes to survive. The conquering fungus mutated and took over this process, for reasons I cannot fathom. By destroying it, you have destroyed yourself, for when the fungus is dead, the earth will be depleted greatly of its oxygen. Master is a good roboticist but a poor mycologist and botanist. He is also a poor strategist." After saying this, he began to laugh again.

The reasonableness of my servant's logic frightened me. I screamed at him, "And how long have you theorised of this possible outcome? Speak!"

"Since the day we left France."

I then picked up my cannongun and struck him hard, until he was nothing but a mess of rolling gears and dented metal.

✝

Since that day, I have seen this island decrease, I estimate, by nearly six percent of its mass and the process still continues.

I will send this letter with one of the seagull-beasts I have captured, in hopes that it might reach you, *monsieur*, since you are accounted France's greatest mycologist.

I wonder what the new face of the earth will bring with it in the coming years. What catastrophes will come? Shall we all die or not?

My hours I spend now, sometimes blaming myself for our predicament, sometimes blaming others.

One morning, I saw, far in the distance, a great mound of decaying jelly arise out of the ocean. It looked like a volcano. It erupted and threw millions of spore-like things far into the sky. What this could mean I know not.

Though, that night, I did dream I walked the fungal island at night, alone. As I looked at the sky, I saw a horrendously large and pulsating moon, all green and dripping green slime. I pictured it as an eye looking down at me. With this thought, I covered my eyes.

*July 23, 17_*

✝

THE PEARL IN THE OYSTER AND
THE OYSTER UNDER GLASS

By Lisa M. Bradley

↑

Lisa M. Bradley's fiction has appeared in *Cicada, Brutarian, Escape Pod* and other venues. Originally from South Texas, Lisa has now lived in Iowa for almost twenty years. She believes, as Oscar Wilde wrote, "The truth is rarely pure and never simple." She tells her impure, tangled truths at cafenowhere.livejournal.com and tweets little white lies @cafenowhere.

↑

ART'S INVISIBLE FUR RUFFLED in the morning breeze. He disguised his shiver as a stretch, meanwhile pulling the cuffs of his hoodie over his knuckles. He was glad he'd worn the extra layer, though it made him feel more conspicuous, like the black spill staining the normally pastel palette of South Padre Island. At six feet tall, Art towered over most people in the Valley and he was one of the few people not unpacking 'shroom rafts on the oil-slicked beach. Add the black hoodie on a soon-to-be scorching day and he became an easy landmark for the volunteers recruited by the Association of Coastal Wildlife Refuges.

On breaks from orienting volunteers, Art assessed the beach with birding binoculars. The "smart 'nocs" couldn't distinguish between oil smears and natural coloration, so, at first, he thought the birds huddled over a distant trash barrel had oil-matted plumage. Turned out they were just Laughing Gulls (quite the misnomer now), their heads naturally dark over cotton-white breasts, their grey wings tipped with normal black. Art also checked out the Brown Pelican perched atop the idle oil-skimmer. The bird had been holding vigil for about an hour, as if disgusted by humans' capacity to muck things up.

Laughter scattered the gulls. Art lowered his 'nocs to find a group of teenagers slogging through the sand toward his booth, making the usual jokes about "booms!" The Brown Pelican ended its rueful vigil and fled for the jetties.

Had these kids gotten permission to skip school to save the world? Art didn't ask, only handed them starter packs, which included water socks, gloves, sunscreen and pamphlets as hastily printed as the Association had been organised.

"I can't walk in these things," a young woman said, trying to hand the socks back.

"Sorry, can't participate without them," Art said. "Trust me; you don't want to be scraping tar off your feet for the next three weeks. It's a carcinogen. Now, anybody have mold or mushroom allergies?"

The flow of volunteers picked up and Art was soon so busy he stopped noticing the breeze through his fur. Half an hour later, when a woman approached his check-in booth from the side, Art had warmed up enough to push his sleeves to his elbows. On auto-pilot, he passed the woman a starter pack without looking, then turned the laminated map on his clipboard in her direction, to show where she was needed.

"Oh, no," she said, amused or embarrassed. Art checked her face and immediately understood, though she went on to explain, "I can't be in the sun. I'm just supposed to help with check-in. I'm Claudia? Ramirez?"

Art stepped back to let her enter. She was more overdressed than he was: floppy sun hat strapped under her chin; long-sleeved blouse; yoga pants collecting sand in the dragging, curling hems; trek sandals over socks.

"Sorry I'm late," she said, stowing her purse under the folding table. "My son was dawdling this morning. I didn't think I'd ever get him out the door and over to school and then there was a rollover on the highway and DPS didn't want anyone driving through …."

"No problem."

Art tried to make himself small — story of his life — but Claudia took up more room than most people. It wasn't that she was a mix-skin. The grafts gave her face and hands a lumpy, quilted appearance, but Art knew she wasn't contagious or anything. The CDC had squashed the flesh-eating bacteria at Memorial Hospital within days of its outbreak and that had been ten years ago.

Still, Claudia was daunting. Art guessed she was five-two and maybe a hundred-twenty pounds, but she seemed set to "steamroll" even when standing still. If she were a cloud, like her name implied, she'd be a storm front. Art couldn't imagine the whole Department of Public Safety stalling her, let alone a child.

"Let me take care of this couple coming in," he said, "and then I'll answer any of your questions."

Once he'd sent the volunteers on their way, she held out her hand. "I didn't catch your name …?"

"Art," he said, shaking her hand. There was a fleshy seam under his thumb; he consciously worked not to rub it.

"Bart?"

He smiled. That was the name of an Alaskan Kodiak who'd been in movies. He thought about not correcting her. She wasn't a regular volunteer; he might never see her again. But he felt compelled to say, "No, it's 'Art.' As in, Arturo … Villanueva."

She nodded, struck her temple in that self-deprecating gesture that meant, "*Mensa!*" before asking, "Are those 'boom' things really made out of hair?"

Art nodded. "And other stuff," he said, squinting at the long tubes bobbing on the water. They formed an artificial reef of sorts. Below the surface, curtains cascaded from the tubes all the way to the sea floor, creating a semipermeable barrier. "Supposedly, hair's good at absorbing oil and what the booms don't absorb, they corral so the skimmers can vacuum the oil off the water."

"*Que grosero.* I'd rather be on *hongo* duty than handling tubes of hair. Wouldn't you?"

Art followed her gaze up the beach. Sweat-sheened volunteers toted straw rafts from the back of a truck in the parking lot all the way to the high tide line. There, other volunteers stripped off the biodegradable plastic and used it to stitch together the rafts, which — according to the pamphlets Art had been handing out — were packed with lab-enhanced *Pleurotus corticatus* spores. *Myco-remediation,* it was called. The mushrooms would feed on the oil, thus cleaning the water, and later be harvested and sent back to the greenhouses. There, they'd be churned to compost to produce another generation of fungal warriors.

Some of the rafts already rippled with snowy crests of oyster mushrooms. They'd erupted *en route*, right through the plastic. Other rafts had actually burst apart from the proliferation of fungus, whiter than sea foam.

"I don't know," Art said uneasily. "It's not just mushrooms. Once the rafts are all connected and anchored from the high tide line, someone applies a souped-up bacterial compound to the straw."

"But it's safe, right?" Claudia looked up at him. "They wouldn't put it in the water if it wasn't."

"Oh, of course. It's just a turbo-boosted version of bacteria that are already present in the ocean. They help break down the oil."

"So …?" she prompted.

Art shrugged. "Guess it just creeps me out, the idea of living things packaged that way."

Claudia's scrutiny intensified. Art felt it like crazy Rasberry ants on his skin, worse than the wind tickling his phantom fur.

"Doesn't look like they suffered any," she said. "I mean, look at those rafts already crawling with *hongos*. It's like they can't wait to slurp up the oil."

"Doing our bidding …. "

"It's just like yeast," Claudia continued. "From the baking aisle at H-E-B?"

But yeast could be harvested from the air, Art thought. It didn't need to be dried out and sealed in an envelope. Fortunately, the deep roar of an engine interrupted their conversation. An ATV equipped with a sand sled trundled along the beach. Heaped in the sled, orange biohazard waste bags rattled with the stiff Gulf wind.

"Is that what I think it is?" Claudia hollered.

Art glanced at her, suspected her face would've wrinkled in disgust if the grafts had been sufficiently elastic. "I'm afraid so," he said. "If we don't collect them the oil company will, and they'll destroy them before U.S. Fish and Wildlife can get a good count."

"Fish?" Claudia said. "And birds, I suppose."

"And turtles, dolphins, jellies, sharks … lots of animals."

Luckily, the ATV motored on to the next dump site without stopping.

"So sad," Claudia murmured in its wake.

Art flipped through the afternoon timeline on his clipboard, until Claudia tsked. "Look at you," she said. "All worried about bacteria in jars a minute ago and then you rattle off dead animals like a shopping list."

"Well …." Art lowered his clipboard, shrugged again. "Those animals are dead. I feel worse about the ones still trapped."

"In the oil," Claudia said, nodding.

Anywhere, Art thought.

↑

Art opened his car door and swiveled in the driver's seat to put on socks and shoes. He'd driven barefoot, unwilling to squeeze his clawed feet into shoes until the last possible moment. After a lifetime of forcing himself into human clothes, he was mostly resigned to fabric squashing down his fur and seams constricting his movement — sweats helped with that — but shoes still tortured him. He usually wore sandals to avoid the sensation of his claws being jammed back into his toes, but he didn't think sandals were appropriate to dinner at someone's house.

He wasn't sure, of course, since he usually avoided human contact outside of errands and his work at the Laguna Madre Wildlife Center. On weekends, he might go more than forty-eight hours without saying a word. When Claudia extended her invite, however, she wouldn't take no for an answer. Anyway, Art thought edging outside his comfort zone might be worth it. Claudia must know what it was like, seeing yourself one way while everyone else saw you differently.

Cold air bumped his muzzle when Claudia greeted him at the door. That, and the aroma of chicken and onions simmering with rice in a peppery broth.

"¿Arroz con pollo?" He stepped inside, careful not to trample her small feet. Only then did he remember it was customary for the guest to bring a gift: a bottle of wine, flowers for the table, dessert.

"You said you were an omnivore," she reminded him, a subtle tease at his word choice.

"I am," he assured her. "It smells great."

She introduced him to her six-year-old son, Moises, who only abandoned his colouring pages on the coffee table after much cajoling.

"It might be your beard," Claudia said apologetically. "He doesn't know a lot of men with beards."

Art realised, abashed, that when Claudia had mentioned her son, he'd imagined a mix-skin. Which was ridiculous. Claudia's skin grafts and scarring were the result of a bacterial infection, not a hereditary condition. Moises had the typically luminescent skin of a child fresh from the bath. His straight-brown hair had dried in some places, others not. He half-hid behind his mom to shake hands.

Art tried not to mash the boy's fingers in his big paw. "I probably look like a giant, huh?" he said. "Nice to meet you, Moises."

Moises peeked out from behind Claudia's loose cotton dress. Not to look at Art's face, but to study Art's paw curiously, as if he saw the same thing Art did: the leathery pads, the sharply curving grey-brown claws, the dense brown underfur and coarser guard hairs. The bear superimposed over a human frame.

Moises craned back to take in Art's full height. He looked higher than Art's human head, maybe at Art's rounded bear ears, and his mouth fell open in awe, revealing a missing front tooth.

"What do you think?" Claudia said, a hand across her boy's shoulders. "Does he look like a giant?"

"No," Moises breathed. "A bear."

The only reason Art didn't break into an itchy sweat was that Claudia's whole house was as cold as H-E-B's frozen food section. At the beach, she'd explained that her grafted skin couldn't sweat, hence her assignment under the protective shade of the booth.

Seemingly unaware of any awkwardness, Claudia laughed and pushed Moises back to his colouring. "Finish your homework."

She waved for Art to follow as she charged into the eat-in kitchen. A bowl of salad sat on the table already, with three bottles of dressing and a pitcher of — Art sniffed — hibiscus iced tea. Claudia stirred the chicken and rice, checking for doneness and chattering about a TV show Moises watched that featured a big bear. Meanwhile, Art tried to get ahold of himself. He stared at the damp circle the glass pitcher dripped on the tablecloth until his manners kicked in.

"Can I help with something?" he said, feeling like a bear of very little brain.

"What? No!" She whirled, flinging broth from her serving spoon in the process. "Sit, have a seat, do you know how long it's been since I had an excuse to cook something off the kiddie menu?"

"Are you sure?"

"Well, you know, this needs a few more minutes to simmer," she said, turning to cover the pan. "Are you sure, because I have this light bulb that went out months ago, over the back door, and I can't reach it even with a step ladder, but I bet you can. Would you mind?"

"No, not at all." Art was actually relieved to step outside for a moment. It gave him time to recover.

But when he returned with the moth-flecked compact fluorescent light bulb in hand, the kitchen was empty. He heard urgent whispers in the living room and the whole idea of *Claudia,* of all people, feeling the need to lower her voice struck Art as weird enough that he froze near the swinging kitchen door.

"*Mijo,* what've you done?" She sounded exasperated. "Didn't we read the instructions together?"

"Colour the shapes with the number," Moises recited. "I did, Mama!"

"But here, the key shows you. One is red, Two is blue and Three you leave white."

"That's silly!" Moises said.

"No, that's the instructions."

An uncertain smile tugged at Art's lips. Hard to imagine a colouring page was such a big deal. But, obviously, he wasn't a parent. Before he could be caught eavesdropping, he walked to the counter. He tugged a paper towel from the roll, folded it on the counter and gently placed the lightbulb on top. He was washing his hands when Claudia returned.

"That boy!" she said with forced cheer. "I swear he's trying to sabotage dinner. Like it'll kill him to eat anything but the unholy yellow trinity: mac-n'-cheese, chicken fingers and fries."

"Why take the chance?" Art joked.

Over dinner, Claudia asked about Art's work at the wildlife center, neatly sidestepping the spill's depressing impact. She still managed to do enough of the talking that Art didn't need to wrack his brain to keep up conversation. He reminded himself to glance up from his food once in a while and often caught Claudia tapping a finger near Moises's plate. Art recognised the code for "Eat your food," "Use your fork" and "Stop playing with your glass" from his own childhood, when he'd still acted more cub than boy.

Art took pity on Moises. "Do you like going to the beach?" he asked.

"No," Moises said, taking him by surprise. "It's like a big mouth, with backwash."

Claudia's head slumped. "I'm going to kill cousin Hector for teaching you that word."

"Why do you work there?" Moises asked Art. "Bears don't belong in the ocean. A lake would be better."

"He's not really a bear," Claudia chided. "You know that. Don't you know that?"

Despite Claudia's embarrassment, Art wiped his napkin across his mouth and explained. "Some bears do go in the ocean. Remember polar bears? Their Latin name is *Ursus maritimus,* which means 'sea bear', and they've been known to swim for up to nine days. And grizzly bears, also known as brown bears, they live along the coast of Alaska. You've probably seen pictures of them catching salmon in their mouths, but they'll also hang out in intertidal zones and eat clams."

"But not in Texas," Moises said, his voice curling into a question.

"Not at South Padre Island," Claudia said.

"But you're right about one thing. This bear," Art said, a thumb to his chest, "would definitely prefer a lake. In fact, I'm thinking about buying a house up in Wisconsin or Michigan, one day, something near a lake."

"But we just met you," Claudia teased. "You can't go now! Or is that *why* you're going?"

After dinner, as they cleared the table, Moises asked Art, "Do you know what colour the number One is?"

Claudia turned from loading the dishwasher. "Don't start that again," she warned.

"I'm not sure what you mean," Art said, looking down at the boy.

"He brought home a colouring page of the American flag. It was a colour-by-number assignment. One is red, Two is blue, etcetera," Claudia said. She took Moises's plate from him, trying to capture his attention, as well. "I told you we'd talk about that later, with your teacher."

Art felt Moises's expectant gaze clinging to him. Knowing he shouldn't intercede between mother and child, he still asked, "But you coloured it differently?"

"I coloured it the way it really is," Moises said, greasy lips glistening under the kitchen light. "The paper says One is red, but, really, it's dark green and the number Two is pink and Three is yellow —"

"Ayy … Moises!" Claudia yanked Art's plate from his hands. "Enough! Go wash up in the bathroom. We'll talk about this with Miss Farias at Open House."

"Sorry," Art said, not entirely sure whom he was speaking to. Claudia and Moises both nodded, however, each apparently feeling entitled. Art tried to make himself useful by handing the rest of the dishes to Claudia. His phantom claws scraped the china and set his real and phantom teeth on edge; he resisted the urge to speak louder, over the scratching Claudia couldn't hear — but maybe Moises could.

"I didn't know what to do with the lightbulb," he said, gesturing at the counter when they were done.

"Oh! No worries," Claudia said. Art suspected she was glad to have something else to do with her hands. "It'll just take me a minute. ¡Tantas gracias! It was driving me crazy; for months I'd flick the switch and be confused then annoyed, and I did try several times, pero …. "

Still talking, she yanked open a junk drawer — Art spotted refrigerator magnets, rubber bands, chopsticks — and fished out a thick remediation envelope that also served as a return mailer to the CFL manufacturer. Art twitched. Claudia didn't notice. She popped the bulb inside the envelope, thick as an old bubble-wrap insulated mailer, and sealed the top.

"You probably think I'm crazy, already, arguing with Moises about colouring, for God's sake," she said.

"I'm not really in a position to call anyone crazy," Art said. He phrased it as a joke, but wondered if he'd soon have to come clean. Moises knew something was off, even if the child didn't seem to consider Art's bearhood "off" at all.

Claudia held the remediation envelope between her palms and crushed it flat. Art winced as the bulb shards pierced the dense mycelial mats lining the inside.

"The thing is, Moises is going to have a hard-enough time at school, in the world, with a mix-skin for a mom," she said. "Sorry if that word offends you, but let's not beat around the bush. There's worse things to be called. Anyhow, the point is, *mijo* can't be making things worse for himself by not following simple instructions and being so stubborn about his imagination .... "

As she spoke, Claudia crushed the bulb to pieces. Art flinched at every crackle. Such a brutal awakening for the fungus inside. Spores of the French summer cep, maybe, or gem-studded puffball. Whatever mushroom it might've been, Art sensed another living being — a wild thing — trapped in a too-tiny, human-approved container. Forced into hibernation, engineered to eat garbage, expected to spit back a form acceptable to humans ....

"Are you okay?" Claudia said and Art only heard her because she stopped grinding the glass and toxins into the fungus. "Don't tell me I made you sick! The one time in months I get to feed a friend and I've poisoned him? *¡Que cataclismo!*"

Feeling less sick and more stupid with every passing second, Art realized he could never tell Claudia. It didn't matter that she, too, was trapped in a body that didn't fit her. *Furry* or *freak* or *crazy man* she'd call him, as merciless with her insults as with her self-appointed label.

"What's wrong?" Moises said. He held open the kitchen door with bubble-gum-scented hands, still slightly damp. He frowned up at Art and Art felt a warm puddle of pity under his sternum. Moises's brow was far too wrinkled for a child his age. He wished he could stay.

But Claudia would crush them both into the appropriate containers, all in the name of making their lives easier. And Art knew, beaten down as he already was, he'd succumb long before Moises. He'd not be doing the boy any favours by sticking around.

"It wasn't dinner," Art said. "Promise. Dinner was great. I just …
feel a migraine coming on. I need to get home before it really sinks its
teeth in."

Art narrowly escaped Claudia's maternal ministrations: "You can
lie down on the couch; we'll turn out the lights for you; should you be
driving; are you seeing the auras already?" Once safely in his car, Art
kicked off his hated shoes and sagged in the driver's seat.

He'd been a fool to try to play at being human.

↑

Art stood on the shore, watching the lake emerge from the shadow
of the bluffs as the sun rose higher in the sky. A breeze ruffled his fur,
but elicited no shiver. That morning, the tansy outside his cabin had
sagged with cold dew, but, even shoe-less, he'd felt warmer and more
peaceful walking to his bit of Lake Michigan than he ever had on South
Padre Island. The shards of zebra mussel shells carpeting the sand didn't
bother him, calloused as his feet had grown from wandering the woods
barefoot.

He caught a sparkle in the marram grass and used his pole spear, a
six-foot piece of white pine, to part the rolled leaves. The ladybug trun-
dling over the sand sensed an audience and flitted off, barely audible.
Art's thoughts turned to whitefish or burbot for lunch. Then he'd spend
the hottest part of the afternoon in the woods, collecting wild blueberries
and blackberries. The staghorn sumac was probably ripe for tea. He might
even luck upon some morels. Though he kept hearing about the all-you-
can-eat fish fry at the local "supper club" — a term he'd never even heard
until he moved to the Midwest — Art was content to forage.

The only thing detracting from the Elysian scene was the power
plant that operated atop the nearest bluff. Pewter clouds puffed from
black-streaked smokestacks, casting shadows over the water and dunes.
The *beep-beep-beep* of reversing dump trucks echoed down from the
bluffs and put Art in mind of that rearview mirror warning: *Objects in
mirror may be closer than they appear.*

Art had known about the power plant when he bought this shaggy piece of land, as well as the degree of fixing up his "fixer-upper" would need. But the price had been right and the woods were the exact shade of green that Art had imagined when Moises told him the true colour of One. (He suspected the morning light that spilled through the hole in his screen door was a perfect expression of Two. The tansy hadn't bloomed yet, but, for all Art knew, it would produce buttons of Three.)

After some research, Art had discovered that the power plant was on its last legs. Antiquated, it serviced only half the counties it once had. It couldn't compete with the newer nuclear plants studding the Great Lakes — a mixed blessing, to say the least. Rumour had it the plant was slated for closure in the coming year.

All Art needed was to wait the plant out. After decades of living in the closet, he figured he had patience enough for one year.

But then, one day, the bluff collapsed.

↑

The lake was never meant to hold a trailer, dump truck, backhoe, three storage units, myriad construction equipment and the tons of debris unloaded by the landslide. The vehicles and most equipment could be fished out, though at great expense, both monetary and environmental. But the muted rainbow sheen of fuel on the lake, the coal ash sinking beneath, the rock and soil that left a wake long as a football field, the shore clogged with a cataclysm of heavy metals like arsenic, lead and mercury ...? Art's coworkers at the Great Lakes Waterkeepers talked about "unstepping the butterfly." Art thought it was more like sucking the venom from a rattlesnake bite. That nastiness had to go somewhere.

And so, too, did Art. The spring and summer he'd spent in Michigan had changed him. Never before had his nature felt so nurtured. His land, his woods, his piece of the lake, they'd saved him. He couldn't hide in a booth anymore. Now he had to save his saviours.

Without a thought, he donned a blazer, jammed on shoes, even knotted a necktie. He shocked his coworkers, who'd grown accustomed to his shyness, by volunteering to speak at various town hall meetings about his experiences with the Gulf spill. He designed an ultra-media presentation to optimise attendees' understanding, regardless of their learning styles. He explained skimmers, hair mats, booms, and — despite personal reservations — bioremediation and even myco-remediation techniques. He talked until he went hoarse; he wrote until his paw cramped; he researched until letters jiggled across his closed eyes at night. The letters were different colours and some of them didn't get along, but when he dreamed, he knew he saw them as they truly were.

In the end, it was like *déjà vu*. Art crunched over the frost-withered grass to visit the lake every morning before work. He no longer needed to wait for the late-rising sun to reveal the waves, however.

Bobbing like deformed water lilies, a sea of oyster mushrooms shone white as moonlit ice caps on the autumn-chilled lake. Anchored rafts of the lab-enhanced, climate-sturdy fungus covered the area slammed hardest by the industrial avalanche. If he'd been a lighter sort of beast — a Jesus lizard, perhaps — Art could've run across, raft to raft, shore to shore, his feet never rippling the water.

Since he'd stayed in a hotel in town the week the rafts were installed, Art could almost pretend the layers of gilled white pads had blossomed naturally. Each morning, he thanked the eager "volunteers" that consumed the coal ash in silence, converting neurotoxins into meaty, slightly anise-scented shelves. But when it came time to haul in the disintegrating rafts and harvest the mushrooms, thereby making room for the next generation, Art was elbow to elbow, shoulder to shoulder, with the human volunteers. And rather than ship the bags of frilled fractals back to the labs, Art and the others tossed them into a refrigerated truck bound for the supper club.

Aching by sundown, still a solitary beast at heart, Art nevertheless joined his neighbours in the refurbished veterans' hall that served as the town supper club. There was no menu and no choice of entree. Only coleslaw and all-you-can-eat oysters, all night long. The myco-remediation company insisted that the engineered mushrooms were safe to eat, that they so thoroughly decomposed heavy metals and toxins that people were more likely to get sick from gone-over coleslaw or dirty deep fryers than the mushrooms.

More than any previous tests or scientific findings, the locals looked to Art, his coworkers and the head honchos from the power plant and the outsourced clean-up company to prove the 'shrooms were safe to eat — by demonstration. The VIP table was set at the front of the hall, CFL bulbs shining down bright on glasses of ice water and steel-topped salt-and-pepper shakers.

Art carried his heaping bamboo plate to the long banquet table lined with butcher paper. His chair screeched as he pulled it out over the linoleum floor, no louder than many others echoing through the hall, but subject to special scrutiny.

He sat quietly and took up his silverware. He sliced through the golden-brown breading of the top "filet" on his mountain of oysters. Within glistened a now-creamy, almost sepia-toned flesh. Art hadn't spoken to Moises since he left the Valley, but he thought that particular colour might be the colour of infinity.

The spores of *Pleurotus corticatus* had been captured and tweaked and replicated in a lab. Art released his knife. The new-and -improved spores had been shocked into stasis, embedded in straw rafts and wrapped in plastic. Art lowered his knife hand to the napkin draped over his lap.

Contained, imprisoned in human-approved form, the spores had been shipped to Michigan in October and forced to feed on the poison of human error. Art lifted his fork. The least he could do was welcome the refugee as a brother, set it free of this engineered, unnatural cycle.

Art opened his mouths, both the hidden bear's maw and the obvious human orifice. He bit down on the buttery flesh, chewed with a redundancy of premolars and molars. He swallowed and gave thanks. He was not at peace, but he would eat his piece, and the next, and the next.

↑

LETTERS TO A FUNGUS

By Polenth Blake

✦

Polenth Blake lives where the mushrooms bloom in autumn. She has two pet cockroaches, except on Fridays, when they get to be in charge. Her fiction has appeared in *Nature* and *ChiZine*. Her website lurks at http://www.polenthblake.com.

✦

DEAR FUNGUS,

I'm writing to discuss my concerns about your recent behaviour. I accept that you need somewhere to live, but did you have to litter my lawn with your mushrooms?

I could cope with the wood mushrooms. They were easily removed. But this time, you produced the most foul-smelling mushrooms imaginable and they're attracting flies. If you don't take action, I'll have to report this to the neighbourhood committee.

Thank you for your prompt attention to this matter.

Yours sincerely,
Jane Goodworth

↑

I appreciate you dealing with the flies. Eating them wasn't what I had in mind, but it solves the problem nicely.

However, I'm not happy about your change of abode. When I said I was unhappy with mushrooms in the garden, I didn't mean you could move into my door frames. I admit you have taken care of the house's dry rot issue, but you're not an improvement. Your spores are giving Aunt Mabel terrible asthma. I've kept her from ripping off the door frames and putting you outside, but I can't hide the crowbar forever.

She blames me for touching the wood mushrooms. How could I know it'd upset you so much? All I wanted was a clean lawn.

I'm willing to compromise. You were right. The garden is the best place. I hope we can arrange a relocation plan that suits both of us.

↑

Sorry about the exterminator. I should have given you a final warning. I do think it was a bit excessive to eat him. Were those poison spores you were firing?

Having weighed up the options, I've decided you can keep the house. All I want in return is for you to uncover the front door. Or maybe one of the windows. I know we haven't always seen eye-to-eye, but it isn't much to ask.

P.S. That exterminator wasn't a cheap snack.

↑

You ate Aunt Mabel.

I'm not angry. I never write letters when I'm angry. It would be silly. You're a fungus. It's like blaming a flood for drowning people.

So, I hope you understand why I tried to set you on fire. You left me no choice. No hard feelings.

You've cut off the phone lines. Accidentally, I'm sure. If you could just reattach them, I can call the fire brigade. It's best we go our separate ways, before either of us does something we'll regret.

↑

I didn't know Aunt Mabel liked to draw. She'd sit at the bedroom window looking down into the garden, pad in hand. I assumed she was writing letters about the local children. They're always sneaking into the garden.

At first, I thought her pictures were random dots. Then I realised — it was the old drifts of mushrooms covering the lawn. It's like finding pictures in clouds. The shapes are random, but they're there. Squares and triangles. People and mushrooms. I'm not sure if the person is picking the mushroom or patting it. I suppose you don't know either.

↑

I saw one of my neighbours today. I wrote HELP on a piece of paper and held it to the last uncovered part of the window. He waved and walked away.

I remember him. He's the one with three cats, after one had a kitten. The housing agreement clearly stated a maximum of two. They're a health risk. He should have thanked me when one didn't come home.

And you. I kept the garden nice. I never used weed-killer. It isn't just about looks, after all. The rot can be within. It kills the spiders and beetles, not just the weeds. Next thing you know, pests everywhere with nothing to eat them.

You never thanked me.

↑

Aunt Mabel wanted a mobile. She brought one a few months back, so she could call her bingo friends. I threw it away when she wasn't looking. Mobiles mean unsightly towers. They say it doesn't lower house prices in the end, but I don't believe them. Better that we all write letters, don't you think?

It doesn't matter. However we talk, it's always one-sided. I send letters and no one replies. I phone up and get an answering machine. Aunt Mabel told me I ought to listen first, but I always listen. She was just angry about the phone.

I wish I hadn't thrown it away.

↑

You're everywhere. You've eaten holes in the door. The pattern almost looks like a cowering cat. Do you want me to cower? Is that why you're waiting?

Maybe they're not coming for me, but they're not going to let you slink away. You're too dangerous. They'll kill you. The monster always dies.

We're a lot alike, you and me. No one wants us here. We could have been friends, if only you listened.

↑

There were children in the garden. That girl from next door was singing again. I've talked to her parents before about it. Irritating habit.

A boy called her to look at the mushrooms. I could've shouted to warn them. I stopped myself. You might as well do something useful while you're here.

I waited for the screams, but they never came. Only songs and laughter.

↑

Dear Jane,

I'm writing to discuss my concerns about your recent behaviour. I accept that you need somewhere to live, but did you have to litter my lawn with your neighbourhood?

We could have been friends, if only you listened. You thought my pictures were random dots. However we talk, it's always one-sided.

The rot can be within. Next thing you know, pests everywhere with nothing to eat them. Eating you wasn't what I had in mind, but it solves the problem nicely. The monster always dies.

Yours sincerely,
Fungus

P.S. Sorry about Aunt Mabel.

↑

THE SHAFT THROUGH THE MIDDLE OF IT ALL

By Nick Mamatas

✦

Nick Mamatas is the author of several novels, including *Sensation* and *Bullettime*, more than eighty short stories, and is the four-time loser and one-time winner of the Bram Stoker award. He writes about fungi because of his avid interest in altered states of consciousness. He writes at all for the same exact reason.

✦

JOACHIM LEARNED TO GARDEN from his mother. She kept a nice house and was the biggest busybody in Loisaida. She yelled at the kids on the street when their mischief turned violent, took a broom to a dealer's head once and, when he came back with a switchblade, she faced him down with a butcher knife. All the other tenants in the building on 4th and D knew to take out their garbage and keep their dogs from barking and their kids in school, or in church. And when the landlord sent his sons down from the Bronx to torch the building

221

next to theirs, Joachim's mother woke up and ran up the five flights of steps and down the hallway in nothing but her giant brassiere and girdle, banging on doors and rousing everyone for a general evacuation. Even as the neighbourhood watched the building next door burn, the rumours spread — the landlord wouldn't dare burn down the house Joachim's mother lived in, even though every tenant there was either on rent control or Section 8. It was 1974 and, for many landlords, arson was easier than rent collection.

The rats came, and the needles, so Joachim's mother got the kids together. With a roll full of bills she had maybe been keeping in her bosom for years, she sent them to what she called "the Jewish store" south of Delancey for shovels and trowels and seeds, and launched a community garden in the vacant lot. Joachim had to work the hardest of all. No comic books, no bicycle, no stickball. "I'll work you like the Jews and Chinese work their children," his mother told him, about both the garden and school. She did special things to the soil to make it fertile, things that Joachim didn't understand completely, but he knew enough to know that his fourth-grade science teacher, Mr. Braunstein, would not approve. There were prayers in the night, burning candles, things done with chicken bones, even on nights when Joachim was only served Kraft macaroni and cheese for dinner. Joachim dug and weeded and fertilised 'till dark. That summer, he ate so many tomatoes even pizza seemed disgusting to him. All the neighbours had their fill of zucchini and bell and *Cubanelle* peppers, onions and eggplants in both white and purple. In fall, when the nights came early, his mother had Joachim drag some thick pieces of burnt wood from the corners of the lot into the apartment, where she took them to her room. And the years flew by.

Punk happened and Joachim loved it from afar — the drums were like cavemen pounding on logs in the flickering firelight of their cavern homes. Graffiti and hip-hop, too, but he still danced along to Willie Colón records with his cousins and friends on the tar beach of the building's rooftop. The city smelled so sweet up there, thanks to the garden.

The garden got famous and white people moved into the neighbourhood. First, they were stringy junkies and fat women with more children
than teeth, but then came the college kids, the artists, the faggots. He
couldn't even tell the difference between a gay man and a Hell's Angel
half the time. Some of them bought a chain link fence for the garden
and stood around amidst the rows. His mother grew fatter and older,
and had to have a foot removed. "A sacrifice," she called it, with a philo-
sophical shrug of her shoulders. She told him to look under her bed for
two logs and to take one down to the garden, to sink it into the black
dirt. It was a strange thing, covered in waxy blobs and smelling like wet
feet, but Joachim was a good boy and did what he was told.

Whatever that log was, the neighbours didn't get to have it, not at
first. The neighbourhood was changing and the same landlord that had
torched his building 15 years prior wanted to rebuild. Studio and one-
bedroom condos for $400,000 apiece. Joachim's mother still paid $400
a month rent on the place she had lived in since coming to New York.
The neighbourhood white people had meetings and invited Joachim
to attend, to talk about his mother's garden. He got his photo in the
Village Voice. He was hugged and cheered and spat on, and called a
"fag spic cocksucker" while standing on Houston Street and collecting
signatures to send to the mayor himself. An old man with a long white
beard — one of the first in the neighbourhood — invented a special kind
of wheel. He pushed it like a wheelbarrow and it painted the sidewalks
and the street crossings with a trail of green footprints. Those footprints
covered the Lower East Side and the East Village, luring the curious
back to the garden.

Two things happened. His mother had a dream of a ship sinking,
only to be raised again with a bony crew of skeletons scaling the seaweed-
choked rigging. And someone slipped an envelope under the apartment
door one morning while Joachim watched NY1 and ate Eggos straight
from the toaster. In it was two thousand dollars in one-hundred-dollar
bills and a Post-It Note reading, "Please Stop." His mother was moaning
in pain in the other room, so Joachim took the money and stopped. He
paid his John Jay tuition, got some painkillers for his mother.

Some of the white people — ones who never had much time for the garden, actually, except when there were so many tomatoes they threatened to rot on the vine — decided to chain themselves to the gates of the garden. They were pepper-sprayed and beaten where they hanged, then clipped free and dragged away. Then the bulldozers moved in and tore the garden to pieces. The city was swimming in money again. It took only a few weeks for the foundation to be poured and the skeletal steel frame to go up. Then winter was hard and the construction slowed.

One dark night, Joachim's mother summoned him into her room. He left his college homework on the kitchen table and slipped into the tiny bedroom. Candles in glass jars painted with pictures of saints were everywhere. His mother was still in the bed, but the shadows danced on the ceiling.

"Those fuckers," she said. She rarely ever cursed and never in English. "Were there any mushrooms growing in the garden when they ruined it?"

"No, mama," Joachim said. He had worked in the garden every afternoon till the day the white people chained themselves to the gate, ironically keeping everyone out of the ground on which they had made their stand. "Not that I saw."

"All those people were acting crazy out there, no?"

"No more than usual, mama," he said. "Can I get you a glass of water, or coffee?"

"No, you can get under my bed. There's a log there, specially treated and prepared. Put it in the other building. Throw it over the fence then climb over after it," his mother told him. "Find the air shaft they're building — I know there's one. I look at the damn building going up every day. They ruined my garden, but I've got something for them."

Joachim didn't say anything for a long time. His mother finally huffed and said, "What?"

"If I do this for you, mama," Joachim asked, "will you die?"

His mother sputtered and gasped. "Die! Are you trying to send me to an early grave?"

"No, no … it's just so —"

"Go!"

Joachim went. It was easy enough to climb the scaffolding with the log and then climb back down into the construction site proper. The security guard was an old friend from high school. Joachim showed him the log and told him about the garden and his mother.

"There ain't no bomb in that log, is there?" the guard asked.

"You can check it out if you want," Joachim said, presenting the log, his arms outstretched.

"Just tell me," the guard said, his own palms up.

"Mama had another one of these that she planted in the old garden."

"Aw, I guess it's fine, then. Ain't like I'll have a job once this place is done."

Joachim picked his way through the site till he found what appeared to be the frame for the air shaft. Avenue D was gentrifying, sure, but, in Manhattan, even the gentry are crammed into tiny apartments. Even tenement apartments must, by law, have a window that faces open air, thus shafts. When he was a kid, Joachim was even jealous of friends who had shaft windows. They threw paper airplanes across the gap at one another and got to watch the shadowplay fuck shows parents and fags put on behind the cheap, landlord-issued blinds. Burying the log in the dirt under a waxing crescent moon, he was glad he didn't have one now. And the years flew by.

Joachim's mother didn't die. Joachim stayed with her. He finished his criminology degree at John Jay then started working for the city, crunching numbers to make the cops look good. The garden was a distant memory. The *Voice* article tacked up on corkboard in his room turned yellow, then brown. The rent slowly climbed to more than $600 a month, which was still a steal. He forgot all about the log. Girls came and went.

Then a folder landed on his desk at work. And another one. Lots of 911 calls to the apartment building next door to his own building. The system flags that kind of thing — it usually means that someone's dealing drugs out of an apartment, or domestic problems, or a cranky old person needs company and likes excitement. But these reports were different. Random. Public masturbation in the hallways and on the stairs — only unusual, really, because the perps were women the same age as Joachim's mother. And self-mutilation. One man gouged out his own right eye and tried to replace it with a bright-blue robin's egg. He had another on his coffee table and another big spoon, too, but the cops broke down the door and stopped him. A neighbour had reported the screaming. According to the 911 transcript, the caller had said, "You pigs gotta hear this shit," and apparently held the phone up to the door. All strange stuff and Joachim was amazed that he hadn't heard any neighbourhood gossip about it. But the residents of the new building did keep to themselves. Joachim and his friends were the undesirables, the poor people who shopped at the corner market instead of Whole Foods, who drank water from the taps as though the municipal government could be trusted. Who were home by 10 pm, even if it was just to get together and dance on the rooftops. The closest anyone in the new building had come to dancing on the roof was falling down the shaft with a bedsheet parachute tied to her wrists.

"Ah, yes, the shaft," Joachim said to himself.

The building was much harder to get into now. He knew no tenants and nobody responded when he rang the bell. There was video security — the tenants could see who was calling. Not like in Joachim's building, with its primitive buzzer system. The few people who entered or exited were quick to close the door behind him and glared at Joachim for loitering. His city ID meant nothing. Some snotnose from NYU even made a crack about "late-night emergency chi-square tests."

There were still garden supplies in the basement of Joachim's building. He grabbed some bungee cords and a ladder, and went from his roof to the roof of the new building pretty easily. There was just a one-story difference. The plan was to lower his smartphone, in camcorder mode, down the shaft, but he didn't need to. Its walls were covered with mold all the way down to the bottom. None of the windows were open, but the air smelled like the inside of a sock. He got down onto his belly and reached into the shaft to scrape some of the gunk off the brick with a drugstore club card. He knew a guy in the city's police lab. But first, he'd ask Mama.

She smiled when she saw the stuff and told him to sit by her. "On your very knees," she said. She pointed to a brazier among the statuettes and candles on her crowded bureau and Joachim brought it to her. She fished an old Key Food matchbook out of it, then scraped the mold into it and lit it afire. She spoke words older than Spanish as the smoke filled the room, and something wonderful happened to Joachim. It was like a story he had read once. About a guy in a basement who saw something that let him see everything: "the multitudes of America ... a silvery cobweb in the center of a black pyramid ... a splintered labyrinth (it was London)," but what Joachim saw was not even of this Earth. It was a deeper thing, and wiser, and it wished him and his mother both well. There was a path like a labyrinth, like a silvery cobweb, like a long tunnel that bored down through the middle of it all, to another better place. One day, Joachim would be able to follow it like he could still follow the faded green-painted footprints on the streets outside to the step of his home. He'd like to take that long walk into the starry starry night one day, he thought.

Hours later, when Joachim's mouth could work again, and when he was sure that his mother was still alive, he asked her, "The log?"

"Yes, of course. It's hard to grow that mold in a climate like this, but when you put your mind to it, you can do it. It's so beautiful. That's why I wanted it in the garden. To feed the people the same wisdom, to teach them the words I know to say when the fire burns and the mold enters the breath. Words I'll teach you."

"But what about the second log? The one you made me plant next door in the shaft?"

"Without the words," his mother said. "Something different happens." And then she smiled and slept.

↑

GO HOME AGAIN

By Simon Strantzas

✦

Simon Strantzas is the critically acclaimed author of *Nightingale Songs*, *Cold to the Touch* and *Beneath the Surface* — three collections of the strange and supernatural from Dark Regions Press. His award-nominated fiction has appeared previously in the *Mammoth Book of Best New Horror* series, *Postscripts* and *Cemetery Dance*. He still lives in Toronto, Canada, with his ever-patient wife and an unyielding hunger for the flesh of the living.

✦

SHE REMEMBERED SO LITTLE of her father, but what she did was vivid, crystalised in the fractures of her psyche. His sour breath, his distended gorge rising and falling as he stared at her, licking his razor lips. If she closed her eyes, she could almost hear his slurred voice bellowing at her cowering mother. The phantoms of his presence surrounded her. She knew this was so because every part of her wanted to break down into sobs. But she would not offer even his memory that satisfaction. In hindsight, she could remember his withering face, his jaundiced skin, his waning strength, but none of these things struck her as abnormal. She was blind to the truth and perhaps always had been. Even when her father disappeared for good, she did not question it. Ives knew nothing more of life than that, believed the world was one way and no other. Even if she could not express the thought, she understood that nothing was permanent, that everything in the world tended toward chaos. It was the reason fathers died and black mould infected the only tangible proof they had ever existed at all.

Afterward, once bruises healed and wounds scarred, once Ives was old enough to understand, her mother told tales of her husband, of his generosity, of the feats he had accomplished before his death, but Ives understood those notions could not be reconciled with the shade that haunted her memory — the man who had glared at her between crib slats, the man whose skin seeped terminal foulness. They were the true memories, and Ives would be the keeper of them if her mother could not.

The return to the house had been slowed only by Ives's reluctance and a basement window swollen shut. So many years spent fleeing only to return and find nothing had changed. Nothing beyond the creep of fungus across the walls. Ives shined her flashlight as she carefully trod, part of her scouring the rubble for any mark of her late father's passing, but she found none. Instead, only gravity's constant desire to unmake them.

The noxious mould had spread across vacant rooms, swirling around broken fixtures and outlets. It was a bizarre pattern, one she very nearly understood and yet one that remained frustratingly beyond. Part of her longed to touch the spreading cancer, as though that would somehow reveal what had been so deceptively hidden, but she resisted. It was a trap: Touching the growth offered no reward she might want. And yet, again, the longing was there, like the ache to leap from the edge of a bottomless gorge, or to thrust a hand deep into the flames of a fire — that urge to experience death, even while running fleet-footed from it.

The floating spores were so thick in the air that Ives could barely breathe. They coated her mouth, slipped down into her lungs — the mere thought scratching her throat, wanting her to cough. Instead, she bit down and stifled the sensation before she inadvertently launched more spores into the air. Her eyes filled with tears, tears for no one but her, for nothing but what life had brought her on a platter and tried to convince her was fruit. But she was no fool; if it were, it would not be so terribly bitter.

Anchorless, her pale mother floundered. With no forethought, she moved them from Montreal to Ottawa, where she believed a new beginning awaited. But her anxieties made the trip along with them and those few places where she found employment were impossible to maintain. Ives had no better luck entering school mid-stream — her English was poor and their living arrangements were far too mercurial for any allowances to be made. Instead, she remained with her mother and feigned happiness in hopes it would inspire the same. But her mother was not her. She was not strong and she could do little to keep food on their table, or a roof over their heads. Ives was barely nine by the time she was sleeping in a parked car with her mother, and nowhere near ten when her mother left to get food and never returned. Ives waited patiently in the car for days, staring at the buildings along the street. It was between their brick she saw the first sign of her life's infection, a small vein of darkness that broke through the mortar like a snake from its skin.

The house fared worse. No one had stepped foot within its skewed walls since Ives and her mother had left in tears. What once was solid became less so — a phantasm fading from notice, invisible to the world around it. Ives, too, nearly passed it on her approach, the overgrown landscape obscuring the drive, and it was only the tug of memories unburied that caused her to slow enough to spot it.

Artwork from Ives's young hands remained affixed to the broken refrigerator, but what shapes she once drew had become a mystery. Lines, spirals, blobs, each so carefully delineated, some arcane pattern whose purpose had been long forgotten. A sorrowful atmosphere pervaded. Within it, a faded table and set of chairs materialised, as though from

Ives's half-remembered past. She ran her finger across the surface and left marks in the dust like scars, but the colours beneath were no less muted. She shined her flashlight on the kitchen wall where the black mould expanded outward like a web, spiralling from the cracks and into others, glistening in the harsh light.

Ives imagined the tumours had been black and tuberous, poison growing inside her father, and her mother's loathing for life could have been little different. Both stole everything Ives had and abandoned her with no hope of survival. But she did survive. The abandoned car was her shelter, her home, and though she knew somewhere deep inside that her mother would never return, she continued to wait. Even when she was discovered by a parking officer, even when she was taken back to the station by child service workers, she silently waited. It was only after she was given a room with other children, asked to sleep and eat and wait with boys and girls whose parents had lost them, that she saw the dark entirety of her life in full relief. She was nothing like those children. She remained alone in her cot, staring at the corners of the walls, no longer waiting for something she finally understood would never come.

What she would not reveal was what she witnessed while inside that locked automobile, waiting for her mother to bring her food. People of different shapes and ages walked by, most ignoring the old car, some peering in the windows. For these, she did as her mother instructed and hid beneath a blanket, remaining perfectly still until she was sure they had gone, and then waiting a time longer. There was more outside the car to worry over, more than scarred men and staggering, hard-faced women. There was a presence in the cold, peering from the darkened alleys and discarded refuse, spying from between bricks and mortar. It wanted her, wanted her as she had never been wanted before. Had she known where to go, she might have run and not looked back.

Dim salvation came in the guise of an aunt she never knew existed, summoned from Sherbrooke by the call of the police. Ives was collected into open arms and taken away, back to that small town to be given the sort of life she never thought possible. There, she was safe, impossibly loved by a woman who had given up on a child of her own, and yet Ives still could not scrape her soul of the crooked house's stain. She lay awake at night in her soft, painted room, wondering whether it was back there that everything had begun to go wrong, if it was there that her infinite choices had been constricted, leaving her but one foul path to travel. One path that led back to a single devastating place.

Was that decaying house any different than her? Sickness grew along its foundations, ate away its support, spread in ever-widening circles so as to consume everything around it. Fingers of mould reached out like shadows across the walls, the ceilings, the floors. She could see them quiver in the beam of her flashlight, struggling to be cloaked once again so they would be free to move, to touch, to explore. If she closed her eyes, she could imagine them wrapping around her throat, trying to choke the last dregs of life from her battered body.

She stood at the foot of the uneven stairs to the second floor and felt awash in evocations of childhood more vivid than any before. The flashlight's small circle climbed the treads before her. Ives found herself surprised it did not light the face of her own younger version, perched on the stair halfway between floors with stuffed toy in hand, staring up at what loomed at the summit. A cold chill ran along Ives's legs, the spectre of something behind her, but the flashlight found nothing — no haunting spirits of the past, no memories made flesh. Instead, there was an empty sitting room, the plaster of its walls crumbling with neglect.

Three bedrooms with open doors waited at the top of the stairs, but she had no desire to enter any of them. The air smelled of stale earth and she wondered if she had not erred in returning to the house. What hid in the corners of that forgotten hallway? Were they mere shadows or masses of that black mould, expanding from the bubbling walls as though it were more than simply a fungus, as though it were something from *beyond* trying to force its way through? Part of her sought an explanation that would bring some modicum of sense to all she had experienced, but inside her head was another voice, wiser and unfamiliar, that wanted her to leave the house and never look back. It was that voice she almost obeyed.

But one door, one room, would not be dismissed. She could feel a force within it drawing her, wordlessly promising the answers she had so long sought. The air had so congealed with dust and spores, as dense and sickening as honey, that she had to push her way slowly through it. With each step forward, her hesitation increased. Every fibre of her being warned her, but she continued, despite knowing she would find nothing to bandage her suffering wounds. Closure was a lie the world wanted to believe. But there could be no closure, no ending. There were no circles, only lines, each with a beginning and an end. And there was nothing between.

As though Ives's vision had once been fogged, suddenly the shape at the centre of the room snapped into focus, though Ives did not believe it was possible. It was a crib, *her* crib — she would forever recognize those slats — but its once-protective shape had been corrupted by teeming black mould. Ives shined her flashlight and saw the mould had spread everywhere, across every wall, every surface, strains of it in a Fibonacci spiral, each tendril recursively spiralling until every surface was inhabited. The black mould pulsed underneath her flashlight like veins of a body, pumping dark ichor throughout. When she traced them back, each strand clearly originated from a single place, one colourless position in the middle of the room. The place where Ives's blackened crib stood.

She could not resist coughing any longer, the dense air accreting in her lungs, and the echo that reflected did not sound proper. It was as though it emerged from another, one who both mocked Ives while striving to *become* her. Colder, deeper, it lacked any of the nuances of human speech. It was alien. When she turned around once more to point her flashlight beam at what stood behind her, what she found was not merely spore-filled air but something far worse.

It was a shape, darker than the shadows around it. It had no face, no real head of any kind beyond a formless lump. There were no eyes, but it saw her nonetheless. She *knew* it saw her, for it choreographed its movements with hers. The thing stood nearly her height, was wider than her by half. Where might have hung arms instead grew a bundle of long tendrils, each pulsing and stretching into the black course that erupted from the crib. The surface of the shapes bubbled like molten rock, cauliflower protuberances covering its body. It was not human, but it wanted to be. Wanted to grow legs and arms and a face. Wanted to look her in the eye for some unfathomable purpose. The smell was utterly repulsive, but it was that odour that clarified its origins, led Ives to understand what it was that slouched toward her, waiting to be born. Holes pockmarked its body, visible only in the light's reflection off its glazed surface, and those openings shrank with each advancing step, its strength growing. Terror strangled the words in Ives's throat, but her fractured mind finally put the pieces together. Despite her horrible choking fear, she managed to scream aloud, "Daddy! No!"

But the words aloud revealed their wrongness. The black mould had tricked her, betrayed her, for what reached out and entangled her in its approximate arms was not her father. It *could* not be. What embraced her in a malodourous grip did so not with anger or resentment, disgust, hate or vengeance. What took her in its arms was something else. Something so foreign to any of those that she did not know if it had a name. But it took her, regardless, and though she struggled like a demon against it, she knew it was too late. She had been infected. The black alien spores within her had finally taken root.

She remained an eternity in its embrace, time itself slowed by the solidified air. Thoughts coursed through her suspended mind, visions of the past feverishly rushing by, stripped of all meaning. She had no control, her resistance paling in the face of the sickly mould's control. She could not breathe, her body struggling for air but unable to expel the mass of spores from her lungs. The tendrils that bound her absorbed her convulsions. As though in defense, her mind detached itself and fell into a warm state of delirium.

When consciousness returned, it did so gradually. It was only when she finally opened her eyes that the briar of tendrils that trapped her loosened their grip. Ives fell the floor, breathless, black decay spewing from her lungs, and looked up to see that half-formed grotesquery before her start to liquefy, the dark ooze seeping into the cracks between the warped floorboards. Coughing, she found herself reaching toward it, but, as her hand pressed into it, what remained burst like a thin membrane and rained the rest of its foulness onto the thirsty floor.

When Ives finally found strength enough to stand, she did so on wobbly legs. Her chest still burned from what she had experienced; her head ached, full of unsettled memories. She retrieved the flashlight from where it had fallen and used it to discover that no trace of the half-formed thing remained. But there was more that had disappeared. The dark crib in the middle of the room had gone as well. As she shined the light on the walls around her, she saw that the mesh of fungus no longer glistened as it had before. Its colour dulled, pieces had already begun to fall away. It was then Ives experienced the vivid realisation of how utterly empty the house really was, how devoid of anything that she might care about. It was the debris of another life, remnants of another world that fell further away the faster the warming spores inside of her multiplied and grew. Pieces of wall crumbled around her like an avalanche, but she uneasily stepped over the debris and toward the rickety stairs. With each step she took, more strength returned, her once stumbling steps becoming confident strides. As her fear ebbed, the house's walls began to shrink, returning to a shape more ordinary than her memories once painted. Pieces of the house rained down around her as she strode to the front door. When she reached it she threw it open, letting a flood of daylight sweep into the house.

She stepped outside and marvelled. The sun had risen, something the mould-coated windows could no longer keep secret. She stared up at the hanging orb. Though she wanted to look away, she could not. It was too large, too overwhelming, and she felt its intense heat. It burned away the last part of her taking refuge in the crumbling house of her childhood, a house she had built from the bricks of her past. She walked away from it and never looked back.

↑

FIRST THEY CAME FOR THE PIGS

By Chadwick Ginther

✝

Chadwick Ginther is a bookseller who lives in Winnipeg. His novel *Thunder Road* was released this fall. In addition to this anthology, his short fiction has appeared in *On Spec* and *Tesseracts*. He refuses to eat mushrooms.

✝

"FIRST THEY CAME FOR the pigs; then they came for their masters."

The men's expressions told the tale. They glanced at the corpse, with its piss-yellow skin and toadstools sprouting from its eyes, its mouth, its ears and nose. The mushrooms swayed, though there was no breeze. Straining against their roots, reaching. As if hunting for me.

I shuddered and all eyes were back to me. They didn't believe me. How could they? It was too terrible to fathom. These were not men of a scholarly bent. These were street toughs. The best — or should I say worst? — Khyber had to offer, lured to my home with promises of wealth. I rubbed at my face; I needed to make them see the threat. All of my wealth would be meaningless if the attacks continued. There was no one left for them to take.

No one but me.

I settled my hand upon the braided silver Goodson's Noose about my neck. He hung from the Wall and faced heathens to win his father's favour. Surely, I could face these ... men.

They came from all over the city of Khyber. Which meant they came from all over the world.

"Who," asked Coal, the ebony-skinned Garan, "are they?"

He was dressed in the colourful robes common of his desert-dwelling people and towered over the assemblage. I, myself, barely came to the man's chest. Furs swaddled him beneath those robes, peeking out here and there, making him seem all the larger. He shivered as if he could not get warm, though we were in Khyber's High Summer and I felt the sweat gathering at my brow. He cupped his hands around a bowl of tea, taking a sip. A spider's web of bright orange scars wound about those large hands, glowing like embers.

"This," I said, gesturing at the toadstool, "is they. They walk like men, hunt like them. Kill like them. But they are not. Not men! Not beasts! They took my stock, but were not satisfied. I've lost my factors in every ward in Khyber. My seneschal! Even the bloody razor guild won't take my coin for guard duty, now!"

I tried to calm myself. Such outbursts were unseemly, even among the lowborn.

Wei, an inscrutable Xiou, leaned against the wall, pushing his broad hat above his eyes with the tip of his staff. He pursed his lips, but said nothing.

"Not even Old Wyrd would expect me to believe that," Hraki, a giant Valkuran from the North Sea, bellowed, jabbing at me with a sausage-thick finger, each jab forcing me to retreat a step. "And he's a bigger liar than any god in Khyber." Hraki was almost as broad as the Garan was tall, a fury of hair and iron.

"A Garan sorcerer could have worked such magic," Coal said cautiously, as if daring the others to accuse him. When they did not, he continued. "Though at a terrible cost to himself. He would need to give up his humanity to take the same from his victims."

Hraki crossed his arms over his burly chest. He spat upon my rug. I was glad now that I'd had the foresight to remove my treasured woven Rusan rugs before I had invited these ruffians into my home. Like Hraki, they'd come from the barbaric far north. Unlike him, they were irreplaceable.

"A witch or hex, nothing more," the Valkuran insisted.

"You're all wrong, yeah?" a cheery voice interjected.

Wheeling as one, we saw a slight man leaning against the doorframe. He picked at something between his teeth, regarded the prize, and then discarded it upon one of my tapestries.

I winced — *those* I'd forgotten to store away, more concerned about the muck on my ... guests' feet.

"Mushrooms out of everywhere," the stranger spoke, gesturing at what was once my seneschal. He shuddered, too, though I felt he was exaggerating the gesture with false disgust. "Glad you kept that one's pants on, yeah?"

"*You.*"

All of my dangerous men said the word, each with a different inflection. Anger from the Valkuran, suspicion from the Garan, amusement from the Xiou.

"Who?" I asked, curious, echoing Coal's earlier confusion.

"Needle," they answered at once.

Then, separately:

Coal added, "A thief and liar."

"A dead man," Hraki growled.

And from the Xiou, "An adequate tailor."

Needle threw back his hood, revealing a tanned, smirking face. He nodded at Wei. Were it not for the smouldering mischief in his eyes, he could have been any man in Khyber.

"It's the creeping rot, it is. Cygaricus, god of shit and muck and what things grow there. It's the Vile Truffle, luv. That's your culprit."

He spoke with the quick brogue of a Khyber native, though I could not quite place from which quarter his accent originated. He was also utterly unconcerned by his less-than-welcome reception.

"I've never heard of this 'creeping rot'," Hraki said.

Needle canted his head, rolling his eyes. "Take a closer look at your prick, then, and you'll have an idea, Hraki Hard-Sailor. Only thing hard about you is how damned hard it is to get your fat ass in a boat these days."

"I should've killed you," the Valkuran said through bared teeth.

"Well you didn't, now, did you? And it's too late to go back."

"Never too late to try again." Hraki's hand tightened on an axe handle.

"Please, please," I interjected, trying to forestall a brawl in my sitting room. "This is not necessary. There is no time."

Needle smiled, ignoring me. *Odious little man.* He had a dirk in each hand. I hardly saw his hands move to draw. "See how far you get, luv."

"I'm not your *luv.*"

"Aye, that's what your sister said, though she bent over just the same."

"She asked me to bring her your manhood."

"I *knew* she still fancied me."

Wei's staff slapped against Hraki's chest, holding the Valkuran back from rushing the intruder. When he spoke, it was in a hard, clipped tone. "I think he may take more than a finger this time."

This had gotten out of hand. I needed to wrest control of the proceedings back from these ruffians before they killed each other in my home.

Gathering myself to my full height — not much in the face of these warriors, but it *was* enough that I could look down upon this Needle — I glared at the thief as if he'd tried to pass me a wooden coin.

"I ... we do not appreciate your intrusion."

"You'd best appreciate me," Needle shot back. "And by that, I mean, you'd best be following me through the Undercity, or you won't be coming back up out of the dark. The Truffle wants back what's his; that's the word I've been hearing. You need to bring that body or they'll keep coming. I wouldn't trust even fire to kill this rot."

"I do not respond well to threats —"

He snorted. "Of course you do. Something bad hit one of your operations. You didn't like the smell of it and so, you found —" He looked at each of the men in turn. To Coal, "The biggest." To the Xiou, "Baddest." And, finally, to the Valkuran: "Smelliest shankers you could find. Only flaw was leaving one out, yeah?"

"Which one might you be?" I asked, dubious.

"The best, luv. The best."

"Prove it."

"Well, I got *this*," Needle held up a greasy-looking leather pouch, bouncing it on his palm and smiling at Hraki, "from that one."

Hraki growled and made to snatch the pouch back. Needle darted back a step, wagging a finger.

"Please, you great hairy lummox. I've been nabbing purses longer than you've been preening that beard of yours — and that's a roll of years, it is."

The thief dipped a finger into the pouch. Recoiling immediately, he grimaced.

"I thought as much. *Vala* Mushrooms. Working for the Truffle, are we?"

"They're sacred," Hraki said.

"They're foolish, is what. Only a great fucking fool would eat a mad mushroom before facing the bloody god of fungus and rot. Poison to the mind, luv." Needle tapped at his temple. "Once they get in here …. "

"It is a gift that'll prove more useful than your quick fingers. Or mouth."

Hraki tore the pouch from Needle's hands, though, I felt, he was allowed to do so.

"Oh, aye," the thief muttered. "Always useful to have a mad Valkuran, frothing at the mouth, chopping up anything that moves. I'm still moving and I plan on staying that way."

✦

I didn't like it.

I didn't know this man and those who did gave me little reason to want to. Assurances that he could handle himself in a fight, or that he knew the Undercity as well as any man alive, did little to ease my troubled conscience.

I liked that I had to accompany them even less. With my trusted guards and factors gone — taken — who might I trust to prove to me they had succeeded?

What were our choices? Going gate to gate in Khyber, and the bribes and graft that would accompany such a journey, would drain even the Lord General's purse, and I was nowhere near so wealthy as that. For better and worse, I had assembled my chosen elite and there were wards that would not allow a Garan to walk through. Others had the same taboo regarding Xiou or Valkurans. Needle, the crafty bastard, had me.

I needed him.

I fought to keep my cheek from twitching. I fought harder to show a smile.

"It seems we can use you, after all."

His grin terrified me.

"Never doubted it, luv. Never doubted."

✦

The Undercity was a labyrinthine world of sewers, cisterns and ruins buried under Khyber from the days when the city was young. I had prayed to the Goodson that I would never see its blackness again. There are ... things that live in the dark. Men, and what once wore the forms of men, worship fell masters where they hope the One God's eyes cannot find them.

We descended into the darkness of the Undercity through a bolthole that Needle proclaimed as his own. It was a tight fit for my own belly and I must assume that Hraki was only able to push his bulk through due to the benevolence of his heathen god, Wyrd. He had scrapes all along his arms. Blood had dried red where he'd rubbed his flesh raw on brick. Needle laughed and I wondered then if he'd led us there because it was closest or because he wished to leave Hraki behind. I must assume the former, as the small man seemed to enjoy taunting the Valkuran. Almost as much as he enjoyed reminding us of his prowess.

Coal's hands flared and flames rose from them as if the man himself were a torch. I jumped back, a hand at my chest. I could barely hear the fire crackle as it burned over the man's skin, but did not consume it. All this time, I'd thought him a mere arsonist. I would have to watch myself. He was a sorcerer. A Garan sorcerer meant but one thing: He'd made a pact with the Goodson's opposite.

But, Goodson preserve me, I would follow even a heathen's light in this dark, dark place.

Water dripped from the ceiling, drops spattering over cisterns, a cacophony of little noises that seemed to roar in my ears. It was hot down here. I mopped at my brow with an already sodden sleeve. They had made me drag the wrapped body of my own seneschal as if I were their pack mule.

Outrageous.

They were to be working for *me*.

I grimaced, but there was little I could do in the face of their hard stares. Not a one would touch Kavin's body. Wrapped or otherwise.

It felt wrong, this heat. Sweat dripped from my nose in time with the rain falling from a brick sky.

"Nervous in the service, then?" Needle japed, suddenly behind me.

I ground my teeth. "I do not like this place."

He smiled. "Be worried if you did, luv. Be worried if you did. But it does grow on you."

It was interminable, the slog through these horrid, labyrinthine tunnels. But the little thief never wavered, turning at every intersection without hesitation as if he were merely walking to market.

"Why won't you be taking any payment?" I asked.

"Kindness of me bleeding heart?"

I snorted.

"Bug-eating cultists always have a trinket or two worth a rub and a tug. I'll take my share from what they have." He looked sidelong at Hraki and whispered, "I don't need to be paid up front before facing danger. Neither did his sister."

The last was not a whisper.

↑

"Fuck me," Needle cried. "But that's a bloody great mushroom!"

The cistern it occupied once would have held enough water to wet the lips of an entire ward of Khyber. No longer. Only the columns supporting the arched ceiling disturbed the mass of the fungus. Yellow clusters of smaller — almost tumorous — growths dotted the bright purple mass where the columns lanced upward. It was luminous, glowing softly with a shifting, pulsating light.

I touched the noose about my throat. Had the Goodson ever seen such a thing?

I looked to the Garan, but he shook his head.

"Even my flames would take days to burn this to nothing."

Days we might not have.

"I'm not crossing that," Hraki said.

"You must," I insisted.

A mistake. One does not insist a Valkuran Dragonman do *anything*. Not unless one is prepared to back words with steel and shield.

"Another word from your fat mouth, Coinpurse, and I'll have you."

244

I swallowed hard, nodding. I knew how to use a sword; I did. A paper-thin protection that blade felt now, facing the Valkuran's shaking axe.

"And since you're so insistent," Hraki added. "*You* may go first."

I swallowed again. Yes. An act of courage, of leadership, might make me seem more to these men than a walking coinpurse. The great mushroom had swelled to take up so much of the cistern that there was no place where I could walk that was not atop it. At its centre, where it rose toward the ceiling, I would have to crouch and scrape. I looked back at the men. Hraki stood with his scowl and set jaw. Coal looked impassive. Wei's face showed concern, or at least what I took for concern. Even Needle's smirk seemed to have been diluted to a nervous smile.

"Go on, then." Needle gestured towards the cistern entrance. "Don't keep the precious beard waiting."

Screwing my courage to my breast, I breathed deep and stepped upon the great carpet of fungus, towing Kavin's body behind me. The surface gave only slightly beneath my sandals, my feet sinking deeply enough that I needed curl my bare toes for fear of touching the great unclean thing.

Fear was not a luxury I could allow myself. Not amongst this rough company. Another step. Another. I would not let this ... this thing unman me. I was used to being the master. I would show them. Garan, Valkuran and Xiou, alike. I would show the smart-mouthed thief who'd felt the need to trod upon my business. Master yourself, I thought and you will master these men. Even if Needle was necessary to reach our goal, there might prove no need for him to return with us.

Yes.

I smiled. 'The best,' he'd claimed to be.

We shall see.

Hraki would be more-than-happy to do the deed. It worried me some. How best to broach the subject? Wei, at least, seemed likely to side with the thief. Reputation was not enough to keep one alive in Khyber, let alone below it. Needle might have cards left to play, dice left to roll.

Many players in this contest — if, indeed, we all played the same game.

My musings had distracted me long enough that I had made my way far onto the great mushroom. I wanted to look back, but dared not. A sign of weakness, that. Let them think I cared not whether they dared to follow me. When I — a fat coinpurse, as Hraki was so fond of calling me — was across the terrible thing, they would need to follow.

Of course, if they did not, if they left me, there would be no one to naysay their courage above. Should the vile creatures that came for my followers come next for me, only these four would know their shame and cowardice.

Not a comforting thought.

This was something I could believe of Needle — and perhaps the Garan. Hraki, though, would not. Honour, courage, these things were far too important to Valkurans, even one so far from his home. No place in heaven for them unless they died with a blade in their hands. I shuddered, touching the braided silver noose about my throat, and happy that the Goodson required no such sacrifice from His believers.

"Come on, you lot," Needle's annoying voice echoed over the chamber. I winced at its volume. I couldn't help it. "Light a fire and leap smartly, yeah? Coinpurse is getting away from us."

A surprise that Needle would be the first one demanding the ruffians follow, but I shrugged, accepting the strange fact. Anything that would get my men moving was comfort to me. It was also a reminder of how far I had travelled away from them and just how exposed I was. Were anything to come for me now, none would reach me in time. Even were they so inclined.

I could feel their footsteps behind me. Strangely, I felt I could almost tell which steps belonged to which man. The power that emanated from each grudging step of Coal's advance. Needle's cocky strut, so brash despite such a light touch. Wei, who barely seemed to brush the surface at all. Hraki's angry stomp sending shocks up my spine. I slowed my progress, hoping they might catch up to me, hoping I was not being obvious.

Hoping to hide my fear of being caught alone.

A large cluster of the yellow growths blocked my path. This time, there was no column rising from their centre. I stopped, peering deeper into a yawning circular chasm. I wrinkled my nose at the smell wafting from within. In the eerie purplish light that emanated from the horrid thing, I saw one of my factors, ripe with decay. He was unrecognisable but for the pendant bearing my house's sigil. No skin visible that was not covered in the foul growth of swaying, hungry mushrooms.

The body stirred and I leapt back with a cry.

He was dead, but he had moved. My bowels went to water. I meant to turn back. To run. But the angry yells of my men-at-arms told me there was no safety to be had.

From beneath my factor, they rose up, standing like men, but they were not. Their broad caps narrowed to points and would have been almost comical, were it not for phosphorescent pricks of light where a man's eyes would be, glowing like a devil's fire. Stalking us, their forms undulated bonelessly. More birthed through small openings, like stool squelching free of the bowels of their master.

From behind me there was a rush of air and a crackle of flame, as if oil had been poured upon a fire. Coal was accessing *his* bargain with his heathen god. The cistern grew bright, almost as bright as day, as the Garan's dark hands burned white with heat.

"Wyrd cast his baleful eye upon you all." Hraki poured a great dribbling handful of something vile and black into his mouth.

I held my noose, clawing for the protection of the Goodson, Khyber's true and proper God, no matter what the cults believed. My breath caught as the silver cord tightened about my neck.

"Begone!" I croaked.

They stopped in step, regarding me queerly before they broke against the symbol of my faith, like a wave in the harbour. My men-at-arms were not so lucky. The creatures bypassed me, pouring toward the others. It was almost heretical, but I did hope the Goodson would see fit to offer my heathen guards the protection they needed to survive. I might still need them, after all.

Fire flew from Coal's hands. Where it struck the creatures, they wilted and fell.

Hraki stood, as if rooted, shaking, though I sensed not with fear. I could almost feel the rage wafting from the Valkuran. His mouth frothed, his eyes rolled back in his head, and then, only as the creatures surrounded him, he moved. Axes whirled, like things alive, lopping limbs from torsos. Heads from necks. Splitting the creatures as if they were cords of wood.

"Wyrd! Wyrd! Wyrd!" he screamed. His god's name the only word that seemed able to push past his frothing mouth.

At first, Wei's staff seemed ineffectual. Bludgeoning the creatures did nothing. They swayed, absorbing each blow. The Xiou was unbothered. With a twist of his wrist, the pole came apart and two slender metal blades shone, reflecting Coal's flames.

Of Needle, there was no sign.

"There's a lad," his voice whispered in my ear. "Keep 'em off us."

I turned and the thief was beside me, almost as close as a lover, holding an outstretched-but-unused dirk and watching the creatures slide past us to engage the others.

They fell and they fell, but more rose to take their place. As if Needle's 'Vile Truffle' could vomit out an endless supply, could birth an unending tide.

I had a moment of hope that my chosen instruments would beat back these creatures, that, with the Goodson's mercy, we would send this Cygaricus back to whatever hell had spawned it.

And then it all went wrong.

Hraki locked eyes with me. His body black with ichour, black as the rotten mushrooms he'd swallowed to fuel his rage. Oily spittle pouring from his mouth, he came for me. Cutting through a wedge of the creatures, he thundered forward like an Eryan cavalry at charge.

I tried to cry out, but my throat had tightened. Fear. Shame. I felt the heat of my bladder emptying down my leg.

Coal and Wei, more men than I, stood firm against Hraki.

Entreating the Goodson, I begged my god to intervene for their, heathen lives. A blade nicked across my throat.

"Let's see how this plays out, luv."

An axe thunked into Coal's spine and the Garan dropped, limp. Hraki stepped over him, but there was some life remaining in the Garan. His burning hands closed about the Valkuran's ankle and held, vice-like, as Hraki dragged the prostrate sorcerer over the tumourous ground.

Flames licked up the Valkuran's leg, setting his clothing ablaze. In his frothing turncoat rage, Hraki didn't notice. His traitorous eyes sought only myself.

Agile Wei easily outpaced the burdened — and burning — Valkuran.

Wei hurled one of his blade staves like a javelin. It pierced Hraki's chest and still he came on, kicking the now-dead Garan from his heel. Hraki threw his axes in rapid succession. Wei blocked the first. The force of the throw snapped his last stave.

Splinters burst free and I felt the sting as one imbedded itself in my forehead. The second axe bit deep into the Xiou's shoulder. He grunted. As loud a cry as I'd ever heard the curious man voice.

Staggering, Wei grasped the axe. Hraki had stopped his advance, fallen to the flames of a dead Garan, who, even in death, refused to loose his murderer.

A gobbet of something vile swelled in the flames, bursting free to splatter me. I felt the cutpurse cower low at my back. It burned, whether with heat or poison, I knew not. I wiped blood and worse from my brow.

"That's it for you, then, luv," Needle clucked. He did not seem upset about my discomfort. I have heard that scalp wounds bleed profusely, but this was not something I had ever expected to experience myself.

I tried to wipe the blood from my eyes, but could not stay ahead of the flow. Everything had gone dark.

"Help me," I begged. The wound burned, the filth of this place aggravating it.

"There's going to be no help for you, I'm afraid." Needle didn't sound afraid in the least, nor saddened by his statement.

"What … what do you mean?"

"You're the job, yeah?" he said. As if that explained anything. "Been contracted by the Truffle to bring his boys home."

"What do you mean?" I demanded again.

"Working for spoils? That's a first-time jobber's mistake, luv. Mushrooms grow in shit, yeah? I guess shit-brown eyes and shit-for-brains'll do just as fine."

"No. No. That cannot be. It was a cut. Just a cut."

I could feel the cutpurse's smirk. Glad in that moment that I was blinded.

"The Truffle wants his … children." The word was almost a question. The thief groped for another. "Progeny, then. The ones sprouting out your peepers and maybe some other places, too; not that I'm for looking down there."

I reached forward with a trembling hand. Afraid in my blindness of what it might find. I knew my fingers had not touched skin.

"No."

"'Fraid it's to be yes, luv. You're done for."

I felt a wrenching pull. I screamed. It was as if the bastard had torn an eye from my skull. The pain radiated from the orbit, down my jaw, reaching my fingers, stabbing at my groin and toes. It was as if he had crushed the orb twixt his fingers.

Gasping, "What did you do?"

The words felt thick, garbled. My tongue had swollen. A rumble in my guts and I voided myself, sobbing. What wept down my face was not tears. Goodson help me, I had no eyes. I wanted to wretch. Something came up, spreading my jaw so wide it cracked like thunder. I took a breath.

My last.

As my nostrils closed, I kicked, clawing for air with bloody fingers.

"Extracted my payment," Needle said, smugly. His words grew fainter and fainter. "These fellows grow in your flesh, but it's said that they keep a flash of their food's memories locked away. You have a lot of secrets, Coinpurse, and I trade in them. I doubt the Truffle would notice if I had just a taste ...."

↑

OUT OF THE BLUE

By Ian Rogers

✦

Ian Rogers is a writer, artist and photographer. His short fiction has appeared in several publications, including *Cemetery Dance*, *Supernatural Tales* and *Shadows & Tall Trees*. He is the author of the Felix Renn series of supernatural-noirs ("supernoirturals"), including "Temporary Monsters," "The Ash Angels" and "Black-Eyed Kids" from Burning Effigy Press. His most recent book, a collection of dark fiction called *Every House Is Haunted*, will be available in Fall 2012 from ChiZine Publications. Ian lives with his wife in Peterborough, Ontario. For more information, visit ianrogers.ca.

✦

IT WAS FOUR IN the morning by the time I got to the house. Jerry had called me an hour earlier, knowing I'd still be awake. We both suffered from insomnia — mine was the symptom of an actual sleep disorder, while Jerry's was the result of too much caffeine in his diet. He claimed this made us brothers, of a sort, and I was too tired to argue with him.

Jerry was a real estate agent with a very specific and very unusual area of interest: He only represented properties that were haunted. Houses, condos, farms, stores, warehouses — it didn't matter as long as it had some sort of supernatural taint. It was a niche market, but Jerry was a good salesman and he made out okay. When he wasn't trying to offload the next Amityville Horror, he was usually out chasing women at Toronto's finer bars and cocktail lounges.

I figured that was why he was calling me that night.

"I'm not going out," I told him. "You'll have to fly solo tonight, Maverick."

"Goose," Jerry said, disappointed, "you wound me."

"It's three in the morning, Jer. It's past last call."

"That's not why I'm calling."

"And I'm not coming over to look at a rash on any part of your body."

"It's not that, either."

"Then why can't it wait until morning?"

"Technically, it is morning."

"Then technically, I'm hanging up."

"Wait," Jerry said, suddenly serious. "It's an emergency."

"What kind of emergency?"

"Do you remember that house I told you about last week? The one north of the city, near Barrie?"

"No."

"I picked up the listing a few months ago. Remember? The shitbox-with-a-bad-roof-but-it's-got-potential?"

"Still drawing a blank."

"Okay, it doesn't matter. I need you to come up here."

"Why?"

"I ...." Jerry hesitated, which gave me a moment of pause, because Jerry never hesitated. "It'll be easier to explain once you're here."

"To Barrie? Jerry, it'll take me an hour to get there."

"I said it's near Barrie. It won't take that long. There's no traffic this early in the morning."

I grunted.

"Come on, man. Do me a solid. I helped you the time that woman tried to sue you after her sister got killed by those spooky kids."

I grunted again. Jerry wasn't usually able to talk me into doing things I didn't want to do, but on those rare occasions when he did, I refused to acknowledge him with actual words.

The thing was, I did sort of owe him and not just because of the incident with those "spooky kids". I had learned early on that if you were going to make a living as a detective who specialised in supernatural cases, then it was a good idea to have a lawyer familiar with supernatural law. Jerry had passed the bar years before he started selling haunted real estate, but, these days, he only practised law on special occasions. He was useful when I needed legal advice — or when I required actual representation. Jerry was a tenacious, sharp-minded debater who didn't know when to quit. It was because of these traits that I knew there was no point in arguing with him.

"It's still gonna take me a while to get out there."

"That's okay," Jerry said. I could hear the relief in his voice. "Thanks, Felix. Seriously."

I grunted and hung up the phone.

↑

I don't like being in the woods at night. It's a common phobia among those who have been to the Black Lands. My one-and-only excursion was brief, nothing more than a few steps onto that Plutonian shore, but it was enough to put me off trees and darkness for good.

The place I was headed wasn't very deep in the woods and that was the only reason I didn't turn around and go home. I took the 400 north out of the city, got off at Shore Acres Drive near Cookstown, and was presently bumping along an unpaved road with nothing around except a few trees interspersed between fields of freshly turned earth.

I spotted Jerry's car — a black 1968 Ford Galaxie, fully restored and the only thing Jerry truly loved — parked up on the side of the road across from a small house. I pulled in behind it and turned off the engine. The headlights went out at the same time and my stomach clenched painfully as the darkness came flooding in.

I sat and took a few deep, steadying breaths. I saw the interior light of Jerry's car come on as he got out to meet me.

Jerry was short and bald, with bright, animated eyes and a stubby chin. He reminded me of the manic money launderer Joe Pesci played in the *Lethal Weapon* movies. He was wearing a grey t-shirt and black track pants with white stripes down the sides. His usual preference was for expensive suits and loud ties, but it wasn't the sort of thing one would be wearing at this hour. Still, I was a little taken aback to see him dressed so casually. He looked decidedly un-Jerry-like.

"This better be important," I said, climbing out of my car.

"It is." Jerry's eyes flicked nervously to the side. "At least, I think it is."

"You think?"

I followed his gaze to the house. A car and a van were parked in the gravel driveway. The van had something printed on the side, but I couldn't make it out in the dark.

Jerry said, "I'm worried about Julie Spiro."

The name sounded familiar, but my brain was too foggy from lack of sleep to make the connection.

"She's the interior decorator I hired to fix up the place," Jerry said.

"She the one you're sleeping with?"

Jerry looked aghast. "You mean Barbara? Hell, no. I ended that months ago."

"So, you're not sleeping with this one?"

"Well ...." Jerry tilted his head to the side. "Not yet. She's a work-in-progress."

"Sort of like your house."

Jerry's eyes darted to the side again.

256

"So, why are you worried about this woman if you're not sleeping with her?"

"Because she's not answering my calls."

"There might be a connection there."

"Would you get your mind out of the gutter?" Jerry snapped.

"Did you tell her you're a writer?"

"I *am* a writer," Jerry said. "I've written books."

"Yeah," I said. "Time-Life books."

"Those are books! What, do I need to pump out fucking *War and Peace* before I can call myself a writer?"

"Did you tell her you write Time-Life books?"

Jerry frowned. "No."

I spread my hands as if to say, *Well, there you go.*

"That's beside the point, Felix."

"So, there *is* a point to my being out here in the sticks at four in the morning?"

"There is if you'd shut up and listen."

I gestured for him to go on.

Jerry cleared his throat and smoothed down a tie he wasn't wearing. "I think Julie might be in trouble. I talked to her earlier today — or yesterday, I guess it was — and she mentioned she was going to stay late with the guys she'd hired to work on the house."

I looked over at the van parked in the driveway.

"Julie and I have been working closely together since I picked up the place. We talk on the phone a dozen times a day; we've exchanged hundreds of e-mails and texts; and, after a while, things started to get a little flirty." Jerry put on a face that managed to look both sly and embarrassed. "Then they started to get a little ... dirty."

"Skip to the emergency, Jerry."

"So, anyway, we talked about getting together later tonight, maybe grab a bite to eat or something, once the guys were done. When I didn't hear from her by eight o'clock, I tried calling her, but didn't get an answer. I tried again at eight-thirty, nine, nine-thirty. At ten o'clock ...."

"You drove out here," I finished.

"Actually, I fell asleep," Jerry said, a little guiltily. "I woke up around two-thirty and tried calling her again. I still didn't get an answer and that's when I started to get worried."

"Maybe she didn't have her phone with her."

Jerry shook his head. "Julie's one of these people who has her cell phone permanently grafted to her hand."

"Maybe she's ignoring your calls."

Jerry said, "I considered that," but I could tell from his dismissive tone that he didn't consider this to be a realistic possibility. "I cruised by her place and her car wasn't there. This" — Jerry nodded at the house — "was the only other place I could think of, so I drove out here and found her car. I was about to check inside, but then I saw the work van parked here, too."

"So?"

"So?" Jerry frowned. "This is one of *my* houses, Felix. As in, *haunted*. As in, potentially, paranormally *dangerous*."

"That you're planning to fix up and sell to someone," I pointed out.

"I inform all potential buyers about what they're getting into," Jerry said defensively. "It's the law. Full disclosure of any and all supernatural activity on the premises. Besides, most of the people that go in for this stuff don't buy the properties to live in them. They collect them the way other people collect stamps or baseball cards."

"So, what's the deal with this place?"

"It's a relatively new house, built around twenty years ago, back when the urban sprawl in Toronto was really ... well, sprawling. People were looking for places like this: close enough to the city to commute but far enough away from the noise and crime and general craziness."

I twirled my hand in a let's-move-this-along gesture.

"So, anyway, the couple who built this place had only been living here a couple of weeks when the husband suddenly got up one night and killed his wife and son. I haven't been able to dig up much on the case — this happened pre-Internet — but I do know the same thing happened to the next couple who moved in. Except, in that incident, it was the wife who killed her husband. They didn't have any kids, so the case wasn't quite as sensational as the first one, but, at their respective trials, both of the accused claimed to have been 'possessed'."

"I'm guessing they were both convicted."

"Of course," Jerry said. "You know how hard it is to prove possession by a supernatural entity in a court of law?"

"Only because you keep telling me about it."

Jerry nodded. "It's very hard. Nearly impossible. I can count the number of acquittals on one hand. Hell, until thirty or so years ago, the charge was still being called 'demonic possession', which brought in all kinds of religious implications that don't exactly mesh well with the judicial process. It's hard enough to defend a person in a case that involves paranormal phenomena without throwing God and the Devil into the mix."

"This interior decorator, what did you say her name was?"

"Julie Spiro."

"Why does that sound familiar?"

"She used to have a home improvement show on The Learning Channel."

I remembered now. Not so much the show as the woman who hosted it: a tall brunette with freckled cheeks who looked as good in a crisp suit and heels as she did in a paint-stained t-shirt and cargoes.

"Is the show still on?"

"No," Jerry said. "It was cancelled. Julie still fixes up houses; she just doesn't have a camera crew following her around anymore."

I nodded at the house. "And you didn't check to see if she's in there?"

"I started to ...." Jerry trailed off. "I thought I saw someone moving around inside, but it's hard to tell because all the windows are boarded up. I stood outside, yelling her name, but no one came out."

"But you didn't go inside."

I saw a momentary flash of shame on Jerry's face, then his eyes turned small and angry. "If I'd gone inside, I wouldn't be standing out here wondering what the hell's going on, would I?"

I almost said something snide, but I kept my mouth shut. After all, who was I to talk? The private detective who was afraid to go into the woods at night.

"You could've called the police," I said.

Jerry scoffed. "Yeah, sure. No offense, but if this turns out to be nothing, I'd rather be chewed out by you than the cops." He looked over at the house. "But I don't think this is nothing. I've got a real bad vibe."

"They could be working in there," I said, even though I didn't believe it myself. I didn't share Jerry's bad vibe, but I had to admit it was kind of unsettling to see Julie Spiro's car and the workmen's van parked next to an abandoned house way out here in the middle of nowhere. "Maybe they're pulling an all-nighter."

Jerry shook his head. "I haven't got the power turned back on yet. They wouldn't be working in the dark."

He had me there.

"Okay, we'll check it out. But if this does turn out to be nothing, you're buying me breakfast."

"Deal," Jerry said in a flat voice.

↑

I got a flashlight out of my car and started across the road. I realised Jerry wasn't following me and turned back to see him standing on the gravel shoulder. He looked like a little kid waiting for a school bus that was never going to come. He was staring at the flashlight in my hand.

"Where's your gun?" he asked.

"In my closet at home."

"What's it doing there?" Jerry's voice quivered with nervous anger. "I call and tell you there's a potential supernatural menace in the house I'm renovating and you don't even bring a gun?"

"You didn't tell me anything," I reminded him. "You just asked me to come out here."

Jerry frowned and marched over to his car. For a second, I thought he was going to get in and drive away. Instead, he opened the trunk, dug around inside for a bit and took out a tire iron.

"Okay," he said, "let's go."

There were no streetlights on this stretch of road and the moon had set hours ago. It was dark, but the faintest hint of dawn was creeping up in the east, like a rheostat turned to its lowest setting.

I played my flashlight back and forth across the front of the house. You didn't need to be a private detective to figure out it had been empty for some time. The red-brick façade was faded and crumbling; the roof was slumped and full of holes; and the front lawn was so overgrown that the flagstone path leading up to the front door had become a trench.

As we walked up, I noticed that the windows were covered with sheets of plywood. A common-enough sight at any abandoned building, until I noticed the second-floor windows had been boarded up, too. That was a little more unusual. Kids and homeless people — the two groups most powerfully drawn to abandoned buildings — didn't typically travel around with ladders.

When we reached the front door, I looked over at Jerry. "Ready?"

He gripped the tire iron in both hands. "Ready."

I turned the knob and pushed the door open. The hinges let out a long, drawn-out squeak that was so cliché I was suddenly sure this entire situation was going to turn out to be a silly misunderstanding.

That feeling evaporated the moment I saw the body lying on the floor.

Jerry saw it, too — caught starkly in the beam of my flashlight, it was impossible to miss — and pushed past me into the house.

"Jerry, wait!"

"It's Julie!"

I followed him inside, swinging my flashlight around as I crossed the small foyer and stepped through an archway into what was probably a living room, when there were people living here. Jerry crouched next to Julie. She was lying facedown on the dusty floor. She was wearing a grey suit-jacket and a matching skirt. A single slingback high-heeled shoe hung from one foot; the other was bare.

"Come on," Jerry said, his voice brimming with panic. "Help me."

I knelt down next to him and passed him the flashlight. He directed the beam at Julie's head while I pressed two fingers against the side of her neck. I found a pulse.

"She's alive," I said, and Jerry let out a sigh of relief. "But we've got to get her to a hospital."

I heard a board creak behind us. I looked over my shoulder. Jerry whipped the flashlight around at the same time, revealing two men standing in the doorway. One of them was short with a crewcut; the other was tall with sideburns and a mullet. They were wearing matching grey coveralls, the kind that typically has the owner's name embroidered over the breast. I couldn't tell if these did because most of the material was covered in some sort of fuzzy blue gunk. Their faces were covered with it, too. Only a few patches of skin showed through and their eyes, which stared at us with matching blank expressions.

"Hey, guys," I said. "We could use a hand here."

I didn't expect them to help and I wasn't disappointed. There was something about the way they were standing there, motionless, covered in that blue stuff, that told me there was something seriously wrong here.

As I watched, the workman on the left turned his head to the side, opened his mouth wide and vomited something thick and dark onto the wall. Jerry panned the flashlight over. The stuff appeared to be a syrupy version of the same blue fuzz that covered the workmen.

"What is it?" Jerry said with disgust.

I shook my head. "It looks like some sort of mould or fungus. They're both infected with it."

"And spreading it," Jerry said. He shined the flashlight on the tall, mulleted workman as he bent over at the waist and vomited a blue stream on the floor between his feet.

I picked up the tire iron Jerry had left on the floor and swapped him for the flashlight. "Take Julie into the other room." I nodded at the door behind us. "I'll hold them off."

Jerry stuck the tire iron under his arm, lifted Julie by the shoulders and started dragging her toward the door. "I bet you're wishing you brought your gun now," he grunted under his breath.

When they were safely away, I stood up and pointed the flashlight at the two workmen. "Do you understand me?"

They didn't acknowledge me in any way, except to each take a step toward me. Then another. I kept the flashlight trained on them, as if I could hold them in place by keeping them centred in the beam. They kept coming.

I thought about using the flashlight as a weapon, but I knew I'd only get in a lick or two before the bulb broke. Then I'd be trapped in the dark with them.

I put the flashlight on the floor, directing the beam at the workmen. It only reached up to their knees, but it was better than nothing. I stepped in front of the beam and my shadow leaped across the floor in front of me. I decided to try something and took a quick bouncing step to the left. The workmen turned their heads to follow me, but it was a slow, robotic movement. I felt a small flutter of hope. Whatever was controlling these men, it didn't seem to have the full, quick response of their reflexes. It might be possible to dart around them and make it out the front door.

But I couldn't leave Jerry and Julie to fend for themselves. I didn't have my cell phone. Even if I did, the nearest help was still thirty minutes away. I had to incapacitate these men, somehow; preferably without killing them.

The short, crewcut workman came at me in a stiff-legged shamble with his hands outstretched. The moment he got into range, I turned to the side and threw a straight jab at his face. The workman's head snapped back and blood dribbled out of his nose. He came at me again, managed to loop his right arm around my neck and pulled me in close, like he wanted to tell me a secret. I went along with the motion, turning into his body, then grabbed his arm with both hands and flipped him over my shoulder. He landed on his back with a loud thud, sending up a cloud of dust that hung in the low-angled beam of the flashlight.

The other workman came shuffling forward. He was bigger than me and I wasn't confident that I'd be able to handle him as efficiently as I had his friend. I glanced over at the man I'd just dumped on the floor. He wasn't moving and that worried me. I didn't want to kill these guys. Whatever was wrong with them wasn't their fault and it might even be curable.

With that in mind, I picked up the flashlight and retreated to the other room.

I closed the door and put my back to it. A few moments later, I felt the workman slam into it from the other side. The fungus might have slowed him down, but it didn't take away any of his strength. I panned the flashlight around. I was in the kitchen. The appliances were long gone, but I could see the outlines of where they had once stood. Jerry had dragged Julie Spiro over to the door that opened onto the backyard. He looked at me with wide, frightened eyes.

"One down," I said. "One to go."

"What the hell's wrong with them?"

"I'm guessing it's the house," I said through gritted teeth, as another blow struck the door.

"But it doesn't make any sense," Jerry said desperately. "I've been through this place a dozen times and I'm completely fine."

"That's debatable." I suddenly thought of something. "The people who died here, you said they were killed at night?"

"Yeah."

"Did you ever go through this place at night?"

Jerry thought about it for a moment. "No," he said. "It was always during the day. Julie wouldn't let me take her here at night. She thought I'd try to put the moves on her." He looked down at her sadly. "She was probably right."

"If there's a portal somewhere in the house and it's spitting out this fungus, then it's probably only happening when the conditions are right."

Jerry nodded. "There's no sun in the Black Lands. And fungus grows in dark places."

"Except fungus doesn't turn people into mindless zombies," I pointed out.

"Unless it's a supernatural fungus."

"You're gonna have to come up with something better than that if you're going to put it in your next book."

Jerry looked suddenly worried, as if this were the real problem at hand. I shined the flashlight in his face to snap him out of it.

"Why don't you check and see if Julie's okay?"

Jerry nodded. "Right, right."

There was another blow against the door. I was pretty sure I could keep it closed, at least until Jerry got Julie out of the house and around to his car. Then I could follow them and we could all get the hell out of this place.

I kept the light on Julie as Jerry gently turned her over onto her back. I had seen her before, on her TV show, and I always thought she was an attractive woman. At first glance, my opinion hadn't changed. Then I saw the dark-blue beard that furred her cheeks and chin.

Jerry made a startled gasping sound and recoiled away.

Julie's eyes snapped open. So did her mouth and a blue froth burbled out.

I took a step toward Jerry as the workman slammed into the door again. I moved back and put my shoulder to it.

"Jerry, get out of here," I yelled. "You can't help her."

Jerry didn't hear me or he didn't care. He pulled himself up and leaned over Julie's prostrate form. Her head tilted back and, before I could do or say anything, she spewed a stream of gooey blue gunk all over the front of Jerry's shirt.

Jerry jerked back with a strangled cry. He managed to keep his feet under him and stumbled over to the back door. Julie sat up and started climbing slowly to her feet. Jerry looked at me, then back at Julie.

"Get out of here!" I yelled again. "Go!"

Jerry didn't need to be told twice. Actually, he did. But what he lacked in responsiveness he more than made up for in speed as he turned on his heel and zipped out the door. Julie watched him go with the same blank expression I'd seen on the workmen's faces. Then she turned and looked at me.

I had to move, but I knew the moment I stepped away from the door, the workman would come barrelling through. Then I'd have to deal with two infected people instead of one. But if I stayed where I was, Julie would have me cornered. I had to make a decision, and fast.

I stepped away from the door and waited for the workman to come through. I heard his fists slam against the door and then a thought struck me. I never heard him try the knob. Not even when I first closed the door on him. Maybe he didn't try it because he didn't think of it. Because the *fungus* didn't think of it.

I was brought out of this reverie by Julie Spiro's hands clamping around my throat. They were small hands, but her grip was incredibly strong. I spun around and she turned with me. Her shoulder clipped the wall and one of her hands came loose. I was able to pull her other hand off, push her away from me and escape through the back door.

The back lawn was just as overgrown as the front. I stood in the tall grass and took a few deep breaths of the night air. Except it wasn't really night anymore. The sky in the east was a pale violet colour.

I looked over my shoulder and saw Julie standing in the kitchen doorway. It occurred to me that I could have simply closed the back door and trapped her in the house. It didn't appear as if those infected by the fungus had the mental capacity to do much more than walk around and throw up the stuff.

Now I had to deal with Julie. If I didn't, she'd keep spreading the fungus until the police or the Paranormal Intelligence Agency stopped her. And knowing the PIA, stopping her would probably mean killing her.

I needed to figure out a way to immobilise her until I could contact the authorities.

I raised my hands like a boxer as she shuffled toward me. My gaze happened to drift down and I noticed a dark stain on my right hand. I looked more closely at it and saw a smudge of blue fuzz across my knuckles. At first, I didn't know where it had come from, then I remembered punching the workman. Right in his fungus-covered face.

I brushed my knuckles against my jeans, but the fungus wouldn't come off. I tried clawing at it with my other hand, but it was stuck firmly to my skin. I started to panic and raised my hand to my mouth, intending to chew the stuff off. I stopped myself at the last moment. There were already a few small dabs of blue fuzz under the nails of my left hand.

I was so absorbed by my hands — and images of myself strapped to an examination table in a PIA lab — that I had forgotten all about Julie. At least, until I felt *her* hands close around my throat and start choking me.

I was about to push her away when Jerry suddenly slammed into her from the side and they both went rolling across the ground. I lost sight of them in the tall grass. Then Julie rose up, her hair dishevelled and one of her jacket sleeves ripped at the shoulder. She recovered much faster than the workmen and I wondered if that was because her infection was more recent. I pictured the blue fungus spreading through her body, slowing her down as it filled her up, until she couldn't move at all. I didn't know if that was how it actually worked, but if the stuff on my own hands was any indication, I was going to find out soon enough.

Julie fell upon Jerry where he lay groaning in the tall grass. I was rushing over to help him when Julie's mouth fell open and a torrent of blue sludge came pouring out. It splattered all over Jerry's face, coating it. The sun was coming up and I saw it more clearly than I wanted to. Jerry's groans of pain turned to moans of disgust.

I grabbed Julie around the waist and flung her away. Then I pulled Jerry to his feet. He wiped madly at the wet clots of fungus on his face. Some of it came off, but most of it didn't.

"Felix!" he said in a high, panicky voice. "I can't see! It's in my eyes! It's in my fucking eyes!"

He started to claw at them, but I pulled his arms down and pinioned them to his sides. "Don't, Jerry. It's no use. You can't get it off."

Jerry let out a miserable moan. His body shuddered in my grip and his legs folded beneath him. I lowered him carefully to the ground and left him there while I went back to the house for the tire iron.

I was so angry at that point I didn't care if I seriously hurt Julie Spiro knocking her out, as long as I knew she wouldn't hurt anyone else the way she had hurt Jerry. This had to stop here.

When I came back out, Julie was struggling to her feet. She wasn't as nimble as she'd been only a few moments ago. The fungus was spreading fast. The stuff on my knuckles now covered my entire hand. It was the same hand holding the tire iron, so maybe I shouldn't have been surprised when I pulled back to swing it at Julie, it suddenly froze in mid-air.

Julie stared at me with her blank eyes, then she stepped past me and headed for Jerry. I wasn't a threat, anymore. I was a part of the fungus family. I tried to bring the tire iron down on the back of her head, but the orders from my brain were no longer reaching my hand.

Jerry's eyes were covered in fungus, so he couldn't see Julie stalking toward him. I opened my mouth, hoping my voice wasn't as useless as my hand.

"Jerry!" I screamed. "She's coming for you! Run!"

If Jerry heard me, he gave no indication. The fungus on his face was spreading rapidly; it looked like he was wearing a fuzzy blue helmet.

This was it, then. Felix Renn, supernatural detective, taken down, not by a vampire or a werewolf, but by some blue fungus. I was glad no one was here to see this.

I took a step toward Julie, mostly to see if I could. There was resistance, but I still managed to do it. I took another step, but when I tried for a third, my leg wouldn't respond. My thoughts were starting to feel distant.

I looked over my shoulder — I still had enough control over my body to do that much — and wondered how long it would take for someone to find us. Would we still be here, or would we be out spreading this blue plague to all points of the compass?

It was a terrible thought, but the fungus didn't let me dwell on it. My mind continued to drift like dandelion fluff on a strong breeze. I closed my eyes and tried to hold onto the last thing I had seen: the sun just starting to rise over the distant trees.

Then I felt something. A tingling along my right arm. I opened my eyes just in time to see my fingers suddenly spring open. The tire iron fell out of my hand and landed on my foot. A bolt of pain went racing up my leg. I jumped up and down on my other foot and realised I had regained control of my body.

I looked at my right hand. The blue fungus was still there, but it no longer had that fuzzy, slightly moist look. It was brittle like dried mud, and when I brushed my hand against my jeans it came off just as easily.

I was trying to figure out what had brought this on when I heard someone being noisily sick. I looked over and saw Julie Spiro down on her hands and knees, throwing up thick, ropy strands of the blue fungus. It didn't have the same syrupy consistency as the stuff the workmen had hucked up. As I watched, I could actually see it fade and turn as brittle as the stuff on my hand.

Jerry was pulling patches of the dried fungus off his face. He looked up at me as I came over.

"Felix." His voice was low and shaky. "I thought ...."

I nodded. "It's okay, Jer. So did I."

"What happened?"

"I don't think this stuff likes the sun." I looked over at the house. "I guess that's why it never spread beyond the Black Lands. It hung around long enough to infect whoever happened to be in the house, then, once the sun came up, it was like it was never here."

Jerry looked over at Julie. She was lying on her back and groaning like someone with a monumental hangover.

"Is she going to be okay?"

"Probably," I said. "But we'll need to get her checked out. We'll all need to be checked out."

Jerry suddenly snapped his fingers and blurted, "Vampire moss."

"What?"

"That's what I'm gonna call this stuff in my next book."

That was typical. Jerry was thinking about book titles, while I was thinking about what would have happened if this had been November instead of June, when the sun didn't rise for another hour.

"That's great, Jer. Now do you think you could help me get the workmen out of the house so we can show them the light, too?"

Jerry grinned. "Show them the light? That's not bad, Felix. Can I use that in the book?"

"Sure."

"By the way, you owe me breakfast."

"What?"

"You bet me this would turn out to be nothing. Body-snatching fungus equals breakfast on you." Jerry rubbed his hands together. "A new book, a free meal and a damsel in distress saved by Yours Truly. The day's barely begun and it's already shaping up to be a good one."

"What do you mean *you* saved her? I'm the one that got us out of the house."

"Yes, but if I hadn't called you, you'd be at home asleep right now and there'd be four infected people out spreading blue fungus — excuse me, vampire moss — across Central Ontario."

"How does that add up to you being the hero?"

Jerry glanced over at Julie. "Come on," he whispered. "I need this one. You're supposed to be my wingman, Goose."

I shook my head. "Welcome back to the human race, Jerry. We're glad to have you."

↑

GAMMA

By Laird Barron

↑

Laird Barron is the author of several books, including *The Imago Sequence*, *Occultation* and *The Croning*. His work has appeared in many magazines and anthologies. An expatriate Alaskan, Barron currently resides in Upstate New York.

↑

MY DAD SHOT A horse when I was a boy. The horse, a young sorrel mare named Gamma, slipped and fell while fording a creek way up in the Talkeetna Mountains. Dad had packed her saddle too heavily with supplies. I *knew* the load was too much when he was piling it on, as if we were heading for fucking Mt. Denali, but I was a coward and didn't say anything, not a damned thing. Dad scared me. He had to cut the straps off with a Barlow knife as the mare thrashed in the frigid water, and sprayed them in mud and twigs and piss.

Come on, girl, he'd muttered through his teeth as she fought. My god, she fought. *Come on, baby. You're okay, you're all right.* He danced at the end of the halter lead, a goddamned acrobat dodging those flying hooves. A bearded ballerina in a drover's hat and cowboy boots, shotgun slapping against his back as he leaped and capered. His antics were so hilarious that I laughed through the tears.

Gamma scrambled to her feet again, but, after that, she was never quite right, never quite the same. As summer wore on toward autumn, her health declined and she became sickly and weak. Her left eye went milky and her bones jutted. She stopped swishing the flies with her tail when they gathered in clusters upon her haunches. She stood in place for hours, muzzle in the mud.

One morning, Dad shrugged on his jacket and took down the big lever action rifle. He went into the barn and looped a rope around Gamma's neck and led her down the trail to a secluded spot and blew her brains out. I heard the shot, muffled through the log walls, from my bunk. He walked back into our homely cabin and put the carbine in its rack above the dining table. He sat without speaking at the table, waiting for his breakfast.

Mom poured him a cup of coffee and fried some of her world-famous pancakes. With blueberries she'd stashed in the root cellar. Fresh fruit was a cause for celebration at the ol' homestead, let me tell you. I recall being so grateful that I licked my plate clean. Like a dog.

↑

If Flatworm B eats Flatworm A, Flatworm B will inherit every-thing Flatworm A knew. Even Snopes is on the fence when it comes to debunking this theory. But look. When I speak of *when*, I mean now. There has always been and will only ever be the now. After the rats and the cockroaches succumb, there's another order in the wings. Of course, eventually, there won't be any carbon-based life on Terra, even the teeny fibroid shit that exists inside volcanic vents at the bottom of the sea.

Meanwhile. It's not just the flatworms; it's everything. Gimme a tomahawk, hell, a flat rock, and I'll show you.

↑

About one hundred and eighty-thousand years ago, a hominid slunk into a cave and murdered its brother with a spear of spruce wood, fire-hardened at the tip. The death scream echoed from the cave mouth and the birds in the trees began to chatter.

For reasons unknown, the murderer elected to remain in the darkness. Carrion eaters stayed away. *Everything* that walked or crawled stayed away. A vast and fecund mushroom bed existed within the depths, a portion extending unto the surface world in the manner of a gray tongue drooling from a slack jaw. In the hooting, glottal proto-language of the hominids, the cave was referred to as a cursed place. Eventually, an earthquake happened and the mountainside closed in on itself.

Thank you, great worm that encircles all creation.

I eat pancakes, drive a Toyota, go hiking along nature trails. Camping at night in the wild, doing for pleasure what my ancestors did from necessity, I tell myself that stars are clouds of flaming gas, not the eyes of the old gods peeping through a black tapestry.

I tell myself a lot of shit.

↑

I met Erin while attending college at the University of Washington. She worked part-time at the Saturn Theater. Blonde, blue-eyed Norwegian honey with dazzling white teeth and a penchant for Catholic-school-girl skirts. She smiled at me a couple of times as I shuffled past the ticket booth and, eventually, I worked up the nerve to ask her out. We fucked on the third date and the next morning went to breakfast at that little greasy spoon that used to be on the corner of 4th and Payne. Ruby's Grille and Disco. The disco bit was just pre-hipster humour.

We ordered blueberry pancakes with blueberry syrup, if I recall correctly. The café became a weekly hangout. After we got hitched and moved to Olympia, I still took Erin there every spring, on the anniversary of our first date.

A couple of years ago, I read in the paper that the frumpy, dumpy teen waitress who served us in the old days got murdered. An exchange student who came in for hash and coffee each and every goddamned morning developed an unrequited crush on her. The guy was a math whiz from Vietnam. His family pawned their souls to ship him stateside for a shot at the major leagues. He tracked the waitress to her house and chloroformed her when she answered the door. Supposedly, her choking to death was an accident. The guy decided not to face the music and snuffed himself in the back of the patrol car with a baggie of chemicals he'd stashed in his sock.

Ruby's went under with the recession, so I didn't have to make an excuse to Erin why we went elsewhere to celebrate our happy day.

↑

Gamma died in a hollow. Scraggly spruce trees laced in black moss tangled together like teeth, marshy ground, stagnant water. A breeding pit for mosquitoes and gnats. Winter had come and gone. The birds and the flies and the worms had come and gone. All that remained of her were bones encrusted with verdigris mold sunk in the muck of a mushroom bed. Some of the mushrooms billowed as tall as my thigh.

Not sure what drew me there months after Dad killed her. I remember sitting in the shadows of the trees, as summer sweltered the mountainside, and I remember the hum of a light aircraft traversing the eastern sky. I remember thinking Gamma's skull was an abandoned palace of the ants, a museum of toadstools. I hadn't read any Baudelaire, but, wow, fuck, it would've resonated, would've blown apart my brain, just like Gamma.

What I couldn't grasp, or didn't want to, was that there were too many bones in that pile. The moss and the fungus obscured the mess, but, down deep, I knew the shape was wrong, knew I'd stumbled upon a dreadful secret, and I decided to play dumb.

The moss rippled and the ferns shushed with a passing breeze that warbled, flute-like, through Gamma's eye sockets, while the gray and black and yellow-capped mushrooms dripped and oozed. The mushrooms whispered to me.

↑

Fact or fiction: In 1951 the CIA secretly poisoned a village in France with a hallucinogenic fungus. The Company was interested in studying the effects of pharmacological mind control in the field. Some villagers died; others were sent to asylums due to lunacy. A royal fustercluck, as my grandma would've said.

Fiction. The CIA had its hands full developing a smallpox delivery mechanism at the time. Yes, mind control and pharmacology were the original hot topics down at R&D, as the MKULTRA project testifies. Yes, there was a fungus involved and, yes, numerous villagers went berserk. However, it was simply a batch of bad bread that gummed the works. The baker's snot-nosed assistant fell asleep at the wheel, as it were. Blame him. Not the CIA and certainly not H.P's bat-winged pals from icy Yuggoth. Pay no attention to rumours about them. No government has ever made contact with an alien species, much less colluded with it regarding human experiments. It was the baker's apprentice in the mill with a sack of moldy flour.

Moving along, moving along.

↑

For a while among certain fringe circles, the Cordyceps discovery got scientists' hearts all fluttery. "The zombie fungus," some called it. It hailed from before the days of the trilobite. Method of proliferation was to zap various insect species with spores, ants being the most infamous example until late in the 21st century, when a rather horrible discovery was made at a monastery in northern Italy. Anyway, the lunatic fringe suggested doomsday might come in the form of a sporulating organism awakened from hibernation, or worse, adapted by one pharmaceutical company or another for military or private sector application.

The nutters were wrong about poor, innocent Cordyceps, but they had basically the right idea.

Lake Vostok was the epicenter of the latest and greatest extinction event to visit the planet. You know, the lake far beneath Antarctic ice sheets at the quaintly dubbed "Pole of Cold", where the Soviets built a station, back when there were real live Soviets. Vostok Station. The Soviets stuck it out there and, after they left, the Russians got ambitious and started digging and digging. No money for bread, no money for car fuel, but plenty of rubles for military adventures and boondoggle science projects that included digging.

Into the ice.

That ice is thousands of years old near the surface and it just gets older until you reach bottom and there's a big, prehistoric lake teeming with ... life. What kind of life? Oh, don't be coy, motherfucker. You know what kind.

The ha-ha part is, that "hypothetical" rogue star would've done the job down the road when it kicked loose that planet-killer asteroid and sent her tumbling our way. Every twenty-six million years. Look at the Yucatan; look at the *Grande Coupre*. Just look. Every twenty six-million years. Like a clock. Goodbye, lizards great and small; goodbye fish; goodbye, you little troublemaking primates. Goodbye.

Except, it wasn't, isn't, goodbye this time around. It was hello, baby. The living and the dead and those in between all merged. Separation no longer exists. Gives the old phrase "stuck on you" an entirely fresh definition. May as well resign myself to my new niche on the food chain. I got the feeling nothing is going to change until Nemesis swings by again.

↑

Contrary to Mama's predictions, I didn't die in a hail of bullets.

My wife, I forget her name, slept with an English teacher at her school and decided he was an upgrade. She patted me on the hand and said, *Sayonara, sucker,* or words to that effect. I left my happy suburban home and wandered the world for a while. It didn't cure my ills.

I read about this poor bastard over in Germany. He was so depressed that he answered a personal ad from a psycho killer who was looking for a willing victim. The depressed guy went to the psycho's apartment and played the role of sacrificial lamb. A few glasses of burgundy laced with sedatives and Depressed Dude was unconscious. The psycho cut his guest's throat and cooked the muscle of his shoulder for supper. Yeah, there was some sick, insane shit for you. But, but … in the end, I sort of got where the depressed guy was coming from. The urge to self-annihilate occasionally overwhelms the best of us. Exhibit A: the atom bomb. Exhibit B: love.

Dad and Mom had moved on to greener pastures when I was still a teenager. Upon my return as a middle-aged wreck, I discovered our homestead in the mountains had fallen to ruin. Roof caved in, yard overgrown. Nobody went up there into our private valley. It surprised me how easy Gamma's death hollow was to find and how little it had changed relative to the obliteration of Dad's handiwork and the nearly-erased trails that led there.

My God, my God, the bones, or *some* bones, remained in a calcified pile, webbed in a strange skein of blue and yellow that clung to everything, dripped from the branches of the trees. Those mushrooms were bigger than ever — cyclopean giants the girth of my torso that oozed dark sap. Thousands of insects and birds and squirrels were embedded in the webbing, the stalks of the towering fungi. Mummified, slightly shriveled.

The horror I felt was surpassed by a crushing sense of inevitability, of *rightness*. I hadn't come home with the conscious intent of suicide, so I hadn't brought a proper tool. No gun, no knife, no rope. When I tore a spruce branch from its trunk and rammed the jagged tip through my chest, I was very much taken by surprise. I collapsed into the bed of slime and muck, and waited for the agony to be replaced by the smooth, eggshell perfection of the void of death.

The creeping appetite of that wilderness grave subsumed me over a span of decades. I remember every moment. Although, I am frequently confused. Instead of skewering myself with a homemade spear, I am staring down the barrel of my father's rifle and into his cold, dead eyes as he squeezes the trigger.

↑

If visitors should arrive here from some distant constellation, they will find this a quiet, peaceful place. Nothing stirs except the water and the wind, the fronds and the blades and the stems of the plants and the fungi that cover everything from sea to scummy sea, from polar cap to polar cap. If the visitors are smart — and, surely, to travel so far from home, they will be quite advanced — their equipment will safeguard them from spores and pollen and the crawling molds that have become ubiquitous. However, I doubt such visitors will ever become aware of me trapped in eternal amber, peeping at them from every keyhole, from every nightmare version of a sundew, a redcap, a pitcher plant. I doubt they will detect that the hiss of the grass, the drip-drop of sap, are the outward expressions of my cries of lament. They will gather their samples and mine their data, and leave, never guessing they've trod, not a graveyard, but Sheol itself. I will watch them depart and I will not twitch, no matter my anguish. I am in hell.

And by *I*, I mean *we*.

↑

CORDYCEPS ZOMBII

By Ann K. Schwader

✦

Ann K. Schwader is a Wyoming native exiled to suburban Colorado, USA. She is the author of *Twisted in Dream* (Hippocampus Press, 2011), Bram Stoker Award finalist *Wild Hunt of the Stars* (Sam's Dot, 2010) and four other collections of speculative poetry. Find out more from her LiveJournal (http://ankh-hpl.livejournal.com/) or at http://home. earthlink.net/~schwader/.

✦

They glittered mystery in the desert night,
those sparks from space we came to know as spores,
but saw at first by childhood's light: each mind
its own myth-maker. So contagion spread
as evils always have, without intent
beyond some impulse to perfect one's life.

Humanity's quixotic quest for life
outside our homeworld orbit stopped that night,
successfully. Forever. By intent
or otherwise, our fate lay with those spores,
drawn deeper with each sleeping breath to spread
their threads of hunger & ensnare the mind.

Why did the notion never come to mind
that loneliness was safer? Surely, life
elsewhere might have its own agenda, spread
itself upon the star-winds until night
exploded with new constellations: spores
enough for legions linked by one intent.

Unceasing motion seemed the sole intent
sustaining the infested. Maimed in mind,
they roved as little more than meat for spores
of future generations. Aping life
no longer theirs, these shamblers by night
soon burst with fruiting death as terror spread.

From continent to continent the spread
accelerated, fuelled by good intent
turned tragic as a shotgun in the night
unthinkingly deployed. Each spattered mind
released in turn its epitaph to life
as we once lived it, innocent of spores.

Adrift in this necropolis where spores
abandoned us at last, survivors spread
a thousand warning satellites for life
that might approach our planet. Yet, intent
undoes us still: each thread-infested mind
cries out in siren welcome to the night.

So life perfects its own malign intent
until the stars are merely spores that spread
in mindless currents to the curve of night.

↑

A BRIEF LIST OF FUNGAL FICTION

WHILE WORKING ON THIS anthology we asked readers of Innsmouth Free Press to send us examples of *fungi* in all types of media. The result is this list, where we present some samples of fungal manifestations. It is not intended as an exhaustive compilation, but it may serve as a lead into other mushroom wonderlands.

↑

Stories

- "The Voice in the Night," William Hope Hodgson (*Blue Book Magazine*, 1907)
- "Fungus Isle," Philip M. Fisher (*Argosy All-Story Weekly*, 1923)
- "The Whisperer in Darkness," H. P. Lovecraft (*Weird Tales*, 1931)
- "Spheres of Hell" (aka "The Puff-Ball Menace"), John Wyndham (*Wonder Stories*, 1933)
- "The Shunned House," H. P. Lovecraft (*Weird Tales*, 1937)
- "Come Into My Cellar" (aka "Boys! Raise Giant Mushrooms in Your Cellar!"), Ray Bradbury (*Galaxy Magazine*, 1962)
- "Gray Matter," Stephen King (*Cavalier*, 1973)

- "A Cabin in the Woods," John Coyne (*Alfred Hitchcock's Mystery Magazine*, 1976)
- "Fruiting Bodies," Brian Lumley (*Weird Tales*, 1988)
- "The All-Consuming," Lucius Shepard & Robert Frazier (*Playboy*, 1990)
- "Growing Things," T. E. D. Klein (*999: New Stories of Horror & Suspense*, 1999)
- "Leng," Marc Laidlaw (*Lovecraft Unbound*, 2009)
- "The Black Mould," Mark Samuels (*The Man Who Collected Machen & Other Stories*, 2010)

Novels

- *The Boats of the "Glen-Carrig,"* William Hope Hodgson (1907)
- *Saint Peter's Snow*, Leo Perutz (1933)
- *The Wonderful Flight to the Mushroom Planet*, Eleanor Cameron (1954)
- *A Scent of New-Mown Hay*, John Blackburn (1958)
- *The Hendon Fungus*, Richard Parker (1968)
- *The Fungus*, Harry Adam Knight (1985)
- *Love and War* (a *Doctor Who* tie-in novel), Paul Cornell (1992)
- *Shriek: An Afterword*, Jeff VanderMeer (2006)
- *Finch*, Jeff VanderMeer (2009)
- *Spore*, John Skipp & Cody Goodfellow (2011)

Movies

- *The Unknown Terror*, Dir. Charles Marquis Warren (1957)
- *Matango*, Dir. Ishiro Honda (1963)
- *Nausicaa of the Valley of the Wind*, Dir. Hayao Miyazaki (1984)
- *Shrooms*, Dir. Paddy Breathnach (2007)
- *The Whisperer in Darkness*, Dir. Sean Branney (2011)

Television

- "The Voice in the Night," Dir. Arthur Hiller (*Suspicion*, 1958)
- "Boys! Raise Giant Mushrooms in Your Cellar!" Dir. David Brandes (*The Ray Bradbury Theater*, 1989)
- "Field Trip," Dir. Kim Manners (*The X-Files*, 1999)
- "Episode #3.5," Dir. Mark Everest (*Primeval*, 2009)
- "Alone in the World," Dir. Miguel Sapochnik (*Fringe*, 2011)

↑

ABOUT THE EDITORS

Orrin Grey writes stories of the supernatural and macabre, which have appeared in a number of Innsmouth Free Press anthologies, as well as other venues like *Bound for Evil* and *Delicate Toxins*. His first collection, *Never Bet the Devil & Other Warnings*, is due out from Evileye Books in 2012. His fascination with monsters and fungus, and fungus monsters, is longstanding and shows no sign of waning any time soon.

↑

Silvia Moreno-Garcia's stories have appeared in *Imaginarium 2012: The Best Canadian Speculative Writing*, *The Book of Cthulhu*, *Bull Spec* and a number of other publications. In 2011, Silvia won the Carter V. Cooper Memorial Prize sponsored by Gloria Vanderbilt and *Exile Quarterly*. Silvia was also a finalist for that year's Manchester Fiction Prize. She has co-edited the anthologies *Historical Lovecraft*, *Candle in the Attic Window* and *Future Lovecraft*. Her first collection, *Shedding Her Own Skin*, is due out in 2013.

CPSIA information can be obtained at www.ICGtesting.com
Printed in the USA
BVOW05s1649140814

362931BV00002B/160/P